LIMELIGHT

An NSB Novel By
Alyson Santos

NSB Series, Book 4

This novel is a work of fiction and intended for mature readers. Events and persons depicted are of a fictional nature and use language, make choices, and face situations inappropriate for younger readers.

Names, characters, places and events are the product of the author's imagination. Any resemblance to actual events, locations, organizations, or people, living or dead, is entirely coincidental and not intended by the author.

PROLOGUE

Limelight. Right, let's put the elephant in the room out of its misery. How many ways can we say overrated? Yep, frontman Jesse Everett is easy on the eye. And I reckon his voice could be a contribution to the musical landscape of our time, but that means bugger all if you can't handle your own gift. Amid rumours of drug abuse, including one "alleged" incident on their last tour where Mr Everett was found zonked out cold on the streets of Newark, it's no wonder this once up-and-coming band will only ever be a could-have-been, two-hit-wonder flop for mega-label SauerStreet Records. The proof is in the pudding, Limelight. Let's not dress this up. A local garage band does not a stadium band make.

Sorry Jesse, wasted talent is the name of the game when you play with the big boys. Time to dust off that old CV, mate. Your "limelight" has officially dimmed.

Burgers anyone?

You heard it here first—Mila Taylor, over and out.

I: FEUD

Overhyped. Exaggerated. Overestimated. *There are your fucking synonyms, Mila fucking Taylor.* Shit.

I drop my phone on the mattress and throw an arm over my face. What do I even care anymore? SauerStreet was going to drop us anyway. All she's done is validate their betrayal.

"Mila Taylor is one of the most influential music bloggers in the industry. While her opinion is certainly not the leading factor in this decision, it illustrates the challenges... blah, blah, blah."

I stopped listening at that point. Why can't anyone ever say what they fucking mean? Just say it, assholes: *You're a piece of shit failure not worth the paper that contract was printed on.* There. Was that so hard?

You're. Done.

A cold draft skims over my chest as I stare at the water-stained ceiling of my bedroom. Muffled voices drift through the crack under the door, and I'm sure the guys are discussing the "news." Whispering because, after twenty-three years of fighting for survival, they still think I'm too fragile for life. It's Parker's fault. The dude suffers from Big Brother Syndrome.

It's why I love him and want to lay him out at the same time. I'll always be eleven years old to that guy.

"I can you hear you!" I call from my mattress.

The mumbling fades into footsteps, and sure enough, my brother's mop of blond hair pokes through the doorway. "You okay, bro?"

"Fucking brilliant. Why wouldn't I be?"

"She's a bitch. That post was bullshit."

"Does it matter when you have a hundred million followers?"

"Damn, she has a hundred million followers?" Derrick, ever the insightful one.

"I don't know, dude," I groan, "I'm making a point."

Parker silences Derrick's follow-up with a glare. "We'll find another label," he says to me.

"Is that even what we want?" My question leaves two stunned faces in its wake. Seriously? One big tour and they're ready to sell out again. "You really want some bastards in a boardroom telling us how to do our music? We hated it."

"Jess, I get why you're upset, but let's wait a few days to decide what's next." Big Bro, always lobbying to be the voice of reason. You'd think he'd give up after twenty-three years of me ignoring it.

"Do we have any food?" I push myself up for a better view of the disaster that is my room. I'm surprised Parker hasn't gone through it with a blowtorch yet. Roaches, mice, fucking ferrets—I don't know what he fears. Ever since we reached the promised land of Philly's Mt. Airy neighborhood he's become a freaking menace.

"Still some pizza left." Reece. I hadn't even noticed him in the hallway.

"Nah, let's grab something at Benson's," Parker says, eyeing me like a cornered suspect. Even big bro can't tell if my sudden hunger comes from the need for food or a subject change. I nod and launch a long stretch to prove how much I don't care about any of this bullshit.

Derrick slings a pair of jeans at me. "Dude, put some clothes on."

"*Dude*, stop checking me out."

"He can't help it. Those abs!" Reece snickers.

"Fuck off," I say, tugging on my jeans. I'm fishing through a pile of clothes for a shirt when Parker shrieks.

"Shit! You responded?"

I cast a dark look. "She deserved it."

"That's 101-level, Jess! You don't respond to criticism. Dammit!"

He turns his phone so the rest of the band can share in his horror.

Hey @MilaTaylorRocks, thanks for the burger invite but insecure pretenders who rip others apart for cash aren't my type. #getarealjob

Hey @JesseEverett99, that's great because I'm not into immature whiny children. #soreloser #enjoythebarcircuit

Their eyes tell me they're not thrilled I picked a fight with one of the top bloggers in the biz.

"She's going to bury you, dude. What the hell were you thinking?"

"What's she gonna do? Get me fired? Oh wait."

I flip them off on my way to the bathroom.

"How about make sure you never get signed again?" Parker barks after me. He's pissed. He should be. I fucked up his life too.

For fifteen years it was *Parker and Jesse*. Through seven foster homes, who knows how many shitty couches, hungry stomachs, black eyes, and shattered hearts, it was always the two of us against the world. We had each other's backs because we learned early on that no one else did. We learned not to hope. That life is cruel, unforgiving, and no one gives a damn about your sob-story. At least, I thought we did. Parker wears optimism like a bullet-proof vest.

The bathroom door swings open to reveal my brother's anger. "I'm not buying it."

"What the hell, dude? A little privacy?"

"Cut the shit. You care. I know you do. You've bled for this band. You sold your soul to get us that deal with SauerStreet. I know it's killing you that they trashed you without a second thought."

He blurs through my narrowed eyes before I turn them back to the mirror. I look like a man who hasn't slept in days. A washed-up wannabe rocker who can't admit he cares because once that floodgate opens... I splash water on my face to mask the evidence.

"What that chick said was brutal," he continues, tone soft like compassion actually fixes shit. "It wasn't right, and it sure as fuck wasn't true. You're amazing, Jess. You know that. You have something special, and we're going to figure out how to share it with the world."

"Yeah? Gonna be hard to do that flipping burgers."

Parker knows better than to respond. There's no getting through to me today. Probably never on this particular subject.

I wipe a towel over my face. "Are we getting food or what?"

∞∞∞∞

Overrated. Garage band wasted.

I balance on the edge of my bed, eyes clenched shut in the darkness.

Talent-jaded. Faded. Hated.

Other voices clash outside my window. The neighbors' never-ending conflict pounds against the pane, and I strain to focus on their shouts. Sometimes they can drown out the ones in my head.

Wasted. Wasted. Overrated.

"You slept with her, you asshole!"

"I didn't!"

"Then who's skanky bra is…"

Failure sated, grated, inflated.

I grip my hair to cover my ears, but that only strengthens the internal screams.

FAILURE. HATED. OBLITERATED.

Two AM. Hours left for my brain to torture me. I suck in air and shuffle to the window, savoring the icy pricks that stab my forehead when I lean against the glass.

Told you so. Told you NO. Garage band hopeless. Choke us. Break it off. Break it off.

"Break it off with her!"

"I told you, there's nothing to break off!"

"Oh really? How about if I call her right now, huh? Should I call her?"

"Go ahead, whore!"

"It's all right in the candlelight..."

The lyrics slip from my lips in a low hum, January frost soothing burning flesh.

"Whore? Oh, I'm the whore?"

"Not bright enough to see my scars..."

"You heard me! What about that bastard from the gym?"

"Who... Frankie? Ha!"

"Just *another night in the candlelight.*" My pulse eases beneath the soothing whisper of verse. *"Just enough to fight, hold tight. It'll be all right."*

My eyes tremble from holding their ground.

"It'll be all right. It'll be all right."

The song is just a brush of air in the stale darkness now.

"It'll be all right."

I sink to the floor and wrap my arms around my legs. Head on my knees, I find sleep for the hours left until I can call Natasha.

∞∞∞∞

Chipping paint billows in the wind, swirls in a gorgeous swatch of blue tints. My lips twist into contentment at the soothing rhythm of my bedroom ceiling. Each color practically sings in choreographed perfection. Such a contrast to the horror of the night.

"Ocean tile, welcome home, you beautiful thrust of life."

"What's that, babe? Are you singing?" Warm fingers trace my bare chest in demanding streaks. The blaze moves lower, *stronger*. Natasha wants payment for the good stuff.

"This shit is amazing. You get it from DJ?" Peace. Freedom.

My goddess nods, red lip summoning as she sucks it between her teeth and climbs on top of me. Her knees lock around my hips as she leans in, and my hand reaches into her hair on autopilot. I shove her hungry mouth into mine. Currency for my beautiful high.

Her groans activate my body as she rocks against me. Slow at first, grinding deep with each wave of desire. I want to contribute. She's earned it. If I can just find that damn ceiling again. I squint past her arching chest for a glimpse of blue perfection.

"Ocean bliss, endless kiss of soul-renewing—"

She grips my face and centers it on hers. "Are you seriously getting off to your ceiling instead of me right now?"

"It's so incredible. Once-in-a-lifetime, you know?"

"You're impossible."

"I can multi-task."

"You better," she mutters against my mouth. "If you want to see your sexy ceiling again."

∞∞∞∞

Natasha is gone when I wake up. So is my ocean ceiling. I'm still naked and only vaguely remember our time together. I hope we were safe. Pretty sure, and I feel better when I spot the condom in the trash. I run my hand through my hair to keep it out of my face as I search for clothes. After sliding on a pair of gym shorts, I make my way to the kitchen to soothe my throbbing head.

Parker is at the table with coffee and his disapproving *you got high again* look. He's learned not to comment. Besides, the alternative isn't exactly pretty.

"Yeah, yeah. I got a new song idea from it though." I fish a mug out of the sink and give it a quick rinse.

"That right?" I swear the dude is twice his age the way he sips his beverage and peers over his laptop at me. All he's missing are drugstore readers sliding down his perfectly straight nose. I have the same nose—from our mother's side we're told. Honestly, it's the only thing we share. His head is covered by a thick layer of short, sandy hair. Mine is dark, wavy, and just long enough to tuck behind my ears when I'm concentrating. Parker says I have a natural *profound* look. Don't know what that means, but it's nicer than most of the shit he's called me over the years.

"Yeah. Working title is 'Ocean Ceiling.'"

His middle-aged accountant expression tightens further. "For real?"

"You'll see."

"Right. Let me guess. It's about getting high?"

"At least I wasn't trash-talking bloggers. What are you doing anyway?"

"Trying to book us some gigs."

My hand tightens on the mug handle as I suck back shock in a hard swallow. "Booking gigs? Why? Barry dropped us too?"

His look confirms it, and my perfect ocean ceiling starts to collapse around me.

"He called last night. Said he needs to reduce his artist list."

"By one Philly-based alternative band, I'm guessing."

"We were going to tell you. We just wanted to give you time to process the whole Mila thing."

"Oh, it's fucking *processed*."

Big Brother Stare Down means he's freaked I'm going to do something stupid. I've earned that signature pose.

"What? I haven't even touched my phone since yesterday." Doesn't seem to appease him.

"We'll find a new manager," he says because that's so easy when Mila Taylor hates your guts. "Until then, we can do this ourselves. We've been here before."

"Well, minus the fact that we're failed has-beens now."

"Really, man? That's how we're playing this?"

I shrug and dump way too much booze in my coffee for eleven in the morning.

"Oh and breakfast drinking now too? Great."

"Most important meal of the day."

Even *Vinegar Face* pinches a smile at that. "Whatever. Just stay off your phone. No more revenge posts."

"Me? Never."

I don't tell him it's way too late for that.

∞∞∞

My Dearest Mila,

I woke up this morning with thoughts of you on my mind. Thoughts like, "wow, thinking about that woman feels damn close to a bad hangover or food poisoning." How's your day going? Ruin any other careers with your bullshit? Feast on any kitten and baby brains? Hey, is it hard taking a shit on that self-righteous throne of yours?

Forever yours,
Burger Chef Jesse Everett

* * * * *

Dear Burger Prince,

I'm so flattered that I'm the subject of daydreams for a D-list legend like you. To answer your question, I like my kitten brains grilled, no onions, and extra mustard. I'll have chips with that. As for the throne, you're the expert on producing shite.

Much love,
MT

I smirk and follow the link to her site. The profile picture is a shadow with sultry eyes that scream queen-of-sass—a penetrating stare I feel throughout my body. I tear my gaze away. Has to be fake. Mila Taylor is probably a sixty-year-old man who lives on a couch with a laptop balanced on his potbelly. Miles Taylor, I bet. And he's bald, missing four teeth, permanent cheese curl stain on his fingers. Only friend is Junior, his golden retriever. No wait, toy poodle. Yeah.

Hey, Miles Taylor. Fuck you. One day I'll be running *you* out of town.

My phone interrupts my throw-down with no one, and I sigh at the caller. Luke Craven: the one person on my automatic answer list.

"Hey, Jess. How you holding up?"

There's no point in playing games with an industry legend like him. I learned that hard and fast on our joint tour when he rescued me from the now-infamous Newark fiasco.

I shut the door to my room and fall back on the bed. "Fucking sucks, dude."

"Yeah, I bet. Mila Taylor, huh?"

"Shredded me."

"How did the Label take it?"

"They're dropping us."

"Fuck. You serious?"

"Our manager too."

"No way."

"He's downsizing."

"Right." I hear the sarcasm in his voice. "What are you going to do?"

"Shit, dude, I don't know. Maybe I should flip burgers like Mila suggested."

"Mila. She had plenty to say about me too. You can't let it get to you."

"Yeah, is that what you did?"

"Hell no. She came at me two months after Elena's death. That's what sent me into hiding."

"Really?"

"One of many things. Hey, if you need management, give me a ring. I'll talk to TJ. I'm sure he knows people."

"Thanks, Luke. Appreciate it."

"Anytime. You know how to reach me if you need to talk through shit. It happens to all of us. Don't let it break you."

Right...

I hang up wanting to believe him. Luke has lived it, fought his way through hell and back, so if anyone has permission to offer unsolicited platitudes, it's the Night Shifts Black's frontman. But I'm a whole new level of dysfunction.

Eyes closed and head pounding, I flinch at the bang on my door.

"Come out with us," Parker belts into my room.

"I'm good. You guys go."

I feel his disappointment when he lets himself in. No look necessary.

"Natasha coming over tonight?" *Are you getting wrecked again?*

"Don't know."

"Just come with us. We're checking out that new spot on Broad Street. See if it has potential."

"The sports bar?"

"It's not a sports bar. Technically."

After the last few nights, I'm definitely using help to get through the next one. "I trust your judgment."

"Jess..."

"I have to work on my resume."

He shakes his head, *probing* melting into *pissed.*

"So is this it, man? This is your life now?"

I shrug. "Apparently."

"Well then, fuck you, because it's not the one *I* want."

I'm surprised he's not worried about the health of the door when he slams it on his way out.

∞∞∞∞

Tonight's mental tirade is... *yeah.*

I present two middle fingers to the shadows with a slow grin. They can't touch me thanks to a few tiny pills.

Overra—ra—ra... Ha! Can't even threaten.

"It's all right in the candlelight..." My voice is barely audible, a feather tickling the cobwebs in my brain.

It's all right. It's all right.

I close my eyes and allow the waves behind my eyelids to soothe me to sleep.

LIMELIGHT 18

2: FREEDOM

A former rock band fills my room, shifting its weight in nervous anticipation.

Parker clears his throat, arms-crossed all authoritative-like, and I force my groggy attention to him. "We want to start recording again."

Part of my brain bursts into laughter. At least it doesn't make its way to my throat. "Sounds good. Have fun."

"C'mon, bro." Oddly enough that comes from one of the guys who isn't my brother.

"There's no Limelight without you, and you know it," Parker says. "Get your shit together and start writing."

"I have."

"Not that Ocean Ceiling crap. Real music. One homerun, man. That's all we need to get relevant again."

"That's it? Just a chart-topper?"

"You know what I mean. Something to get us noticed."

"Oh, well, if that's all."

Angry face now. Wait, *freaking pissed* face. "The grieving period is over, Jess!"

Asshole. He knows I don't get that luxury. I tug the blanket up to my neck.

"So what, you're just going to spend the last fifty years of your life stoned?"

Talent-wasted. "Doubt it'll be fifty."

He bristles. "Enough. Fucking *do* something!"

A notebook flies at my face, and I block it just in time. The others stare, the air heavy with uncertainty. I'm unpredictable. A genius and an underachiever. I read it in their hesitation, their fear that I will bring them down my dark hole. And I could. Parker's right. There's no Limelight without me. I'm the songs, the voice, the passion, the pain. I'm the failure. Their curse, because they can't let go of our potential. God knows why I'm still here and not dead already.

Parker softens. "*Do* something, Jess."

My eyes rest on a notebook that's been through hell. Its tattered pages tell the story of my journey, every trial, every painful victory. I'm running out of pages and will need to replace it soon. My gaze travels across the room to the guitar propped against the stand.

Maybe *soon* is now. Maybe soon is never. The guys wait for the verdict.

"I need some air."

∞∞∞∞

Air comes in many forms. It can be fresh air—good. Hot air—bad. Poisonous air—good or bad depending on the poison. This kind is good.

Natasha couldn't stay today. Something about a job interview. She smacked me when I snickered, but come on. I asked if she wanted to use me as a reference. She smacked me again.

Now, I'm draped over my mattress, staring at the floor instead of the ceiling for once. I'm not sure why I don't engage the rustic wood grain more often. It's way more insightful than the blue ceiling I've grown so fond of in recent days. There's history in this floor, a story I want to know beyond all reason at this second. I wonder if you can Google floor pedigree in the Philadelphia area. You can Google anything, right?

I'm starting to come down now. The worst part of the cycle, when the oblivion fades and dumps you right back in your mess—with the added bonus of guilt.

I swore to Parker I'd never get into the hard stuff, and I've kept my promise. The problem is our definitions aren't exactly in sync. There's a list of shit I won't touch; his list is much longer. Whatever. I know my limits. I've only crossed into trouble a few times. Like Newark.

Parker loves to hold that night over my head. A wakeup call, he says. And yeah, it kind of was. When Luke Craven has to personally get involved in your rescue, maybe you stepped over the line. I didn't mean for it to happen, but now I have a shitload of consequences to keep me company. Our manager Barry was pissed, and even though the guys will never say it, we all know what happened that night was a factor—read: *the* factor—in dropping us as clients. I'm not a big enough paycheck to be worth the headaches.

Party smart, Luke had said after tracking me down in a shady park and dragging my nearly unconscious ass back to the tour buses. It became my mantra since then. Finally, someone cracking me over the head with rules I could actually follow. And I have. God knows I have, which is why I forgive myself for escaping when necessary.

Do something.

I close my eyes against the voices, the pressure I can't satisfy.

Do something. One homerun.

Deep breath. A push up from the bed. A pause until I'm able to shake the voices off.

Food. There's never enough in our house when I emerge from hiding, but way too much Parker. Funny how that works.

"I didn't write anything," I say as I duck into the fridge. I feel his sigh from the table and snap a look back. "Dude, why don't *you* write something for once?" *Yeah, I'm a jerk.* It's like asking why he doesn't try having green eyes instead of brown.

"I'm not good at that and you know it." Every thread of his glare is knitted into his tone.

"I know." I let out a breath and straighten. "I will man, okay? I just need time. It's not an on-demand thing."

It is for a lot of musicians. I hear it in the silence, but I'm not them. I do music because it's all I have. It was never a choice. It's who I am, and sometimes that's not enough. I'm a slave to my nature, waiting for it to show mercy and drop a gift in my lap. I wrote "Candlelight" in forty-five minutes. "Nothing I Want" poured out in just over an hour. "Dragonfly" was the outlier and took me three. That's my process. Nothing, nothing, nothing, and bam—chart-topper. As annoyed as I was over Parker's comment, he was only reciting history. Three #1 hits on our debut record? Yeah, that's why he thinks I have a gift.

But they don't get it. It's a curse. Expectations fucking suck when you have no control. The music chose me. I'm its victim not its gift.

"Just..."

I meet Parker's gaze when he stops and read the rest. *Be careful? Don't crash/break/implode this time?* All valid. All screaming in the silence. *Don't be you, Jesse Everett.*

Except he needs me to be me and he knows it. Everyone fucking needs it no matter how much damage it does to me. It's why they'll never seriously stop me from swallowing, snorting, and smoking.

"Come out with us tonight. Just for a little? Clear your head."

"Fifty-cent wings?"

Relief colors his smile. "And five dollar pitchers."

∞∞∞∞

Wings, booze, and the dissolution of our relationship with SauerStreet Records: the perfect formula for a mock celebration.

Parker holds up a shot glass. "To freedom."

We toast and swallow our liquid release.

"I also have an announcement," Parker continues while I signal for another round. "You know that festival in Allentown?"

"The week-long thing?" Reece asks.

"We're in the lineup."

"Seriously?" Derrick is amazed at everything on the planet. The weather? Yep. The new signing by the Flyers? Wow. The dog statue beside the hostess stand? Epic.

"Yes, it's official." And Parker is damn pleased with himself, except...

"Isn't that in August?" Not trying to be a dick but we'll probably have to eat in the next eight months.

"Well, yeah."

I force a half-smile because deep down I do love my brother. "That's great, man. Gives us plenty of time to prepare." If we haven't starved by then. Biology's a bitch.

"I'm in talks for some other stuff. Plus, not all of the promoters have backed out. Some of our dates are still on."

"Like?" Me again playing the asshole.

He taps his fingers on the table. "Harrisburg."

"The glorified lawn party?"

"Poconos."

"The poolside thing?"

"Dover."

"Oh, that super-fun bowling alley." So much for not being a jerk, but come on.

"It's not a bowling alley." Parker's glare has its own personality. "Anyway, the point is we still have dates. If we add some new tracks to that, we can get back up."

"As long as we're doing local shows, our costs should be low too," Reece adds. The silver lining is way more their thing than mine.

Parker's arms cross again because he's so freaking right about this. "Exactly."

I shake my head and throw back another shot.

∞∞∞

Overrated. Talent-wasted. Do something! The bar's assistance was good for a few hours of sleep, but alcohol is a disloyal companion. Especially when it passes on its wrath as payment for its assistance. Head pounding, stomach churning, mouth dry from...

Failure. Hated. Wasted.

Wasted. Heh.

My phone buzzes with a notification, and I hold it up, a spotlight streaming down to connect my squinting eyes with its critique.

Bad news about SauerStreet @JesseEverett99. Never mind duck, I've heard there's dough to be made in kids' parties.

Fucking... Really? A spark tears through me. Fire.

You'd know with your thriving clown career @MilaTaylorRocks #nicecostume

My blood pounds right along with the satisfied smile that stretches across my face. I wait in the darkness, hoping she bites back.

3: ENGLEWOOD

Our first gig without a label also means we're back to a trailer and our own biceps for moving our gear. Reece pulls the van around and double parks in front of the building that houses our practice space. It shouldn't be too much of an issue at this hour. Avoiding parking violations is a big part of our tour schedule.

The rest of us have already started piling cases and amps on the curb so Reece can work his Tetris magic inside the just-big-enough box hitched to the back of our van.

"Yo, D! How about you not throw my shit around like that?" Reece shouts as he leaps down from the driver's seat. Derrick returns a middle finger and disappears inside for more stuff. I start moving boxes and stacking them by the entrance of the trailer.

"We're using the in-ear system, right?" Reece asks, scanning our remaining pile.

"Yeah. Want to give me a hand with this?"

He meets me on the sidewalk and hoists the other side of a heavy case. Together we work our way through the legally parked cars to our soon-to-be ticket if we don't get our shit loaded.

"How many seats at this venue?" he asks.

"Are there seats?"

He snickers and backs up the ramp with his side of the crate. "We need to get a case with wheels."

"We had one until Derrick decided to ride it down that ramp in Seattle."

"At least he broke his nose to go with it. Idiot."

"Let's have no injuries today. We can't afford medical bills right now."

Reece grunts and starts strapping down the cases. I go back to the curb for another load, just as Parker and Derrick stack their latest with the pile.

"That everything?" I ask, grasping the handles of a couple guitar cases.

"Yeah. We hitting Wawa on the way?" Derrick asks.

"Duh," Parker says and points to the drum cases. "Reece needs those next."

We finish loading, lock the trailer, and pile into the van.

"Everyone good?" Reece asks, turning the ignition.

"Let's do this," Parker says. He tosses me a grin that takes us back five years. No Mila. No Label drama. Just four guys and a thing they had to do to keep breathing.

Gotta admit, the feeling in my gut doesn't suck.

∞∞∞∞

After playing a stadium, Englewood Pub feels like a great aunt's living room. It's a tight fit, but we manage to cram most of our equipment on the tiny stage. Reece called it *quaint* because he's the least cynical of the bunch. He changed his mind when we didn't have room for his extra bass.

"What am I supposed to do on 'Candlelight'?" he whines, inspecting the clutter of equipment for an empty space we missed.

"Dude, it's Englewood Pub. I guarantee no one is going to notice the difference in your tone," Parker mutters. "You ready for a sound check?" he asks me.

"In a sec. Something's up with my pedal board." I crouch down to investigate. "Shit, it's the compressor." Parker joins me and starts poking around as well.

"Fuck. You removing it from the chain?" he asks, even though I'm already rerouting cables.

"You'll have to take the intro to 'Dragonfly' now."

"Yeah, no problem. Just play rhythm."

"Okay, got it. Let's go."

We straighten and settle in front of our mics. I adjust the boom stand to the right height and toss Parker a thumbs-up. Then we wait. And wait because this venue is supplying their own house engineer, and Reece is back at the booth arguing about something.

He stomps toward the stage, and we huddle together to brace for bad news.

"So apparently, the *engineer*, is the owner's nephew. I gave him specs on how we like our levels and he's refusing."

"Let me guess, doesn't want to ruin their equipment," I grunt.

"Bingo."

Drummer Derrick curses, and we give him a collective warning in the form of a stare-down. He holds up his hands. "I know, I know. I'll back off the volume."

"Gonna have to tickle those babies in a space this size," Reece corrects.

"Should've brought the shield," Derrick jokes. Shit, we barely have room for the kit.

"We'll make it work," Parker says, returning to his mic. "Let's get a sound check to set our monitor levels at least."

∞∞∞∞

The set goes as well as can be expected. We actually have a blast rocking a small crowd again, and we're a big enough name that they're appreciative. Fully engaged, even, especially the scantily-dressed cluster of women hovering just offstage.

I'm not surprised by their approach immediately after we close our set. Flirty eyes are universal, and I'm still pulling the guitar over my head when I hear my name.

"Jesse, right?"

She's tall, curvy, straight black hair. Yeah, okay, I'm game.

"That's right. Nice to meet you," I toss back as I balance my guitar on the stand. I jump down from the platform and offer my hand. She takes it with a coy smile and risky stroke of my thumb.

"You guys are really good."

"Thanks."

"None of us agree with all the stuff they've been saying about you."

"Yeah?"

"Dude, you packing your shit up or what?" Parker barks from stage left.

"Just a minute," I shoot over. "Sorry about that," I say to... this person. "What's your name?"

"Maria."

"Hi, Maria. Thanks for coming out."

She studies the action behind me. Cases clicking, cables being wrapped into coils. "You guys leaving right away?"

"Probably. We have to get back to Philly."

Her eyes brighten. "You live in Philly?"

I nod and climb back on the stage.

"Me too. I'm a junior at Temple."

"No, shit. What are you doing down here?"

"Her birthday," she says, pointing at our audience of giggling women.

"Wish her a happy birthday for me."

"Thanks. She'll love it."

I give her my famous smile and start back to the equipment before my brother's head explodes.

"Wait!"

I look back, and she's holding out a scrap of paper. *Well, okay then.* I take it from her and let my grin spread.

"You know. If you're ever bored," she says, lashes thick as they lower over striking dark eyes. Damn if I don't have a thing for eyes. Soul-windows and all that.

"Thanks." I shake the paper in acknowledgment and tuck it in my pocket. Maria. Hmm.

My gaze drifts over to her table several times as we tear down. And each time hers locks directly on mine.

"Who's that?" Derrick asks as I help him pack his kit.

"Maria."

"Damn."

"Yeah."

"She gave you her number?"

"Yeah. She goes to Temple."

His eyes widen in a more intense search of that side of the room.

"Dude. You're just going to leave it like that?"

"I have her number."

"Yeah, but…"

I cast a subtle look back at the table. I've seen that expression often enough. "She'll wait."

∞∞∞∞

Hey @JesseEverett99, saw this today and thought of you. #yourewelcome

Well, look at that. I stare at the photo of a "now hiring" sign in the window of a fast food restaurant. This one actually makes me chuckle.

"What's so funny?" Reece asks without looking away from the road. The other guys are asleep in the back. I was almost out too until my screen lit up.

"Nothing. Just more shit from Mila."

He shoots me a glance. "Seriously? She's still ripping on you?"

Doubt he sees my shrug in the dark. "Yeah."

"Damn. That's not right. Sorry, man."

"Whatever. I'm over it."

Enough to type back:

Thanks @MilaTaylorRocks. You get an employee bonus for referrals or something? Tell your boss I'm free for an interview.

4: Buzz-Chasing

I wait five days to text Maria with the location of a local gig we're playing. This one is bigger than the Englewood living room where we met and a venue we've hit a couple of times before. They also let us use our own audio equipment so we call our buddy Jay to run front of house for us.

"Been a minute, huh?" Jay says, approaching our trailer as we unload.

"Hey, man! Good to see you," Parker replies. Handclasps and back-pounding all around before our guest asks what he can do.

"We're still unloading but most of the audio stuff is inside if you want to start working on that," I say.

"You got it. Anything I need to know? Now that you're superstars and all."

I huff a laugh. "Right. For about fifteen seconds. Nah same equipment as before, just a new IEM system."

"Plus I run two guitars now," Reece adds. Ah yes. That too.

"I'm using a seven-piece kit tonight," Derrick calls over.

Jay salutes and grabs a couple cases on his way inside.

"Damn, I missed that guy," Parkers says.

I smirk. "Yep. Another reason labels blow."

"Tommie was fine."

"Yeah, but he's not Jay. I swear even by the end of the tour, the dude still didn't get our music. The playbacks were brutal."

Parker doesn't bother arguing. We'd spent enough hours collectively lamenting the loss of Jay to make further defense impossible.

"Well, regardless, we've got him back and tonight will be epic," he says.

Shiny dark hair and suggestive brown eyes flutter through my brain. Yeah, it just might be.

∞∞∞∞

The room is too big, too crowded for me to find her, but she finds me by pushing up against the stage. I add a targeted grin to the lyrics when I spot her during "Nothing I Want." Definitely the wrong song for our visual reunion, but I'll make it up to her after the show.

Her gaze locks on me, travels over my body with blood-pounding intensity. She stokes the surge of stage adrenaline already gusting through me. Her expression has us clawing each other at the after party. Or in our van. Or—honestly, I don't give a damn. I'd follow this girl back to her dorm room if she insisted.

"Stop beggin' for the hunt, babe. You've got nothing I want.
Hey—
Keep checkin' for clues, cuz I refuse your bait.

Just wait. Your games were a mistake. Hey—
Maybe your lies work on other guys but this one's checking out.
You've got nothing I want.
Nothing, no, no, nothing I want."

I love hitting the tag at the end with a sick run. Why? Because I can. Because it makes girls shiver and record execs shit themselves at the thought of what we could be if only we had their guidance. But right now, it just feels good to let go. Luke once told me the music always comes first, but even he never understood what that means to me. How dangerous it is to give it unchecked power. On stage though? In the heat of the lights and internal electricity pulsing through my bloodstream, music is everything. It's infinite, transformative, and for a few minutes I do get lost. I not only believe Luke is right, but that I can actually live that motto. I can survive the music.

It's after we're packed up and I crash from that natural high that my dependent brain demands inferior replacements. I'm not naïve. I get it. I'm just too weak to fight on my own.

Will. Power.

What a messed-up combination of words when it's a trait that can measure zero. Zeropower. That's Jesse Everett.

∞∞∞∞

Party smart.

Maria's plan seems harmless enough. The campus isn't far and her roommate is away for the weekend. The topic of substances comes up, but that's standard after-party small talk. I tell the guys where I'll be and ignore Parker's *cautious uncle* look.

"Almost there," she purrs, curving bright red lips while tugging me through a maze of hallways. I've been to the Temple campus several times, and apparently, I misunderstood the plan. Her apartment is off university property.

The building is sketchy at best, and suddenly *party smart* becomes an obnoxious sign flashing in my head. Is it smart to follow a relative stranger back to an unknown location for an unknown activity? This is almost exactly what happened in Newark. But my willpower works best on shooting *down* red flags.

Exaggerated bass lines thump through the hallway long before we approach an open door crammed with drunken college students.

"This okay?" Maria shouts back to me, still gripping my hand.

I shrug and let her pull me through the human gate into every other college party I've been to. This is the kind of event where connections are made on a visceral level. It's too loud for conversation, too dark for meaningful looks.

We fill plastic cups with vodka, and she drags me to the living room where couples are engaged in a wide range of interaction. Maria takes a healthy gulp of her drink and loops her arms around my neck. Her body rushes against mine, connecting us in all the right places. I adjust to swallow some of my own booze.

We get a few looks, but no obvious star-gazing. It's dark, and honestly, I'm not big enough to be recognized out of context. It's only happened a few times, at after-show bar breaks where fans expect to find us.

Now, though. I don't know. Something feels off in this moment. Maria takes some serious liberties with my body for someone I've spoken thirty words to—not that a hot girl's attention is something I'm against.

Her aggressive hands become aggressive kisses, and I'm wondering if she expects to get down to it right here. We wouldn't be the only couple. I'm seriously considering it when she starts pushing us through the crowd and into a vacant bedroom.

"Is it weird that this room is empty?"

Her grin is all naughty rebel as she shoves me on the bed. "No. No one's allowed back here."

"And yet…"

"Except me."

"Ah. And who are *you*, exactly?"

"I'm the girl you won't forget."

My eyes sift over her, reading clues, evaluating history. "Really. That's some serious confidence."

"Not confidence—a promise."

"Hmm." I flip her on her back so I can test those flimsy bra straps. "Show me."

The satin fabric slides away to expose smooth skin that's begging for a taste. Her soft moan—*damn*. She reaches for my shirt, and I help shrug it off. She tastes like a color. Strawberry-red. It's been a while since I've tasted red.

"Wait, don't you want to get high first?" she breathes against my neck, hands sliding down my chest. "I'm prepared."

Blood competes with the bass pounding in my ears. "Huh?"

"It's cool." She shifts away and reaches for something.

"Nah, thanks though."

I tug her back to the bed and take another hit of her skin instead. Deep, sweet. Maybe more like pomegranate red. Intoxicating.

"You sure? I got it just for you."

I stiffen and notice the bag in her hand. She shakes it with a grin that carves into my stomach. Who is this girl again?

"Is that blow?"

"It's legit, I swear."

Right. I push up from the mattress. "Thanks, but I should probably take off."

"Are you bailing?"

"I have an interview in the morning."

"Seriously? You're turning down sex and a good high?" She holds up the bag.

I reach for my shirt. "It's not personal."

"No? I thought you loved to party. Is it because my stuff isn't good enough? Do you need something better? I can get whatever you want. You like oxy, right?" She's sincerely asking me that question. The fuck?

"No, it's because I don't know who the hell you are and I'm not a fucking junkie." Thankfully, the door is well-within reach.

"Jesse, wait!" I study her hand on my arm before meeting those lying eyes. "I'm sorry. Just, don't go."

"What is this? You a dealer or something? A cop?"

She seems too shocked to be either. "No, of course not. I just thought..."

"You thought what? Go ahead. Finish your *thought*."

She quiets with the look I've seen too many times.

"Don't believe everything you read," I say, and leave her alone with her "bait."

∞∞∞∞

"You're home."

Parker's a freaking detective tonight.

"Yep. That okay?" I pull open the fridge and search for a beer.

"Of course. Just didn't expect you when you left with that hottie from the show."

"Yeah, well, that *hottie* wasn't actually interested in me."

"What? She was all over you."

"She was a buzz-chaser. Not even a good one."

"Ah... Sorry, dude."

"Whatever. What are you working on?"

"Englewood wants us back."

"Oh yeah? Can we bring Jay this time?" *Irritated Accountant* look again. "What? It's a legit ask if they want us back."

"Maybe we should be grateful someone even wants us."

"What about the killer lawn party and bowling alley we booked?" He typically doesn't find me as funny as I do.

"Asshole. How's that new song coming?"

"I'm thinking key of B."

"And?"

"That's as far as I got." Apparently, that's not funny either.

"Not a great pitch, Jess. 'Our new track will be in B.'"

"Or not. Can't nail down the key until it's written."

"'Our new track *could* be in B.'"

"Ocean Ceiling is still up for grabs."

"Pass."

My phone buzzes, and I glance down.

Have you seen the new ranch-flavored kitten brains @JesseEverett99? Delicious. #soworththecalories

Unbelievable. Parker is back to his laptop and misses my glare.

Wow @MilaTaylorrocks. Hope you have a gym membership. #dotheycomeinbulk

"I'm gonna go write."

Parker's skepticism turns to approval when he sees my face. "Good."

5: NOT WORTH THE PAIN

I didn't get far last night before crashing. The music knows I'm a fraud and doesn't appreciate when I rebel. I crawl toward consciousness to find a text from Maria that doesn't help either. She's sorry and wants to see me again. I'm not surprised, but it's also not the first time someone's treated me like shit because they thought they knew me from the tabloids. I ignore her plea and reach for my guitar instead.

Last night's scribbles are crap. Garage band lyrics, not a stadium masterpiece. The key of B is a hard no. D might work if I had words that didn't make me want to gouge my eyes out. I need to *own* Mila Taylor with this one.

What a joke. Own her ridicule maybe. I rip the page out and hurl it on the floor.

Minutes become hours. I only know this from the periodic interruptions that are getting harder and harder to ignore. The pile of lyrical trash on my floor is now a full-on monument to my failure.

I flinch at the latest thump on my door. "Hey, man, you eating today?" Reece this time. Do they have a *Bother Jesse Schedule*?

"Nah. Hey what do you think of this?" I play the progression I've been working on, the last branch of hope for this wasted effort. His face echoes my thoughts. "Yeah. It's shit, right?"

"No. It's just…"

"Shit."

"Average."

Which is worse than shit.

"But it could still work!" he rushes out. "I mean—"

He quiets at my glare. "Don't." I tear the page out and add it to the pile. The music is laughing. Fucking cackling in the shadows at my pathetic attempts.

"You've been at it for a while. Come take a break."

I hear him, but I'm too busy slamming new words into the paper. My pen works mainly in protest because it's only transcribing incoherent thoughts at this point.

Swing, fling, ring.

I read through the new lyrics that blow even more than the last ones. I don't know when Reece gives up, but I'm alone when I finally check the door.

Cling. Sling.

I press my palms against my eyes.

Bring. Wing.

Been, wind, sin. Stars glisten behind my lids. I push harder. *Drink, sink, think.*

Sin. Sin, sin, sin.

"Fuck!" This time it's the entire notebook that flies across the room.

I thread my hands through my hair and pull. Who the hell am I kidding? Maybe they're right about me. I'm no genius. I'm a pretender who got lucky.

Overrated. Talent-wasted.

I reach for the bottle tucked between my bed and the wall. It's emptier than I remember and not nearly enough to get me through the day. I don't even want to think about surviving the night.

I call Natasha. I need my ocean ceiling back.

∞∞∞

Click. Click, click, click.

I squint toward the annoying tick and try to swat it away. It only intensifies into voices. Fingers. The clicking becomes fire on my face. And again. A third time until finally, images materialize in the darkness.

"He's waking up."

"Jess, hey." Another sting, and I mutter a curse.

"What the hell?" I try to push myself higher, but my limbs rebel.

"I knew we should've made him take a break. You know how he gets."

Damn hypocrites. They beg me to write, then freak out when I commit.

"Yeah, but he seemed good Saturday night."

Saturday night?

"What time is it?" I groan.

"You mean what day is it?"

I'm starting to sober up enough to read emotion, and Parker is concerned. Also pissed. A few more seconds and it becomes *pissed-concern.*

"I just needed to take a break."

"Well, you fucking got one. Almost eighteen hours, dude. You were moving and mumbling crap, which is the only reason you're not in the hospital." Now, he's just pissed.

"Thanks for being patient, man."

"Patient? Fuck you, Jesse! This has to stop!"

What's the word for beyond pissed? My brain isn't working yet. Fortunately, the other guys retreated from the inevitable brother fight once they confirmed I'm alive.

"Sorry. Must have been a bad mix."

"No, you know who's sorry? I am. This is my fault."

A most insincere confession if ever I heard one.

"Yes, that's right. I blame myself. I never should have asked you to be the person you could be. The person we need! Because I get it now. You can't be that person without fucking yourself up, can you? You can't separate the art from your wounds. The magic is in the darkness, your fucking *ocean ceilings*, so what are we supposed to do? What do we do with that, Jess?"

I can't tell if the numbness is from the substances still assaulting my nerves or my brother's explosion of truth. Mostly, I'm surprised he's only figuring this out now. I thought it was pretty obvious I'm destined for a tragic end since the day I was born. I don't live—I function. And create. If I can't create, I stop functioning. It's an impossible cycle and a battle I've been losing for as long as I can remember. His fists clench as if he wants to melt them into my face. I wouldn't mind a good blow or two to wake me up.

"I'm not worth the pain, brother." I push the conclusion of his truth into the silence, immobile as my words soak the air around us. His fiery eyes train on me, then soften. It's a long look, filled with history and two lifetimes of pain.

"It doesn't even matter if that's true. Don't you get that?" His expression is laced with too much for my foggy head to interpret. "You're my brother. You're all I have. I don't get a choice, so fuck you for choosing this for me."

He doesn't wait for a response. I'm still breathing today. That's where his standard is now.

It's the worst possible moment for my phone to buzz.

Hiya Burger Prince,

Loving the tour schedule on your website. You got many birthday parties in there? You might as well offer a pizza and drink package to take advantage of the upsell.

xo
MT

* * * * *

Hey Mila,

Fuck you.

J

* * * * *

You wouldn't know what to do with me.

MT

I could block the address. I should block it. But if I did that, who would be around to remind me of the truth everyone else seems too fucking scared to admit?

6: REGRETS

The guys manage to get me out of bed for our next date. When we pull up to an old mansion straight out of a Poe story, maybe I'm even looking forward to this one.

"Dude! Check this place out." Derrick is excited. No surprise there, but then, he might be onto something. Shimmering tiles checker old stone walls. The gothic-looking building even has a mossy cape cascading down its left side. Legit turrets jut from the roof and have me squinting through cloudy glass in search of a princess or something.

"This is a museum?" I ask. Parker seems damn proud of himself as we climb out of the van. Four hours straight of driving leaves us all stretching our limbs on the parking lot, gazes drifting in evaluation of our latest venue.

"Do you think it has a dungeon?" Derrick asks.

"It's Pennsylvania," I say.

"So?"

"So... never mind." I turn to Parker instead. "Who's our contact?"

"Stella. She said to go in and ask for her at the desk. She'll show us where to set up."

The building doesn't seem big enough to pay what they are—until we go inside. Far from the undersized rooms of typical historic structures, this one opens into a vast wonderland of medieval fantasy. Giant tapestries hang from a cathedral ceiling and stained glass spreads up most of the eastern wall. I'd give up my Les Paul to see a sunrise in this place.

"Pretty sweet," Parker says, tone reverent as he pulls up beside me.

"It's incredible." I know my wide eyes probably make me look five years younger, but this is—

"Dude, swords! Let's go fight some dragons and shit." Derrick.

I send a glare toward the anachronism. "I don't think they want us touching their exhibits."

"We need to set up anyway," Parker adds. "I'm going to find Stella."

Which leaves me free to explore.

Paintings, weapons, furniture, clothing. This place is designed to fill a cosplay cult's wet dream. Hell, I'd participate just to rock one of those suits of armor.

"Amazing, isn't it?"

I flinch at the interruption by a gorgeous redhead.

"Jesse, right?"

"Hey."

"I'm Stella." She's wearing a tight black top and ripped jeans to go with a smolder that wreaks havoc on a guy's dick.

"You work here?"

"I do. Not what you were expecting?"

I can't help but smile at that—and the way each of her curves competes for my attention. The fire in my groin wants all of them.

At least my head remembers previous business. "The guys are looking for you so we can set up."

"They already found me. Now they're looking for you."

"They'll manage." I turn back to the armor I'd been admiring. She moves close enough to cement herself in my awareness. God, she smells good. "Do you think this getup would rust in the rain? You know tinman in the *Wizard of Oz* style?" My voice is intimate, like we've had lots of conversations like this.

She squints at the intricate clasps connecting the metal suit. "Certainly would take some of the magic out of the joust if it did."

"I bet this thing weighs a ton."

"You could handle it. I watched you unload your trailer and carry your equipment."

Damn. No chance she's the groupie-type, but the way her stare travels over my body…

"Yeah, we've been doing this for a long time."

"How long?"

"Depends. Technically, six years."

I'm not sure why she seems surprised by that. "Really? You look young."

Are we doing this? Right here in front of the ghost of a 14th century knight?

"Well, with the start Parker and I had, it was either music or prison by the time I was seventeen. We decided to go for it. We had nothing to lose."

"You started your band at seventeen?"

I shoot another quick glance. She's hanging on strong to these disclosures. Tight, like that thin piece of fabric clinging to her incredible chest. I'm not used to interest in the non-rocker part of me.

"No, that's when we started touring and trying to make it. We started the band when I was fifteen. Parker was out of the foster system by then, and I moved in with him."

"Foster system?"

Tinman is as confused as I am about why my story is exploding out to this woman. "Anyway, I need to go check in with the guys and help set up. It was good to see you."

"Mind if I tag along?"

I don't actually have an answer to that, a fact Derrick makes irrelevant.

"Hey! ...*you*. You're the girl."

"Or Stella. Whatever," she says, holding out her hand.

Derrick kisses it. Inspired by the surroundings, I guess? "It's a pleasure, *my lady*." Yep.

"Are they ready for us?" I interrupt, because what the hell?

Derrick's little jig is just as confusing. "Reece, Parker, and Jay are still unloading. They sent me to find you. Dude, did you see the chamber pot collection? So sick!"

There's a lot more information to be known about the chamber pots as we make our way back to the great room, and Derrick doesn't hold back. Stella and I exchange a commiserating look when he finally gets distracted by our gear—which also requires the museum jig, apparently.

She studies his animated movements. "Wow. He's..."

"A lot."

She snickers. "I should check on everything and make sure we're on schedule. I wasn't involved with hospitality for this event, but let me know if you're missing anything."

"You mean free parking? That's about the only rider we can get through since our epic collapse."

Her gaze settles on me. "What do you mean?"

I thought that was pretty self-explanatory. "I mean, since our label dropped us we have no leverage. We're back to where we were five years ago."

"Oh? Your brother didn't mention any of that when we confirmed last week."

"Yeah, well, that's Parker."

"In what way?"

"He still believes in shit."

"And you don't?"

"Nah. Music is in my blood. I play it because I have to. The rest is bull." The way she's considering my words—so confusing. "Hey—"

"Yo, Jess! You helping or what?" Parker shouts over to me. "T and A is for later, dude!"

"Nice, Park. Sorry," I say to Stella whose furrowed brow has smoothed into a grin.

"I'll go check with catering to make sure your water bottles and pretzels are ready."

I laugh. "Thanks." Our gazes linger through a smile that suggests this conversation just started.

∞∞∞∞

The house is packed. I expect the crowd to be stuffy socialites putting their trust funds to benevolent use, but there's actually a good mix. A few guests hover around the perimeter cocktail tables, while the rest gather in anticipation of the eruption about to come from our makeshift stage. With Jay running sound they're sure to be transported to a new dimension. Stella is off to the side, shooting me knowing smiles that scream, "I'm special in this crowd." She's not wrong.

Derrick counts us off, and it's through the pulse of our opening intro that I croon a greeting to the room. The crowd roars in response and the volume stays hot. This is just how I like it. Loud, passionate chaos that fills voids and erases history.

I dig hard into "Candlelight," a classic that never fails to draw a response. At the second pre-chorus, I shove the guitar around to my back and yank the mic off the stand. The crowd tenses in anticipation at the build, and I play it up for the ultimate eruption into the chorus.

Derrick hits the downbeat and...

Wham!

Bodies jumping, baseline raging, Derrick slamming toms, cymbals, snares, and kicks. Yeah, we're epic again. I hold the mic over the crowd and our music explodes from the impromptu fan choir on the floor into the rafters high above our heads. I pull the monitor out of my left ear so I can disappear into the echo I'd typically despise. This place is a nightmare for acoustics but it *feels* like magic. It's here that I can let go. Forget I'm not good enough and actually believe my soul is locked in the right place at the right time. I'm safe. Real. Past, present, and future connect in one euphoric moment where the universe makes sense. That's "music" to an unwanted Philly boy who's never had anything else.

The music comes first.

I pull the mic back, singing, screaming, pouring my soul out for myself as much as these paying witnesses. It's obstinate, and beautiful, and glorious, and then it ends. The encore fades out, the lights come up, and suddenly you're just a Philly boy standing in a crowd of strangers.

My smile is trained for this moment. Adoration is a gateway drug. Once you taste it, the music stops coming first. Adoration comes first. And when it's sucked away—

Crash.

"Hey, you okay?"

I rip my fake smile from the current face and shove it toward the new one. It falters at Stella's searching gaze. Why isn't she smiling? This is the part of the night where everyone smiles.

"Fine, why?"

"Jesse Everett! Omigod!" A troop of fangirls shoves its way between us, pens and flyers waving.

"We love you!"

"You were amazing."

"Will you sign this?"

Will you?

Will you?

Smile. Smile. Smile.

"Thanks," I say through auto-scribbles. The squeals continue after I shift my fake smile to the next in line. This smile gets me an invitation to go out and a request for a photo. I'm game for the photo. Then the next. And the next.

Stella's attention is palpable through the groupie barricade separating us, and it's getting harder to maintain The Smile. I don't like that she sees through it. My gaze keeps finding its way to her against my will, each time helping the hypocrite inside claw its way to my face. I block her to preserve the Smile Session.

It feels like hours before we're finally free to retreat to the space converted to a green room. The remaining fans groan as we wave goodbye, but there's only one way to empty a venue like this. I let Stella follow us back.

"Hey." She grabs my arm before we reach the others. They're already laughing and attacking the beer inside.

I turn, but she doesn't speak. Instead, it's those eyes again, looking for something. *Saying* something I interpret but don't want to accept.

"Have fun?" I ask.

My deflection doesn't work, and the fingers on my arm slide down to lace with mine.

"You're complicated," she says.

I swallow the lump of truth knotting in my throat. "Aren't most musicians?"

Her hand tightens in response. The other finds my face and directs me toward her. "No," she whispers, painted nail tracing my jaw. Her gaze locks on my lips; mouthwatering curves press me into submission. I'm all about museums.

∞∞∞

We barely make it to a vacant room before I have her shoved against the door. Her top peels off to expose the most incredible gems swelling from dark gray lace. She moans as I work my way down her neck and free them.

"You too," she says, fists crushing my shirt. I help her drag it over my head, and she smooths the hair from my eyes.

It's a second that takes days, weeks, as unspoken messages pass between us.

I lean in and brush my lips on hers. "Is this really what you want?"

"You?"

"In a storage closet?"

"I'd take you in a bathroom right now," she murmurs.

I'm on fire, harder than I've been in a long time. "You taste so good, baby." She does. Raspberries. Intense, dark red, and I'm dying to know what I'll find beneath those tight jeans.

"You were amazing," she says.

"Mmmhmm." Her skin, her hair, her mouth. I want it all. I drop down, sliding my hands along firm thighs, and unhook a clasp.

"I mean it, Jesse. Something happens to you when you perform. You transcend." She grips my hair and tilts my head back so I absorb her words.

"I told you. Music is all I have. It's what I am."

"I believe you."

Her gaze falls to her fingers absently tugging a lock of my hair. "You make people feel. Things they're not supposed to."

Concerned, I straighten and tip her chin up. "Hey, you okay?"

She bites her lip. Sucks in a breath. There's a gloss in her eyes that shouldn't be there. Not in a moment when we're supposed to be flushed with need.

Her head moves in the wrong direction for this scenario.

"I'm sorry," she whispers.

"Sorry for what?"

Her lashes squeeze shut. "This. I can't... You're just so... Ah!"

She slips from my arms, turns away.

"Stella." I pull her around and brush her wet cheek with my thumb. "What's going on?"

"I'm so sorry! I... I'm seeing someone."

Oh god.

"I have to go!" The words stumble out as she pulls open the door.

"Wait!"

But she's already halfway down the hall.

"Dammit!" I punch the door in frustration.

∞∞∞

I find a lingering groupie to finish what Stella started. I'm polite and attentive, but yeah, it's just a Smile Session for my dick. She doesn't seem to mind. She doesn't seem interested in anything except discussing how hot I am and how much she disagrees with Mila Taylor.

I close my eyes when she finally commits and stops talking. Except now it's Mila Taylor in my brain as this girl rewards me for being *so so hot*. I let her enjoy her fifteen with a rock star. Hell, I even return the favor a few times because I'm not a total asshole.

Her name is K-something. She works retail. She says a lot of other things I miss while we're cleaning up and I'm consumed by thoughts of Stella and Mila.

"Want a drink?" I ask. Again, polite.

"Wow! Seriously?"

I'm not sure what she thinks I meant by that, but it's clearly not what I'm offering. "Sure. I have some things I need to finish up, but you can chill in the green room if you want."

"Ahhh!"

I force a half-smile and lead her to the promised land. She becomes Parker's problem when I toss him an apologetic look and duck back out of the room.

My phone buzzes and I glance down to find an e-mail. A hurricane rips through my veins at the name, and I draw in a deep breath.

Hiya BP,

I've not heard much from you, I was getting worried. Just wondering if you'll send me a pic of you in your new uniform.

Ta.
MT

* * * * *

I'm starting to think that's not really the pic you want.
J

7: TRAITORS

"What do you think of a beach tour?"

This must be today's random Tuesday morning topic brought to you by Parker Everett. Derrick is crunching down the biggest bowl of children's cereal I've ever seen; Reece is changing his strings.

"A beach tour? Is that a thing?" I ask, dumping coffee down my throat like it's my new job. Heh, Mila's got me planning now. Jesse Everett: Barista.

"You know what I mean. We line up a bunch of clubs and bars down the coast and —"

"It's January." Minor detail, apparently.

Parker grunts. "Do you have a better idea?"

"Sure. How about anything that doesn't include the beach in the dead of winter?"

Eye-roll from Parker. Clearly, I'm not seeing his vision. "I'm not talking about Wildwood, obviously. But what if we go down south?"

"Oh right, because the retirees totally dig our music." I earn a flat-out eye-*dart* for that one.

"I'm trying here, Jess. We need something."

"What about a ski lodge tour? Or maybe we could open for Santa."

Derrick snorts through his fruity crap and shrugs when Parker turns the glare on him. "What? A sleigh tour would be sweet. I bet even Reece would get laid."

"Shut up," Reece barks from the couch. "I have a girlfriend."

"Oh right. *Gina*." Derrick sings her name like he's suddenly an opera house baritone.

Reece's face scrunches into defensive mode, a common reaction when this mysterious girlfriend we've never met comes up. I'm with Derrick. Gina is imaginary. Or a dude he met on the internet.

"What about a Caribbean tour?" Reece suggests. I guess throwing out stupid ideas beats defending *Gina*.

"Way too expensive," I say.

"We could just sit around the house like losers for the rest of our lives," Parker mutters.

I pour another cup. "Now you're thinking practically. I like it."

Parker doesn't and shuts his laptop. "Jess, we need to call Jonas."

My blood pressure instinctively climbs through my body. "Hilarious."

"I'm serious."

I snap my gaze to his and meet stony resolve.

"Not a chance in hell."

"What choice do we have?" Desperation is not a good look on Parker—especially when it involves the man who donated his sperm to our existence.

"Okay, I'm out. Catch you later." Derrick practically throws his bowl in the sink as he flees to *anywhere* else. Reece turns up the TV in the next room.

"Have you lost your mind?" I ask the remaining bandmate. My limbs suddenly feel so stiff I have to lean against the counter for support.

"He knows people, Jess."

"Yeah? So do we."

"He got us the deal with SauerStreet."

Parker could have just punched me in the stomach. That would've been way more pleasant. "That's your argument?"

He sighs, big-brother-style. "No, sorry. What you did for us — the band — it was epic, and he... It pissed me off too, but, dude, this is different. He's different, and we need another push."

"Not from him."

"He wants to make things right."

My spine straightens into a steel rod, blood pounding through my head and driving furious eye-bullets toward my brother. "Are you kidding me? You must be fucking kidding me right now."

"Jess, it's been a couple years. He's — "

"Wait, have you been seeing him?" My voice is a growl now, my hands shaking. He's not looking at me which makes my stomach churn. I'm not a volatile person. You have to care about shit to get angry, but right now. Yeah, this might be the one thing I care about.

I shove away from the counter. "Fuck you, Parker."

"Jesse, come on! Let's just — "

I don't hear the rest. I'm already in my room, door slammed behind me. I lock my fingers on my head as I pace from one creaky floorboard to the next. Betrayal. That's the word that flashes through my head.

TRAITOR.

"Fuck!" I scream, flinging the first thing I grab across the room. A tattered notebook slams into the wall and flutters to its death on the floor. I stare at the feathered pages for a long time. Marked and scarred they taunt me from their grave, reminding me of all the moments I felt this pain. I hate them. Love them. Need them. Because that's when the words come. They shoot up my limbs and lodge in my brain as a parasite until I can free them into music.

Today I'm infected.

I stomp across the room and yank the pages from the floor. My desk is a disaster of lazy moments, so I fish out a pencil and drop to the bed instead. I draw in a deep breath, brace myself for hell—and write.

∞∞∞∞

Time is irrelevant when the music comes. Days, hours, minutes—I have no idea how much I've lost.

Eyes rounder and redder than any drug-induced reaction stare back at me from the mirror above the sink in the bathroom. Dark hair is carelessly tucked behind my ears with lost strands drifting over my face. I look like a man possessed because I am. The music owns me. Unhealthy? Maybe, but it was never a choice. *Jonas* made sure of that when he fathered a clone and abandoned him to fight the tortured artist gene alone.

*Little light of mine. Flicker, flicker burn, until I learn to slay the
ghost of hope, the fucking joke you've made of me.*

*Little friend of mine. Don't be kind when you grind our past
into lasting crimes that might just be the end of me.*

Traitor. Fool me once.
Traitor. Fool me twice.
That knife you hold is so damn pretty.
How's it look in my back? Hey hey

My reaction time is lacking
No backtracking now that you've got me on the prowl
Hey hey
I'm looking at you, traitor, faker, promise-breaker,
Re-arranger of the lies we've tried to bury
Hey hey
I'm looking at you, pretender, mender, truth-blender
Defender of the game I thought we ended
Yeah, yeah, I'm looking at you

My arms brace on the sink in faulty support of my body.
Traitor. Faker. Promise-breaker.

Flashing lights. Ashy skin stretched over sharp
cheekbones. *"You'll need to come with us, kid."* Come with us
to a stranger's house. To another stranger's house. And
another. To a fifteen-bedroom prison of other abandoned
teenagers.

Don't be kind. Don't be kind. Don't be kind.

I press my fists into burning eyes.

A needle. A dusty plaque with a gold record hanging in crooked perfection for its owner to betray. A guitar missing two strings. When has it last been touched? Certainly not by the gray, motionless, junkie-hands draped on the floor.

Pretender. Truth-blender.

"*I'm okay, Jesse. I'll be fine.*" Final words from a father to his son before the child became a victim.

Fool me twice.

"Jess?"

I jump at the knock on the bathroom door.

Parker pulls it open. "You—" He stops, stance softening when he sees my face. "You got one."

I nod.

"Is it good?"

I nod again and close my eyes as something hot and wet leaks over my pupils. Then I'm in his arms, secured by the only person who has ever kept his promise.

Promise-keeper.

"What day is it?" I ask.

"Thursday."

Pressure clamps down on my chest. Three days. I've been locked up for three fucking days. I drag in a throat-full of air.

"Can I hear it?" he asks quietly.

I nod against his shoulder. Relief seeps from him at my response.

"What's it called?"

"'Jonas.'"

8: CONFESSIONS

The guys love "Jonas." After one run-through, they want to lay down a work-tape so they can start building their parts. I push for a bass-driven intro that locks in with Derrick on the kick and hi-hat through verse one. The full explosion will come on the chorus when I'll let loose over Parker's backing vocals. There's a subtle trap element to this song, so we'll need more production than usual, but the band is game. We're all about pushing the limits of the alternative genre, and now that we're indie, have nothing holding us back.

"Dude, this song is sick," Derrick says, wiping off the sweat as we finish our recording.

"The crowd will go ape-shit," Reece adds.

Parker evaluates me. He loves the song, but there's a hidden track only the two of us can hear. I force a half-smile.

I'm good.

His eyebrows knit together, and I remove any chance of interference by adjusting to pack up my gear. I'm snapping the case shut when my phone buzzes.

Come over tonight?

A text from Natasha. After the last few days I've had, there's no one I'd rather see.

Give me an hour.

∞∞∞∞

Natasha's grin says it all. My turn this time.

She inhales as I flip her on her back and rip my shirt off. I graze her neck and kiss my way down exposed skin.

Thanks to my visiting angel, "Jonas" hovers far from me now. A distance that allows my frantic brain to breathe again, and I sigh right along with it as I sink into the abyss of Natasha's body. She arches against my mouth. One, two— her fists dig into the sheets.

"Jess…" She groans. I know what she wants. I know this body almost as well as my own. Three, four, and—"Ahh. Jess!"

I grip her thighs to help her ride the high for as long as possible. It's only fair for what she gives me. She threads her hands into my hair and pulls me up for a long, deep kiss.

"I love you," she breathes. "I want…" Her eyes snap open to meet my stare.

Shit.

"Sorry, I didn't mean that," she rushes out.

I push off her and roll to my back.

"I… I'm sorry. It's just… Maybe I want more. With you."

I close my eyes as her words echo through my brain, chip at my peace. She's supposed to know the rules.

"I want to know," she says softly.

"Know what?"

"Everything. What's in here." She brushes her fingers along my temple, and I have to calm the rising panic. "I can tell there's so much going on. I want more than sex."

"Nat..." I rub a hand over my face, suddenly exhausted. Natasha is the courier of my oasis. My break from the weight of existing.

"You don't feel the same for me," she says.

I don't love. "How much do I owe you?"

∞∞∞

I won't call Natasha again. It's not fair to her. I'll have to find a new angel, preferably one who won't be attracted to my mess. My phone buzzes, and I grab it from the floor by my bed.

Parker wants to know if I'm coming out of my room today. Damn, I must be in bad shape if Mr. Intrusive won't even risk a knock on my door.

I'm tapping out a response when another message flashes across my screen.

Hey @JesseEverett99. I'm a tad gutted that you've given up without a fight. Is the burger business so rewarding? #putthatlipaway

Fuck, for real? A fire shoots through my blood with enough force to ignite lazy fingers.

Hey @MilaTaylorRocks. Things are great. We're now serving a "Shite Burger" in honor of you.

Not my best work, but that woman triggers an instinctive response that doesn't leave room for reflection. Heaven knows why I've been given talent I can't control, and it guts me when people like Mila Taylor strike at the core of my battle.

I lay my phone back on the floor and stare at my now-boring ceiling.

Mila Taylor's punching bag. Is that my legacy? I've never been a close follower of her "work," but I'm pretty sure I'm special in her dedication to ripping me down. Did I kick her puppy? Insult her home planet? Have my crimes against music really been serious enough to earn this sentence? Wait until she hears "Jonas." Just...

I'm looking at you, pretender, mender, truth-blender
Defender of the game I thought we ended
Yeah, yeah, I'm looking at you

Another phone alert, and I lean over for a look at the display. *No fucking way.*

I open the e-mail, and sure enough:

>> *I'm starting to think that's not really the pic you want.*
J

*****

You're alright, love. I've found everything I need. You have really enthusiastic fans.

I follow the link she shared and huff a laugh. Photos, articles, more photos. Damn, so many shirtless pictures of me on this fan's public shrine. I don't even remember half of these moments she's immortalized. I'll never get used to this shit.

Blood pounds through me as I look, imagining Mila Taylor searching my name. Scrolling through image after image, and what? Smirking? Or admiring the view enough to drag me back for more.

I clench my jaw. Time to conduct a search of my own. I type in her name and... *damn*. Mila Taylor is breathtaking.

∞∞∞

I don't know how long I stare at her posing on the red carpet at an awards show. The A-list actor beside her looks pedestrian by comparison.

Long, dark hair, almost violet in the light, frames pale skin in loose waves. The couture gown exposes just enough to make my dick covet the rest. Yeah, so many sins in my head right now for a woman I hate. A woman who's destroyed my career and sent me crashing into my latest hell.

My search yields more facts. Mila Taylor is twenty-six and a native of Yorkshire, England where she splits residency with Manhattan, New York. Damn, bet she has a sexy accent. She's a foodie who rocketed to fame as a food blogger and social media personality. Which means she makes and breaks musicians because...?

Oh. She's the daughter of UK rock legend George Conway. Well, good for her.

I grunt, and close my laptop, but I can't get that image out of my head.

I've found everything I need.

What is it that she needs? What's she getting from me that requires constant attacks to keep my attention? I haven't played these bullshit games since Jenna Potter threw mud at me every recess in fourth grade.

Dark hair. Smooth skin. Tight… everything. God, she's hot as a hell. Who knew? Those eyes, windows into something that challenges the shit out of me. I'm not often challenged.

I'm not often alive.

I pull up my phone.

Hey, girl.

Didn't take you for the D-List stalker type. "Easy on the eye"? Should I be concerned?

J

I get a response two minutes later.

No need to worry, love. I like my blokes employed.

Yeah, I legit grin when I drop back to the mattress.

9: JONAS

A strange woman nurses a cup of coffee at our kitchen table when I emerge the following morning. Long hair up in a clip and certainly no natural color on God's green earth. If I had to guess, she's the reason for the grunting and moans from Derrick's room last night.

"What's up?" I say, grabbing a mug.

"Hey. Jesse, right?"

"Yeah. And you are?"

"Mandi. With an 'i.'"

"Ah." I offer a brief smile and return to my coffee. "Where's Derrick?"

"An errand. He said it was fine for me to stay here 'til he got back."

"An errand?" Okay, yeah, this place is too quiet. "Who else went on this 'errand'?"

I didn't think my question was as complex as her furrowed brow makes it out to be.

"Did two other guys leave with him?"

"Yeah. One had blond hair and one light brown."

Shit. "Did they say where they were going?"

"No. Just that I had to wait here."

I'm already heading back to my room as I mumble my thanks.

Where are you? I tap out to the group. *Left me alone with "Mandi"?*

No immediate response.

Hey, D. I told her you were crazy about her. You probably went out for a ring.

Derrick: Shut the fuck up.

Me: Seriously where you at?

Parker: Breakfast dude. Chill out.

Me: Without your fiancée?

Derrick: It was one date.

So not the point. As usual.

Me: I like breakfast. Thanks for the invite.

Reece: You were asleep.

Assholes. Something's up, but I'm not going to get anywhere like this. I toss my phone on the bed and drain my coffee.

I have no interest in another encounter with "Mandi" and stay in my room. Her high-pitched voice squawks through every crack and gap in the house as she blabs on her phone. So much to say about so much shit I don't want to hear. There better have been some fried egg emergency or I'm going to detonate when they get back. You bring a girl home? Don't make her my problem.

I mess around on my guitar to drown out the distraction as much as possible. "Jonas" still needs some work, and I'd love to play with the new direction on our older material as well. If alternative-rock-EDM is our new thing, then let's go all in.

It's a good half hour before I hear the main door. I rest my guitar on the stand and brace for the confrontation about to come.

"I'll call you later." Derrick's voice drifts down the hall, and Mandi's whiny response finally brings relief. She's leaving, thank god.

Once the door crashes again, I know it's safe.

"Hope you losers have a damn good…" I freeze. *The fuck?*

"Jesse…" The man's face is younger, fuller. Cleaner than it should be.

Parker steps between us. "Don't freak out, just—"

"No fucking way," I spit, and tear back to my room.

"Jesse! Will you… Jess!"

Parker's following me, and I don't understand why he's begging for a bloody nose.

TRAITOR. PROMISE-BREAKER.

Traitor. Traitor. Traitor.

The words slam against my skull as I push into my room and grab the first thing I touch. A bottle smashes into the far wall and sprays its wrath over my floor.

I scream a curse and tighten my fingers on my head as I pace the room. A piece of glass slices into my foot, but I barely notice. That pain is nothing compared to the agony in my chest.

"Jess…" Parker hovers in my doorway, gaze pleading for… something. I don't know. I don't fucking know!

"Why? Why would you bring him here?" My tone is as shattered as the bottle.

"It was the only way you'd—"

"No, no, no." Back to pacing, I tangle my fists in my hair.

"Jess, just—" He grips my arm and pulls me to a stop. "Hey."

I shake my head, refusing to look at him.

"Oh shit, you're bleeding."

I follow his gaze and flinch at the streaks of blood painting the floor. Now I feel it. The pain I can measure—fix. It feels safe. Air rushes into my lungs again.

"He's changed, Jess. I swear. I wouldn't have brought him here if I wasn't absolutely sure."

Changed. Such a lie. An irrelevant event. How does that *change* the years of hell we've already survived?

I lower myself on the bed and rest my head on my fists.

"He's clean now, Jess. Over two years sober. He's even producing again."

"Good for him."

"Just—come out. He wants to help us."

"Like last time?"

"That was a wakeup call. That's what sent him into rehab. Jess..." Parker kneels to face me. "He's our father. He's the only family we have. He fucked up. But now we have a chance to put things back together."

I glare at the traitor in front of me. "He didn't *fuck up*, Parker. Sleeping with your buddy's girlfriend is *fucking up*. Backing the trailer into a cop car is *fucking up*. What Jonas did to us—"

"He can hear you, dude," Parker hisses.

"You think I fucking care? Go to hell, Jonas!"

Parker cringes, actually looks wounded. "Please. I know you hate him, just hear him out. For the sake of the band? We spent over an hour going through his plan. It's legit. Next level stuff. Makes the SauerStreet deal look like shit."

"It *was* shit. Thanks to him."

"He didn't..." Parker shakes his head and clenches his fists. "It's not just *your* band, Jesse. It's not just *your* career on the line. We have a say too."

My chest tightens again. "Yeah, you do. If you want to work with him so much, then do it. You'll just have to find a new frontman."

∞∞∞

I knew it would be bad after Parker left. After the door crashed closed. After the daylight passed into darkness. I wasn't prepared for this.

The pressure on my lungs is excruciating. Not even the neighbor shouts interfere with the roar in my head. So many words. So much emotion, and none of it will sort into any kind of manageable shape. No, it's chaos in there. Screams, sobs, blows, and every combination in between.

I curl up on my bed and try to protect my head.

It's all right in the candlelight...

Even my vocal cords won't engage.

It's all right. It's all right.

Bullshit! It's pain.

It's lies.

It's *truth.*

It's—

My phone dings. Parker trying to get my attention and force me back to the surface?

No. A chat request. What the *hell*?

Mila: Hiya, BP. You're awake.

Jesse: No.

Mila: Har Har. Isn't it early in Pennsylvania?

Jesse: You know where I live?

Mila: I know a lot about you.

Jesse: Oh yeah? Like what?

Mila: You're tall, dark brown eyes, brown hair, nice build. And you have a small birthmark on your chest.

Jesse: Very small. You must have studied that nice build pretty hard.

Mila: I've always said you were easy on the eye. Have you only got the one tattoo?

Jesse: That you can see in pictures.

Mila: Ohh, interesting. Tell me more. Where's the one I can't see?

Jesse: Why, so you can rip me up about it in a blog post? No thanks.

Mila: Aw, put that lip away, love.

Jesse: You really didn't have to message me to tell me I have a birthmark. Must be boring over there in Yorkshire.

Mila: You know where I live?

Jesse: I know a lot about you.

Mila: Oh aye?

Jesse: Black hair, blue eyes. Prefers actors over musicians for some reason.

Mila: Oh there's a lot of reasons.

Jesse: I'm sure. Good to know I'm safe.

Mila: Yep, quite safe.

Jesse: Great. What's this about?

Mila: I'd like to propose a truce.

Jesse: Ah. Not used to people calling you out on your bullshit?

Mila: You're a brave man. I'll give you that.

Jesse: Yeah, well, thanks to you I have nothing left to lose.

Mila: And I know you're too clever to say somat like that.

Jesse: Nah, just well-acquainted with rock bottom.

Mila: Yeah right. I'm sure the son of Jonas Everett really had it tough. Let me just get my violin out.

The boulder returns, crushes my ribcage. I clench my eyes shut until it stabilizes.

You're one to talk, I type out.

Mila: Why do you think I started my career in food blogging instead of music? I only want what I can have off my own back. My doing and no one else's.

Jesse: And you think I don't?

Mila: Tell me Pops didn't put a word in and get you that deal with SauerStreet. Great bands work their arses off from nothing to get noticed. You toured with A-list talent from the off. Must have been well hard getting started when your father is an iconic producer. All I did was level the playing field.

Jesse: Fuck you. You don't know a thing about me.

And I log off.

∞∞∞∞

I stare into the darkness for a long time. Confused, furious, and completely turned on. I hate that woman so much it's ignited a fire in my gut. A blaze I can only get from the inferno of the stage anymore, at the pinnacle of locking into the moment. It's a hatred so different than the bitterness I feel for my father. This one rages hot, awakens a fight instinct that shoves my world into sharp focus.

Mila Taylor. That name has become a spark I despise and crave.

I pick up my phone and reopen the chat.

You consider yourself a journalist? Do your research.

I finally fall asleep.

10: Daylight Mugging

I wake up the following morning to a binder outside my door. After leafing through the pages, I toss it on the bed with a grunt.

Parker and Jonas' genius plan. What, I'm supposed to change my mind because they figured out how to use a three-hole punch?

"What do you want to do this weekend?" Parker asks as I shuffle into the kitchen. "Derrick and Reece just headed out on that snowboarding trip."

"How about the same thing we do every weekend?"

"Come on. There has to be something."

"We could cuddle."

I feel Parker's eye-roll in my back.

"I had an idea for Jonas," Parker says.

I'm hoping he means the song not the man. It's too early for a fist fight.

"Yeah?"

"We should layer in some orchestration throughout."

"Strings?"

"Yeah. I don't know. Maybe a simple cello on the verses and then a full-on symphony for the chorus. With that sick groove of the song, it would be cool."

"Maybe. Let's play around with it. Want to work this afternoon?"

"Can't, man." Sly smile. Waiiit...

"You have a date?"

"Maybe."

"Please tell me it's not the chick from the coffee shop."

"What if it is?"

"Two disastrous attempts weren't enough for you?"

"Third time's a charm." He shoves a croissant in his mouth, whole damn thing.

"In a hurry?" My coffee is way lazier in its journey down my throat.

"Yeah. We're doing Christmas shit."

"Christmas shit? Christmas was a month ago." Why did I ask? I don't want to know.

"Yeah, there's some tourist village or some shit up in Bucks that does Christmas forever. She wants to go look at discount wreaths and drink hot apple cider or whatever."

"Sounds amazing," I mutter, refilling my cup.

Parker shrugs into his jacket as he grabs another pastry. "Whatever. She's hot. Sweet too. You'll like her."

Uh-huh. "Well, have fun. Grab me a scented candle or something."

"I will. Anything to mask the stench of weed in this place."

∞∞∞∞

Music blasts through my stereo, filling the gaps in my consciousness. Some band called Clown Irruption, I don't know. All I care about is the pain in the lyrics, the raw agony that claws through my closed eyes and wraps itself around the daggers in my head.

The neighbors are at it again. Early today. It's not even dark yet. The echo of an indecipherable yell, then a crash. This one feels close. Wait, are they in my yard?

I turn down the volume for a better read.

"Anyone home?"

I bolt up from the bed, heart hammering. The voice is in my house, in my foyer.

"Hello?" Moving down my hallway. To my...

I'm shaking when the specter appears. Face drawn and twisted in pain, it studies me slowly.

"Jesse," it breathes out as only a ghost can.

"I'm calling the police," I hiss, reaching for my phone. Jonas grabs my wrist, and I jerk away, eyes wide. "What do you want? Why are you here?"

"Just... hear me out?"

My head shakes, violent in its protest. Instinctive because my mind is a black knot of nerves.

"You deserve better than what you got. Better than... this." His gaze scans my walls, my disheveled desk, my floor still stained with blood from last night's visit.

"Leave," I croak out.

"I'm clean, Jess! I swear it."

"Leave!"

"I want to make things right. I'm sorry for—"

"Fucking *leave*!"

A chair flies toward the door. From my hands? Probably, but I'm not in this scene anymore. No, I'm back in a shitty living room. Backpack dropping from my middle school shoulder. A third-chance guardian passed out on dirty shag carpet and demonstrating once-and-for-all where his son ranks against the synthetic peace in his veins. Back to strangers. Back to caseworkers and group homes and expectations I couldn't meet because I wasn't a normal kid. Only the unconscious bastard on the floor could've understood the weight of every thought and neuron firing through my confused brain. Only he could've helped me tame my torment. But he chose a needle. He chose strike three and the same fate for his son.

Jonas has backed into the hall now. I still see his shadow hovering, watching me from a safer vantage point.

"I'm sorry about SauerStreet," it says.

SauerStreet? Interesting how it ranks its crimes.

"I..."

I'm too impatient for whatever useless defense is coming next. "What'd you do with the money, Jonas? What'd you do with *our* money?"

I already know the answer. Flushed it through his bloodstream. He stole my art, my *soul*, and enslaved me to the corporate suits for a fucking high.

Traitor. Fool me once.

"I screwed up, Jess. I make no excuses. Just please, give me a chance."

"What makes you think I would *ever* trust you again after that?"

"I don't expect you to trust me. Just hear me out. Let me make it up—"

"Get out!"

"Jesse—"

"Out!" I'm shouting now, breaths coming in sharp hisses that can't seem to find their way to my lungs.

It's all right in the candlelight. It'll be all right.

Basement locks. Spider webs. Towers of debris haunting the shadows.

It's all right.

"Stop your goddamn crying! You want a beating too?"

Throbbing cheek. Damp floor. Icy howl through ancient concrete.

"I'm sorry! I couldn't—"

"Shut up, you little shit! No one wants to look at you."
Tattered blanket. Forgotten candle—a flicker!
It's all right. It's all right.
"Jess?"
I blink and pull myself back to the surface.
"Please just go," I whisper.
I'm looking at you, traitor, faker, promise-breaker.

∞∞∞

I can't get the filth of Jonas off me fast enough after he leaves. The memories have jammed every inch of my room, pressing on my head until I'm fighting a scream. I grab my phone and dial Natasha.

Voicemail.

I try again. Voicemail.

Stop calling me, lights up on my display, and I shove my phone in my pocket.

Fuck.

I zip up a hoodie and jog toward freedom.

∞∞∞

"Damn it!" A voice growls from the other side of the door.

My fist aches from pounding against the wood, but it'll all be better soon.

"What do you want?" The shaved head of a late-twenties thug pushes through the crack.

"Natasha here?"

"Who's asking?"

"Just tell her—"

"Jesse? Fuck."

"You know this prick, Tash?"

She nods, dark nails tapping the doorjamb. "Used to." Her gaze scans me slowly as the door opens the rest of the way. "What do you want, Jesse?"

"Can we talk?"

"Yeah right," she snorts. "Get lost."

"Wait!" I block the door with my foot when she goes to close it.

"Watch it, asshole. She ain't interested," Bald Head tells me.

I ignore him. "Just something to get me through tonight. I won't ask again." Her eyes narrow, and yeah, maybe I'm desperate. "Jonas came back."

The tapping freezes as her expression softens. "Shit. Your dad?"

I nod, pleading for one hint of mercy.

"You look familiar," Bald Dude interrupts.

Natasha shifts uncomfortably and moves to block his view. "Nah, he's no one. Just some junkie I used to know."

Bald Dude's stare turns direct. "No no. I know you."

"Not sure, man," I say, and focus back on Natasha. "Please. I'll never ask again."

"You said that last time."

"Yeah well, it's not like I was expecting Jonas to show up at my house."

"Damn. Just out of the blue? What did he want?"

Her companion/roommate/I have no idea is still slicing me up with his gaze.

"Um... just the usual bullshit."

"Looking to score?"

I shrug. "Kind of, but not drugs. He wants to help us he says."

"What?"

"I know. It's fucked up. I kicked him out. Just—"

"That band! You're the dude from that band who used to play The Wharf all the time! Damn, what was it...?" His forehead scrunches in a painful search for information. "Lemon-something. No, wait."

"Limelight?"

"Yeah!"

"No, he's not," Natasha rushes out.

Bald Dude laughs and slaps her arm. "Hilarious, Tash. Why didn't you tell us you were fucking a celebrity? Damn. Come in, come in. What do you need? We got it all, man."

"Trav...."

"Get us some drinks, will ya?" he barks at Natasha who slinks off to the kitchen with a grunt.

"Trav" makes quite the show of organizing two ratty throw pillows on a recycled couch before offering me a seat. VIP treatment for the "dude from the lemon band" I guess.

"Yo, T, guess who's here," Trav calls out.

A younger man shuffles out from an adjoining room, eyelids sagging with sleep and chemicals. Envy, anticipation, that's the burn in my stomach as I will the pleasantries to end.

"'Sup, man," the new guy says, slumping to the other end of the couch.

"This is the dude from that band," Trav says.

"T" raises his hand. "Sweet. 'Sup, man."

I doubt his vocabulary is any more developed when he's sober.

"Hey," I say. He doesn't care which band so I focus back on Trav. By now Natasha has returned with mismatched glasses of amber liquor. Her gaze locks on mine as she hands me one. She's upset? Of course she is.

"Okay, so before we talk business, I just got some new shit in you want to try." Trav crosses to a safe on the floor and pulls out a bag of large white pills. "This stuff is the shit. Here. On the house."

"What is it?"

"Cracked Pearl."

"Never heard of it. Is it like white pearl?"

"Nah, nothing like that. It's new."

He hands me one before I can protest. "Appreciate it, man, but—"

"Dude, I said *on the house*." His smile falters into something darker.

"He doesn't want it, Trav," Natasha cuts in.

"Stay out of it. The guy knows what he wants. Trust me, once you try this, you'll be changing your order."

Fuck. The warning flares blast through my head. Little shoulder-Luke is screaming at me about breaking my rules, but Jonas. The basement. Darkness. Vicious demons that circle and shriek without warning. I can't go back to that empty rowhome without a weapon.

I pop the pill in my mouth and swallow.

∞∞∞∞∞

It's dark when I come to. I groan as I try to adjust to a less awkward position. My body won't move. I squint at the unfamiliar surroundings. A barred window, a door. The only light comes from a distant streetlamp. I'm definitely not in the grimy living room where I left my consciousness.

My head throbs; sandpaper lines my mouth. Cracked Pearl, my ass.

My limbs start to cooperate, and I push up from the bed. The room spins in a manic testimony to my latest screw-up. I reach for my phone and my pulse races. Gone. So's my wallet. *Fuck!*

I stagger to my feet and lurch toward the door. It's not locked, which brings the briefest flutter of relief.

Three sets of eyes greet me from the familiar living room.

"Morning, sweet cheeks," Trav drawls.

"What the fuck was that?" I hiss. "Where's my shit?"

"Relax. We'll give it back once we're compensated."

"Excuse me?" But I'm not confused. No, this relationship is painfully clear.

"Just call your manager or whatever and we'll get this straightened out." He flashes a gun, and my heart hammers against my ribs. I send a silent plea to Natasha but she won't look at me.

"Okay, look. There's been a misunderstanding. I don't have any money."

The men snort. "Right. A big rock star like you? We looked you up while you were out."

"I'm not a big rock star. I'm not even with a label anymore."

"Whatever, dude. Fifty Gs and we're good."

I almost choke. "I'm telling you. I don't have money."

"Well, that's unfortunate. Guess you better get comfortable."

The fear starts to transform into anger. "Fuck you," I spit, heading toward the exit.

Damn, they move fast.

"T" blocks the door, while Trav crowds me from behind.

"So what, you're gonna hold me hostage? Hope your schedule is clear. I'm telling you. I'm fucking broke."

"I told you," Natasha calls over. Her gaze brushes mine before centering on the others. "I've seen his place. Trust me, you're wasting your time." She crosses her arms and leans back. "S'why I kicked his sorry ass to the curb when I found out."

Trav's glare cuts into me. Over to Natasha, then back to mine.

"Dude, you have my wallet. I've got like twenty bucks in there. Any rich bastards you know carrying a single twenty around?"

Trav pinches the bridge of his nose. "Fuck!" He slams his fist into the wall. The next one connects with my side and my vision blurs.

"Travis, stop!"

Natasha screams again when a foot collides with my ribs. My face, my groin. I try to push myself up but the blows come too fast. This is rage. Frustration. The worst kind of motivation because nothing can make it stop.

Until it does.

I'm fighting for consciousness when the violent kicks become violent pacing as the men mumble curses to each other. Natasha sobs from the couch. God, I just want them to finish this.

They grab my arms and yank me to my feet. T opens the door and Trav shoves me into the hallway. My phone and empty wallet come flying after me.

"Don't ever come back here, you fucker," he growls and slams the door.

I almost laugh before the darkness takes over again.

11: MEMORIES

I tell Parker I was mugged. I've got plenty of my own self-condemnation to keep me company and don't need to face his as well. Still, I'm on the verge of confessing if it'll stop the painful compassion.

"You need to call the police," he tells me for the fifth time.

I shift the bag of ice from my eye to my jaw. "What are they gonna do? I didn't even see the guys. They jumped me from behind."

"Still, they can—"

"Park, I love you, but you need to drop it. How was your date?"

"Fine. I got you something."

He pulls a glass container from a fancy paper bag, and a laugh leaks through my cracked lips. "Nice. What scent?"

"Uh..." He examines the label. "Spruce Tree."

"Wow. So no weed-flavor?"

"Want me to light it?"

"Sure, man."

Soon our kitchen is a winter wonderland of bagged ice and evergreen stench. I force more water down my throat to combat the nausea swirling through my stomach. Can't tell if it's from the mystery drug, beating, kidnapping, or near death experience. Just another day in the fragile life of Jesse Everett.

My phone's been buzzing in my pocket the entire time I've been sitting here, but I'm afraid to look with Parker hovering so close. I'm sure it's Natasha apologizing, asking if I'm alive. Maybe even a full-on I-told-you-so since now, in retrospect, she definitely did. I don't blame her.

"We should talk about what happened to you."

"What's there to talk about?" I hide my eyes behind the ice again.

"This is major shit, Jess! You need to share it."

Right. He'd have a whole other opinion if he knew what really happened.

"Jonas stopped by when you were gone," I say.

Parker flinches, and I'm somewhat comforted that he wasn't part of the follow-up invasion. "You're kidding. What did he want?"

"Same as before. To talk."

"And—"

"I didn't. That's why I went out for a walk."

Guilt for someone else's guilt? That's a fun one.

"I'm sorry, Jess. I thought you were ready. I thought—"

"It's over, okay? Just leave him out of our lives." I force myself up from the stool and limp toward my room. "I'm gonna lie down for a bit."

He nods. "Let me know if you need anything."

∞∞∞

Sure enough, my phone is stocked with messages when I check. A few from Natasha, but it's the one from Mila that catches my interest.

Mila: NEC Children's Home, eh?

My insides constrict as always at the mention of that place.

Jesse: You did your research.
Mila: It wasn't easy. I had to dig deep and call in some favors.
Jesse: Yeah, it's not exactly public knowledge. I'd like to keep it that way.
Mila: I'm sorry, Jesse. I didn't know.
Jesse: Most people don't.
Mila: Your father lost custody three times before you ended up in NEC.
Jesse: No one wants the teenage son of a drug addict.
Mila: How long were you there?
Jesse: Two years. I ran when I was fifteen and lived with Parker.
Mila: I bet that was hard.
Jesse: You wanted to know what being the son of Jonas Everett got me. Now you do.
Mila: What was it like at NEC?
Jesse: Right. Like I'd tell you anything.
Mila: This isn't an interview.
Jesse: No? What is it then?

No response. Yeah, because it's bullshit like everything else.

∞∞∞∞

Two AM and I can't stop shaking. The scene replays through my head with fresh clarity. I see every detail of the gun, every fiber of the carpet scratching against my face. The muffled thud of a boot in my ribs and the spray of saliva landing on my skin. Natasha's screams. The paralysis, the terror of waking up in a vacuum.

My eyes squeeze shut on their own, a rebellious attempt to block out the ghosts in my head. But my eyes are weak. Nothing stops the shouting once it starts.

Thud. Thud. Searing pain. Cold, dirt floor that catches me at the bottom of the stairs.

"Stop your goddamn crying! You want a beating too?"

I suck in a ragged breath and force my lids open again. No basement anymore, but the suffocating darkness is the same.

It's all right.

No it's not all right. I'm alive for no reason I can comprehend. I should be dead or worse. I should be...

My brain is shrieking now, so loud I'm afraid it will wake Parker. I bolt up, sweat breaking out over my body. Air filters into my lungs in short gasps. Numbness spreads over my limbs. A gun. A prison. I can't get enough oxygen. Too much oxygen. Oh god, I'm having another panic attack.

I hold my breath and close my eyes.

Another night in the candlelight
Not bright enough to see my scars, just enough to
Fight, Fight
Hold tight tight
Just a spark.
Another night.
It'll be all right.

Just. Breathe.

Breathe.

Sensation starts to return to my hands. The room stills. I grab my phone. 2:17am but...

You awake?

Mila: Yep.

Jesse: NEC was hell.
Mila: I know.

I close the chat and lower my phone to the floor. I just needed someone to know I'm alive.

∞∞∞∞

I begged Parker not to tell the guys about the attack and let them enjoy their trip, but that's not how the dude rolls. I'm not surprised when our house is full again hours after the message goes out. My follow-up assurance that I'm fine had no effect.

I repeat the story at least three times and it gets no more interesting with each recitation. I was jumped. I had no money. They took my twenty and let me go.

Not your phone?

No. Guess they didn't see it.

That's good.

"Dude, did you know it's Groundhog Day?" Derrick announces while scanning his own device. "We should celebrate."

"Who celebrates Groundhog Day?" Reece asks.

"How about we work on 'Jonas' instead?" Parker says. "You up for it?" His gaze traces my injuries before locking on my eyes.

"I'm fine. Let's do it. You wanted to mess with the orchestration right?"

"Ooh strings?" Reece perks up, already heading to the door.

"Want to lay down a track today so you can play around with it?" Parker asks me.

I nod and shrug on my jacket. "What else would we do on Groundhog Day?"

oooooo

I get a big brother stare-down when we take five. Reece and Derrick are comparing notes about the turns and pre-chorus, giving Parker a chance to hunt me down by the mini-fridge in our practice space.

"What's going on?" He accepts the bottle of water I hand him but doesn't open it.

"Not sure what you mean."

"I know you, dude. We lost you for that entire take. You were completely gone."

"I was in the zone. That's a good thing, right?" I wipe the sweat off my face with my shirt. Despite the February chill outside, our little practice room never does well at managing the body heat of four high-energy musicians.

"It would be good for anyone else. Not you."

I shrug and attack my own water. "I got jumped. What do you fucking expect? At least I'm dealing with it."

"You're not dealing with it. You're hiding it in the music like you always do."

The muscles in my shoulders tense. "I'm not hiding."

"No? What really happened, Jess?"

"I told you."

"You got mugged. Right. In broad daylight on Germantown Avenue?"

"What can I say? Thugs don't respect schedules."

"Know what I think?"

"Not interested. Are we going to run another recording or are we happy with the first one?"

"I think you were rattled and went looking to score. I think it didn't go well."

"Fuck you, Parker."

All gazes rest on me as I pull my coat on.

"You're not going to be happy until your dead, Jess," Parker shouts after me. "Don't be selfish!"

∞∞∞

I answer on the third consecutive attempt, mostly to make her stop.

"What do you want, Natasha?"

"Thank god! I was so worried. Why didn't you answer my texts?"

I close my eyes and imagine myself sinking into the mattress until I disappear.

"Why do you think?"

"You're mad."

"That your boyfriend drugged and kidnapped me, then beat the shit out of me? Yeah, I'm a little pissed."

"He's not my boyfriend. And I warned you never to come by. I always went to you for a reason."

"Yeah, well, you weren't responding."

"You said you were done with me."

"I said I didn't love you."

She quiets, and I wonder which part of this conversation she's struggling with.

"Well, I'm sorry about what happened. As upset as I was, I never wanted that. I tried to stop them but..."

Yeah, I get it. I've replayed every detail enough to see it now.

"I don't blame you, just... dammit." I push my fingers through my hair.

"I was so scared, Jess. It could have been so much worse. You get that, right? I've seen it."

"Do they know where I live?"

Her hiss makes its way through the phone and sucks the air from my bedroom.

"I don't think they'll try anything. They're dealers, not criminal masterminds. Look, I'm going to drop something off. Just to say sorry, but that's it then. You have to be careful, okay?"

"Sure."

Careful is my effin middle name.

12: WINTER FEST

Her name is Candi. No, it's not, but it should be. Becca, I think. I know this because she's been hanging at the edge of the stage since sound check. I know a lot of things about Becca I don't usually learn until after a show. She's cute, maybe a little desperate, but it's been a while for me.

I sing "Jonas" directly to her. It's our first live performance of the new track, and the crowd at Crystal Casino's Winter Fest is digging it. We are too, rocking an audience over a thousand for the first time since the NSB tour. It's good to feel legit again.

"…Traitor, faker, promise-breaker,
Re-arranger of the lies we've tried to bury
Hey hey…"

My eyes are deadly, saturated with a biting smirk as I rip up the chorus. Chew it up, spit it out—yeah, feels damn good.

"I'm looking at you, pretender, mender, truth-blender
Defender of the game I thought we ended…"

I'm looking at you.

No, she's looking at me. They all are; this is what I was born to do. This is what record labels lose their shit over until Mila Fucking Taylor reminds them I'm a walking train-wreck off the stage.

Becca doesn't care about that. Neither do the other twelve hundred souls we own for the ninety minutes of our stage time.

Sweat trickles from my temples. My t-shirt is soaked, but there's no slowing my body when there's a guitar in my hands and fire raging through my blood. It's an extreme sport: thrashing and jumping, then rushing back to the mic for an assault on that too. I'm scary when I let go.

Becca's hands run over her curves as she sways in sync with my voice. Eyes closed, body undulating to our sensual rhythm—god, I could take her right here. Right now. She touches and presses, manipulating my eyes and pulse to join her in the seduction. Yep, it's been way too long.

Her lips move along with the lyrics when we rock our hits to close the set. Nice lips, definitely kissable, damn near suckable when they form around my words. The final note can't come fast enough.

We draw it out for a full seven seconds. A thousand voices could be ten thousand with the way their roar fills the room. We'd already planned for an encore, but having it validated with such fury? Yeah, pretty epic, even if it means waiting longer for release.

"Thank you, Crystal Casino! Have a great night!"

The lights go out and we escape to the green room. Last fall our crew would be rushing out to start packing our gear while we chilled with some groupies and booze. Now? A bottle of water and snack from the deli tray until the crowd disperses and we can load up ourselves. Cable-wrapping and case-stacking: the life of an indie rocker.

"Hell, yeah!" Derrick shouts, banging his sticks on the doorjamb. "That's what I'm talking about!"

Even Parker displays the grin I haven't seen in months. Dude definitely deserves it, and maybe it kind of feels good to see him happy again.

Security Joe pokes his head into the room. "Excuse me. There's a woman out here, says she knows you? Becca Saunders?"

"Yeah, she's cool," I say before the guys can react.

Parker shoots a *what*-look as Derrick whistles. "Wait, is that the chick who was eye-fucking you the entire show?"

"Shut up, D," I mutter.

"Knew it! Damn, she's hot."

God, I hope Becca wasn't close enough to hear any of that. She appears sufficiently unperturbed when she steps into the room.

"Hey, rock star," she purrs, homing in on me. I feel the amusement of our audience. Just as long as they keep it to themselves.

"What's up? Enjoy the show?"

"Totally."

Eye-fuck. Yep, that's a thing. Those curves, too. I glance back at the guys who are pretending... no they're not even pretending.

"I'll be back down to pack up." I take Becca's arm amidst a chorus of farewells. If all goes well, they'll each have their own girl by the end of the night. Well, except Reece who remains faithful to his imaginary lady. He'll make a real woman happy one day.

Now *I'm* snickering.

"What's so funny?" Becca asks as we board the elevator.

"Nothing. You cool with heading up to my room for a while? The guys can be a lot to take when they unwind."

"Fine with me." The flirty tone is back. She even takes my arm to reinforce it. "You guys were so so good."

I manage a quick smile. "Thanks."

"I mean it. Like, one of the best shows I've seen."

"Yeah?"

"I've seen a lot, too." She supports this by listing every single one of them as the elevator crawls to the 9th floor. I clench my jaw while counting each number on the slowest climb ever.

"Did you know I bought the songs from your first EP? Even before you were big. I've been talking about you guys for years. Ask Rach."

"That so?" Don't know Rach.

"Yep. Omigod. Look." She pulls down the neckline of her shirt to expose a tattoo on her shoulder. It's the candle from the cover art of our Candlelight EP. "See? Toldya."

I guess she thinks tattoos come with timestamps?

"I'm honored."

Shit. I was hoping for an easy night.

The elevator finally finds our floor, and I motion for her to exit.

"Ooh! And polite too? Such a *gentleman*."

Huh?

"Which is yours?"

"903."

"Omigod. I love that number."

Of course she does.

"You're not gonna believe this but my dorm room freshman year was 907!"

I check my phone but there are no urgent messages to get me out of this.

"You want a drink?" I ask as we move inside.

"Really? Omigod! I can't believe this is happening! My sisters are going to die!"

I force a nod as my brain runs through a quick inventory of recent groupie failures:

1. DEA Girl.
2. Regret and Bolt Girl
3. Natasha — Assault Girl.

With that track record, of course I'm about to hook up with Omigod Girl.

Maybe I need to try celibacy for a while.

I find her enraptured with the minibar when I tune back in.

"They're so adorable! Omigod, look at this one. Ahh! What are you having?"

"Help yourself. I need a minute."

I lock myself in the bathroom and lean against the sink. I can do this. I need this, just...

Shower. Perfect.

"I'm gonna rinse off," I call out, unnecessarily I learn when her face appears in the crack of the door.

"Want some company?"

"Thanks, but it'll be quick."

I click the lock and soothe my head against cool wood. This is my life. These are my connections.

It used to be enough.

My phone buzzes. Wes Alton? Thank god.

"Hey, man. How's life since the tour?" he asks when I answer.

I smirk at that. Tracing Holland's leading man has also been in deep since our joint tour. "Better than yours. I don't have a rap sheet."

"Yeah, well, I don't either. Mila Taylor, man."

"Is any of it true?"

"Just that I left Tracing Holland. The band is still intact. Holland is hiring Sylvie's new boyfriend."

I lower myself to the edge of the tub. No freaking way. "Wait, Shandor?"

"You know him?"

"Yeah. Met him at the Bahamas gig. Cool dude. Guy can play. Total flamenco vibe."

"Flamenco? Holland will have fun with that."

I laugh, trying to imagine the flamenco version of their alt rock angst. "I'm sure if he can play like that, he can manage the rock thing. Plus, she's got Luke and NSB behind her." Oh right. Luke and Wes despise each other. *Nice, Jess.* "Shit. Sorry."

"It's cool. I'm over that. Bigger shit on my plate right now."

"Obviously. What's your next move?"

"That's why I'm calling."

I adjust the phone in surprise. Uh-oh. "You want in on Limelight?"

"Ha! No, dude. I wouldn't do that to you. Remember my sister Sophia?"

"How could I forget? Did she like the swag?" Still can't believe we have international fans, especially connected to rock legends like Wes and Holland. Maybe I kind of get why Parker's pissed I shot us back down to the Englewood Pub.

"Loved it. Listen, I'll save you the background drama, but can you pretend you're playing her wedding in April if it comes up?"

Random. "Um... sure?"

"I know. Totally messed up, but she wants me to play and our family would freak. Everyone would with what's going on right now. Better that they think it's you, then we show up last minute."

"Makes sense. We got your back." My pulse picks up when I start to channel Parker-brain. "Hey, does she want us to play it for real?"

"Seriously?"

"Wouldn't that be better? You can still do your thing, but we'll play too. Then we're officially booked."

Waiting sucks. I press my fist against the wall.

"I'll ask her. I have a feeling she will lose her shit."

"In a good way?"

"In a 'never mind, big bro, I only want them' kind of way."

Hell yeah! "Sweet. We're in. I'll talk to the guys."

"Dude, you're the best."

I manage not to laugh. "You got it, man. Mila Taylor is on my shitlist too."

"Wait, did she go after you too?"

Ha.

"Eh, we'll talk about it another time. Let's just say, right now your sister's wedding might be our biggest show this spring."

"Fuck. I'm sorry, Jess. You guys are legit."

"Whatever." A knock at the door precedes a muffled *you okay?* "Hey, I've gotta run, but it's been good catching up. Send me the details."

"You got it."

Maybe this night isn't a disaster after all.

"Omigod! Should I call for help? Are you sick?" The tap becomes pounding. "Jesse! Talk to me, baby!"

I run a hand over my face.

"All good," I mutter, and drown her out with the water.

∞∞∞∞

A hot shower and booking a high-profile gig do wonders for my mood. I shake the water from my hair and wrap a towel around my waist. I feel somewhat guilty about my harsh appraisal of Becca as I pull open the door, especially when she no longer hovers right outside. Maybe she's not as clingy as I feared. Clingy ones are the worst. Another hard-learned truth that required Luke's intervention on tour.

I cross into the main area of the room and...

"Uh, hi," I say to the four *additional* girls in my room. *My* room. My crowded, invaded room.

"Oh hey, babe! These are my sisters: Rachel, Liz, Elisa, and Lara." They look nothing alike, as in: "Sorority sisters!" she shrieks for the sake of my confusion.

They all laugh at that and—*shit*.

"I hope it's okay. When I told them about us, they just really wanted to meet you. They were at the show too."

Us?

"We love your music. We play your stuff at the house all the time," the redhead says.

"All the time," Becca clarifies with an emphatic nod.

"That's great. Uh, you mind if I get dressed?"

"What if we said yes?" The Blonde's lashes flutter with mischief straight out of a '50s movie. A six-some? Is that even logistically possible?

I force a tight smile, and open my suitcase.

Whispers and giggles scatter behind me like I'm back in middle school. It's not attractive and not at all how I planned for this night to go. No, I'm a pair of jeans and a t-shirt away from returning to the green room with the guys. Maybe they'll be more interested in a college orgy.

"Hey, I've got to get back to help pack up our gear. You ladies want to hang down in the green room?"

"We'd rather hang here."

Becca is *right* there when she says it, and I take a step back. For two seconds I hesitate. They're cute. I'm horny... and then I remember my track record.

1. DEA Girl
2. Regret and Bolt Girl
3. Assault Girl
4. Omigod Girl who's now multiplied into five Stalker Girls

Shoulder-Luke screams: *Is it worth* five *Stalker Girls?*

Is anything worth five Stalker Girls?

Then again, they're cute and I'm horny.

I suck in a breath and grab a change of clothes. "Thanks for the offer, but as I said, we've gotta pack up. You're welcome to join us."

"Aww, you sure?" Becca asks. "We don't mind waiting." Her fingers trail up my arm, and I don't know why I'm surprised by her boldness. She's done nothing but overstep boundaries since the moment we met. I was okay with that until she multiplied.

"Sorry," I say with a shrug, and back out of reach. "I'll meet you down there."

A chorus of whining reinforces my decision, and I'm relieved when they take the hint and file toward the door. I smile apologetically through a veil of disappointed looks as it clears out.

What the fuck?

I lower myself to the bed and run a hand through my hair. I'm twenty-three years old. A musician. Single. Why the hell can't I find a sane girl? Not asking for a soulmate here, just a girl who won't freaking try to kill me or invite an entire sorority house to intrude on our night together. Am I being unreasonable?

As if on cue, my phone buzzes with an update from the Queen of Kingdom Crazy.

Mila: *Can I give you a ring?*

My heart pounds as I stare at the message. It's a strange reaction, but not as strange as the part of me screaming *why the hell not?* That part types "sure" before the rest catches up.

My phone erupts seconds after I give her my number.

"Hiya, BP. Thanks for the chinwag."

"The chinwag?"

My lips curve up. The accent, the slang, the sweet tone, who knew this is how the feared Mila Taylor would sound? Confident. Human. Sexy as hell, actually.

Did I just think that?

"You've never had a chinwag before?"

"I honestly don't know. I can guess from the context and etymology that the answer is yes."

"Etymology?"

Is she impressed?

"I'm not the dumb rocker you were expecting, huh?"

"I never said you were dumb."

"No, just overrated and wasted talent."

"Which implies that you have talent to waste."

"I'm flattered." I'm not.

I can almost hear her smile through the phone, and my own grows. It fades when she draws in a long breath.

"I've been doing more research."

Fuck, here we go.

"Yeah?"

"NEC was shut down three years ago for abusive practices."

The blow lands right in my gut. I close my eyes and lean forward.

"I read reports of children being locked in the basement for days. No food, water, facilities. Beatings, restraints, god it was dreadful what they reported."

Tears push against my eyelids, and I fight them back.

"I... It made me think. I went back and listened to your early songs again."

I refuse the opening she leaves for me. She'll hear the pain in my voice if I speak.

"When I got to 'Candlelight'..."

Thump. Thump. Thump.

"God, Jesse. I just..."

She's choking up, and my dam fails.

"What do you want, Mila? More of my soul to feed to the masses?"

"What? No! I just—"

"You, what?" The anger in my voice doesn't do enough to mask the tears. I scrub at my eyes, blood burning hot through my veins.

"I—"

"Go ahead. Don't be shy *now*!"

"I'm ringing to say I'm sorry."

The air... what air? Her words float through my brain and out into the space around me. I almost see them drifting in wafts around the room.

Sorry. Sorry.

Everyone's sorry. No one's really sorry. Sorry is a tool. Sorry makes you think you won't be thrown down a flight of stairs into a dark basement again. It makes you believe your father isn't selling you to a record label for his own gain.

"Jesse? You still there?"

"What do you want from me? Wasn't destroying my career, my *life*, enough for you?"

"I..."

She what? *What?!*

"I can't stop thinking about you."

The phone freezes in my hand.

"What?"

"Ah! I know, it's just—"

"Is this a joke? Another trick to humiliate me?"

My hand is shaking. From anger? Fear? Hope? Desire? I have no clue and force my fingers into a fist.

"I deserve that. Look, I'm not wrong about people very often, but when I am, I'll admit it."

"That's so nice for you." Why am I so pissed? I knew who and what she was before she knew who and what I am.

"Jesse, please—"

"Hey, thanks for the *chinwag*, but I've got to help the guys pack up from our show."

I hang up before my heavy breathing gives anything else away. My face is slick from a few lingering tears when I run a hand over it and push up from the bed. I shuffle to the bathroom and do my best to wash away the conversation with a few splashes of cold water.

But I'm too angry. Too charged. Too fucking *alive* for the first time in a long time.

My phone rings on the bed in the other room, and I scream a curse.

∞∞∞∞

I wake up to a strange ceiling. Not my comfortable blue one. This one is sterile. It's... shit. I groan and reach for my phone. Messages from Natasha? I delete those. Also, from Parker who's freaking out. Of course he is because it's past checkout, and I never returned to them last night. I dial his number.

"Jess! Where the fuck are you?"

"In my room."

"What? No, I tried that about ten times last night."

"Yeah, must have been asleep."

"Wait, did you get high?"

"Smoke weed in a hotel room? No."

"You know what I mean!"

"Sorry I missed checkout. I'll cover the fee."

"Fuck, Jess! Seriously?"

"Just letting you know I'm on my way."

I hang up and toss my phone back on the pillow. He's not going to make it to forty if he doesn't chill. Then again, I don't expect to make it to thirty.

Getting high is so… relative. I squint toward the window and do my best to adjust to the bright light. Packing my suitcase requires more effort, and I end up cramming shit in until I can close it. A quick scan of the room and I'm headed to the lobby.

I have more than Angry Parker waiting for me. Derrick doesn't say a word, only marches toward our van parked out front. The trailer is attached which means it's loaded and I'm the last item on the checklist.

"Let's get out of here," Reece says, also avoiding my gaze as he moves toward the exit.

So I messed up again, and they hate me. What else is new?

"Sorry, guys," I mutter as I climb into the van.

I strap into the backseat by myself. Parker's up front with Reece and throws on some music while Derrick leans between them from the seat behind.

I dare another look at my phone. Mila called back after I hung up last night. Also sent a message I haven't opened. Why should I? So she can tell me more about the shit history I've lived? Boohoo, my father was a junkie. Boohoo, my childhood was Hell. No one cares about your shit past. I'm not an idiot; I'm a good story. My pulse is already racing and I haven't even opened the damn thing.

Jesse,

I'm sorry. Honestly, I am. I get why you don't trust me. I'm in New York for a bit, can we meet up for a bevvy?

Mila

What? Fuck no! So why's my blood pounding? Why is my heart suddenly deciding to do more than push oxygen through my body?

And why the hell do I tap out: *can you come down to Philly?*

13: JANE

I don't tell the guys what I'm doing. They're still pissed about the Crystal Casino thing, and I still don't understand why I'm even here.

If I'd never seen a photo of Mila Taylor, I would've picked her out of the crowd at Benson's. I almost smirk at the polished, or should I say *posh*, raven-haired stunner seated at a booth in our favorite dive bar. I could have suggested a trendy spot like Estates, but why? She can be cryptic and confusing on my own turf.

Her back straightens when she sees me, exposing the figure I've admired on my laptop screen. Damn. I really should've taken her to Estates. I swallow and remember that I'm getting hard for *Mila Taylor*. I hate this woman. *Hate* her. She's ruined my life, everything I've worked for. I hate her so much she's re-lit fuses I thought were dead.

"Jesse?"

That accent though.

"Hey." I slide in across from her. Shit, there's no avoiding her gaze now. It's full-on lightning and supernova explosions shooting from those icy blue irises. I feel her stare deep in a place no one is allowed. And her scent. Scarlet, almost purple. It flows at me in waves I haven't experienced since my ceiling orgy.

This was a huge mistake.

"Thanks for meeting me."

"For a *bevvy*?" Crap. I'm flirting, aren't I?

Her smile is something I won't forget. "I believe you call it 'a drink.'"

"Right. What can I get you?"

"Nowt. I'm buying."

I raise my brows, eyes drawn to shiny full lips. She scans me slowly as I adjust my position on the bench. When her attention freezes on my mouth, my body rebels. I don't think I've ever experienced anything like this woman.

"Whatever IPA they have on draft, then."

"A beer man, eh?"

I shrug. "Alcohol isn't my vice."

"Not your main one anyway." She adds enough humor to force my inhale.

I'm charged with her. Tension threads through my back, infusing into primed muscle straining for release. At this second, I could handle a sorority house after all.

"What's *your* drink?" I ask. "Let me guess, margarita? Cosmo?"

"Hmm… you'll see."

She slips from the booth, giving me a full view for the first time. *Whoa.* She's a ten. An eleven. The daughter of a British rock legend and supermodel who's had all the advantages and enjoys all of life's luxuries. And here she is, crunching through peanut shells at Benson's to buy me a beer. Because? Guess we haven't gotten to that part yet.

I watch Marcus, tonight's bartender, fumble through a rare misstep in his come-ons. Even he's intimidated. Damn.

I can't help the grin on my face when she returns with our drinks. There's my pint and her… is that a jack and coke?

Of course it is.

"Nice choice," I say as she slides the glass to me.

"Shift up."

And I obey.

Her heat is tangible when she climbs up next to me on the bench. Her smell, intoxicating. Deep scarlet throbs in a halo around her as she shifts until our thighs touch.

I have to stop this before my brain completely fails.

"Why are we here, Mila?"

"I told you."

"A truce?"

"A cleansing. I can't get you out of my head."

This comes with a penetrating stare that smashes through me.

I take a hard swallow of my beer. "Really? I'm so captivating?"

"I had to see you in person to make sense of it all."

"Make sense of what?"

Her gaze traces my features, lands on my mouth again.

"This. You."

She leans in. I'm already there.

Her lips are soft and demanding. They dig into mine, hunting, until I groan. I reach into those gorgeous tresses. Lace and satin on my fingers, I tug to release a whimper from her. She tastes like angels' breath and rainbows and all the things she's not. Her hand threads into my own messy hair and locks us together. I part her lips to find her tongue, so damn ravenous we are. When her palm slides up my thigh and grips me hard, I'm done for.

"Fuck," I let out as she massages to the rhythm of her own breaths.

"God, I wanted this." She attacks my mouth again, shoving me into the wall of the booth this time. Her hand slides into my jeans and time just… stops. The room, the noise, everything is gone. Just a pulsating connection, heavy, thunderous.

Sparks rush through the black space around us, pinging my skin and slicing through to my blood. When I reach under her shirt, she gasps out the most delicious response. I'm starving for the rest.

I run my finger under the wire of her bra, enjoying the way dark lashes respond to the brush of tender skin.

"Going for another headline?" I mean it too. I know this isn't real. I know… I don't know. No, I don't, and I hate this woman for making me desperate for her poison. My brain is already reading tomorrow's post but my body doesn't care. It's experiencing a connection that's worth the pain.

"No! No." She pulls back. Her palms lock on my cheeks and direct me to her eyes. I'm jolted awake with a view of the entire bar staring at us. I still don't care.

"I'm sorry, Jesse. This isn't why I came."

"To seduce me?"

"For a headline."

"So you *were* trying to seduce me?"

She returns my smile, lips hovering just a breath away from mine. I still feel the heat of her embers, even pinker after our collision. I run my tongue over them and draw her in again. She softens into me, her hands running up my back and curving around my shoulders.

"Do you live close by?" she whispers.

"Two blocks."

"Can we go to yours?"

"I live with the band."

"So?"

"So they hate you."

"More than you do?"

She does it again. Draws that smile people don't earn anymore.

"Nobody hates you more than I do. Let's go."

∞∞∞

"This is Jane," I announce as we brush past the guys sprawled out in front of the TV.

A few mumbled hellos drift over, but it's game-time so my roommates barely look up from the screen as I pull her toward my room.

Her sexy smile is back when I close the door. "What's so funny?" I ask.

"This." She waves her hand in the air.

"My room?"

"Yeah."

"It's a mess, sorry."

She shakes her head. "This is exactly how I pictured it." She moves from pile to pile, stopping at the desk for a closer inspection.

"You pictured me as a slob."

She chuckles and holds up my notebook. "No, I pictured you as a mad genius. This is Einstein's lair if he were a musician instead of a scientist."

My amusement fades as her gaze moves over me again before resting on the bed. At least my sheets are clean. Parker has his neuroses; I have mine. Pristine bed: another relic of my NEC days.

"So, is this it?" She holds up my notebook and lowers herself to the mattress when I nod.

She shouldn't be touching that. No one gets to touch that. Even Parker knows better, but here I am watching a stranger I hate rummage through my fucked-up head. She stops on the last page, and my stomach constricts. Her expression, so confident a moment ago shatters before my eyes.

"Who's Jonas?" Her voice is barely audible.

I don't answer. I don't have to. It's not a common name.

"Oh my god. Jesse…" She drops the notebook and moves toward me.

"Jonas Everett did me no favors."

Those glacial eyes melt as her fingers sink into my arms. Slide down until they fasten on my wrists and wrench our bodies together. I don't need more than that.

I grip the collar of my shirt and pull it over my head. Her gaze… turns me rock hard when her surprise transitions into desire. She's seen pictures too, and there's nothing hotter than meeting expectations. Her palms slide up my chest and tighten behind my neck to pull me in again. We're one body now, moving with coordinated friction toward the same goal.

She gasps when we land on the bed. Her grin as I stretch over her… Tantalizing blue fabric becomes heart-stopping lingerie just a shade darker when she unbuttons her top.

Expectations. Can be exceeded too.

I need to taste, touch, sample soft flesh billowing from navy blue lace. Her head falls back, chest arching to meet my mouth with every kiss, every suck.

Delicious, intoxicating. I open the clasp for full access.

"Damn," I mutter, searing her image into my brain. "Alabaster queen of sapphire nights."

"Most call me Mila." Her grin, though. She doesn't hate my poetry.

"Resistant scars ignite the fiercest flames, babe," I mutter against her flat stomach.

She grips my face with both hands and turns my head up.

"You're real, Jesse," she whispers, searching my eyes. "You're special."

No. I'm fucking screwed.

∞∞∞

Sex with Mila Taylor is nothing like I'd imagined. She's soft and vicious. Receptive and forceful in a deadly mix of passion. Sex as a physical act is fun. As a spiritual act? I've never given a woman my mind, body, and soul at the same time before. That's all I want now.

Once, twice, damn even a third, my body doesn't tire of her. She releases the most beautiful moan as I pump the final notes of our latest duet, the perfect harmony for my own rush.

"That was ace," she whispers as I balance over her. "Again?"

Damp hair hangs in my eyes, and I pull it back in a firm grip. "Damn, woman." I push up with the other arm and land on my back beside her.

"Need a break? I thought you rockers could go all night."

I shoot a look, and her smile… She cups my cheek and plants a gentle kiss on my lips.

"I'm kidding. You're…" The humor fades as her thumb moves over my cheek. Her eyes become mirrors, an arctic sea that swallows me.

I want your sea to drown me, baby.
Surround me, baby
Sweep over and devour me, baby

"Jesse?"
"Yeah?"
"Where's your head at?"
I kiss her slowly, deeply. "Sorry."
Her fingertips brush along my face, and I close my eyes.
Heaven help me, I can't swim
I don't want to swim. *Consume me in this one moment I actually want to live.*

Warm fingers entwine with mine and draw me back.

She squeezes my hand. "I'm posting a retraction tomorrow. I was wrong about you and your music. The world needs to know."

"Don't."

She straightens up on her elbow. "What?"

"You weren't wrong."

"You're not a fraud, Jesse."

"No, just wasted talent." I cut her off with a kiss. "I don't want to get into it now. Just—"

"But one post from me and you're on top!"

"Yeah? Maybe I don't want to be."

I pull away and swing my legs to the floor.

"How can you not want what you deserve?"

"And what do I deserve?" I say, twisting a look back at her.

"I don't know. Everything. You're genuine. You're special."

"Special," I mutter, rising to my feet. I clasp my head and stare at the wall.

"You don't think you are."

"I don't think anyone is."

Arms slip around my waist and force our naked bodies together. I clench my eyes shut at the panic starting to move in.

"I've seen loads of frauds." Her voice is so soft against my back.

"Why are you here, Mila?"

"I told you. I—"

"No, why are you *here?*" I face her and force her chin up to search her eyes.

"You fought back. No one fights back."

I kiss her, and she relaxes into me.

"At least, no one fights back just cos they don't care what I think."

I close my eyes. Parker. Derrick. Reece. What do they deserve?

"I was never in it for the spotlight."

"Just the *limelight*?"

I take her in my arms. "Oh, she's a comedian now."

Her hands move back into my hair and pull me down. "I'd do anything to see you smile."

"And a poet?"

"Shut it." Her laugh trickles up my spine. "Please let me fix this."

I sigh. For the guys? I owe them way more than that. "Okay, but..."

"I'll be typing right here," she says, pointing to my bed.

"Oh really? You're optimistic."

"Do you want me to go?"

She makes a move toward the door.

"Not dressed like that! Damn." I pull her back.

I'm totally ready for round four.

∞∞∞∞

I wake up beside a woman.

Mila Taylor.

I wake up beside Mila Taylor.

In the history of *WTF Moments* this has to take the cake.

She snuggles closer when I stretch my arm around her, and hell if I wouldn't mind more mornings like this.

The softest moan leaks from her lips. Sweet, carefree. Everything a guy dreams of but rarely gets.

"You're an enigma," I mumble into her hair.

She takes my hand and secures it to her chest.

"If it keeps you interested, I'm fine with that." She kisses my fingers, and I close my eyes to make it last longer. I still don't know if I believe any of this, but she'll be able to prove it soon.

"So what's in New York?"

"Quite a bit, actually. You should visit."

"Hilarious. You know what I mean."

"This trip is for a meeting with my agent."

"What? No fucking way."

A swat lands on my shoulder, and I wrestle her to her back.

"I do more than write music gossip, you know." Her gaze fixates on mine as I straddle her. *We're all more than we seem.*

"So this agent?"

"Literary agent."

"You wrote a book?"

Another sly grin. Damn. As if I wasn't already hooked.

"Four, actually."

"Four?" I let out a breath and drop beside her again.

"If I tell you a secret will you finally start to trust me?"

"Depends on the secret."

She takes my hand and traces my fingers, lingering longer on each callous. I glance over as she draws in a deep inhale. "My pen name is Nicola Woods."

My laugh comes out as a snort. "Right. And I'm Luke from Night Shifts Black."

Her brows lift as she reaches for her phone. "Eh, you'll be in the same league as Luke Craven before you know it."

I'm still smirking when she places the phone between us and puts it on speaker.

"This is Maggie," says a voice on the other end.

"Maggie, hiya. It's Nicola."

"Nicola! Good to hear from you, hon. Are we still on for tomorrow?"

"Actually, that's why I'm ringing, love. I'm a bit bogged down with another project. Can we reschedule until later next week?"

"Of course, darling. I can't wait to discuss the new draft. Our contact at Bristol Press is going to shit his pants over this one."

"Do you reckon?"

"Definitely. They've been on my ass for edgy women's fiction like this. It's perfect for them."

"Okay. Well, send me a time that works for you. I wanted to pitch another idea as well."

"Oh really? I look forward to it."

"Ciao, love."

Mila hangs up and turns to me.

I'm the one shitting my pants. "No fucking way."

∞∞∞∞

Raising yourself has its advantages. I'm a decent cook and manage a breakfast that even draws the guys from their rooms. Not bad considering I'm stuck with the crap we had in the fridge.

"A girl," Derrick announces, rubbing his sleep-matted hair.

Parker shoves him and holds out his hand to Mila. "Jane, right?"

"Yes," I cut in. "I met her at Benson's last night. Jane, this is Parker and Derrick."

"Nice to meet ya," she says.

Derrick claps as he drops to the stool beside her. "Hot as hell *and* a foreigner!"

"Really, dude?" I toss back from the stove.

Mila laughs. "Yorkshire, actually."

"Not the Connecticut one, right?"

"England."

I shoot Derrick a look, and he holds up his hands. "Just asking, geez."

"What about you?" she asks him.

"Philly. Born and raised," Derrick replies.

"All of us are," Parker adds.

"You and Jesse are brothers, aren't ya?"

Parker nods. "When we don't want to kill each other."

I grunt and pull a toasted tortilla from the pan. "Hot sauce?" I ask Mila.

"Totes."

Derrick practically jumps on the island for a better view of the pan. "Ooh, is that the sausage thingy?"

"Breakfast burrito? Yeah."

"Hell yeah!"

I smirk and throw another tortilla in the pan.

"Weren't you going to the gym this morning?" Parker asks him.

"That was before I knew Jess was having a breakfast girl over."

"A breakfast girl?" Mila asks, eyeing me with a playful glint.

Ah, shit.

"It's not often our boy does breakfast for his girls. Only the special ones."

"His girls?"

"Oh my god, D. Will you shut up?" I say.

He cringes. "Fuck, that sounded bad. It's not like he has a lot of girls over. Just Natasha, really."

"D!"

"Natasha, eh? Should I be concerned?"

"No, no. Sorry," Derrick laughs, waving his hand. "She's not his girlfriend or anything. Just his dealer — with benefits."

"Derrick!" I snap.

The humor leaves her eyes as she locks them on me.

"Besides, I'm done with all that."

Now I have Parker's attention too. Dammit, the entire kitchen is staring at me, and I focus back on giving the egg/sausage mixture a stir. Last time I ever bring a girl home when Derrick's here.

"Natasha is no one," I say as I shove a plate toward Mila. I try not to think about the long string of messages I deleted this morning as I drop the bottle of hot sauce on the island. "I don't know how much you want. Need more coffee?"

"I'm fine."

Damn, those eyes. I'm in for it when we're alone. Fucking Derrick.

Parker is quiet as well, but his attention is more centered on Mila. *Shit.*

"So, Jane. What brings you from Yorkshire to Philly?"

"I'm a huge Limelight fan. I heard you're playing The Tunnel later this week."

Parker smiles at her teasing. "Right. Lots of fans fly across oceans for a Tunnel show."

"At least five hundred, I reckon."

"Seven on a good night."

"I'm here on business," she says seriously. Her gaze crosses to me. "At least I was. Now…"

"It's *pleasure*." Derrick contorts his hands in a universal "pleasure" gesture that only he knows. "Our boy is such a stud, huh?"

"That he is," she says.

I shake my head and shove two more plates across the island. "Eat so you assholes can leave us alone."

My phone buzzes, and I glance down. Parker? I meet his gaze across the kitchen before opening the message.

Mila Taylor? Are you out of your mind?

∞∞∞

"Your bandmates seem fun," Mila says once we're alone in my room.

"Fun? That's generous. Sorry about Derrick."

"He's hilarious." She pulls my guitar off the stand. "Play me something."

"Nah."

She looks disappointed as she sits on the bed and balances it on her lap. "Tell me about Natasha then."

I flinch and grab the guitar. "What do you want to hear?"

"'Jonas.'"

How does that name still have the power to gut me? "I… How about 'Nothing I Want?'"

She leans back on her elbows. "No. I hate that song."

"Really." I huff a laugh. "That's our biggest record."

"Yeah and it's the most derivative. 'Candlelight,' what I saw of 'Jonas'… It's when you expose your soul that your music becomes exquisite."

"Exquisite, huh?" I smirk.

"Why do you think I was so mad at you for buggering up your gift?"

"Wow. Harsh."

"And fair." She adjusts to face me. "Why, Jesse? What are you afraid of?"

"Afraid?"

She doesn't back down. "You're hiding. Behind chemicals, your failure—"

"Hey, my *failure* is because of you." I clench my fists. "You're the one who screwed me over."

"I did you a favor," she fires back. "You don't belong with SauerStreet. They were destroying you. 'Nothing I Want' was bullshit and you know it. That was your father's legacy, not yours."

"Oh right. Forgot you were an expert on my *father*. You really want to do me a favor? How about not telling the entire world how much I suck?"

"I never said that."

"No? Just that I'm an overrated, garage band waste of talent."

"I already apologized! I even offered to fix it."

"Wow. So generous of you."

"Yeah? And now you're proving my point!"

"Fuck you. I think it's time you go."

She jumps to her feet, arms crossed. "Oh okay. Is this where we get the whiny child version of the boy genius?"

"You think because we fucked, you get access to everything about me?"

"No. I think because I care about you and want to understand you, you can open up and be honest with yourself. Heck, maybe that would be for the first time in your life!"

"What the hell do you know about my life?"

"I do this for a living, Jesse. I know a fraud when I see one."

"Oh, I'm a fraud again now?"

"Worse. You're your own assassin." She quiets, anger melting from her face. "You're the only person holding yourself back, Jesse Everett. How do you not see the magic inside you?"

Magic. She has no idea what demons do with magic. "You should probably get back to your real life. Thanks for the drink last night."

I can't read her expression as her gaze moves over me in the silence. "You think you're protecting yourself by pushing people away. You know what you're protecting? The darkness."

My veins burn with self-preservation. "It's not a birthmark," I hiss.

"What isn't?"

"This." I lift my shirt and charge toward her.

She stands firm as her eyes lower to the mark on my ribs. "What is it?"

"You tell me. You're the expert on all things Jesse Everett now, right?"

Fuck her for making this scar important.

"So go ahead. See the truth."

"Stop it!"

"Come on, Mila. What is it?"

She bites her lip and shakes her head, tears gathering in her eyes. Good. She needs to see what I am so she can stop believing in what I'm not.

"Well? Skateboarding injury? Bar fight?"

"You know I don't know."

"What about these?" I'm the asshole who twists around to show her my lower back.

She pushes past me toward the door, and I grab her arm. "What's wrong, babe? You don't want to fix me anymore?"

"Get fucked," she cries, shoving me away.

This time I let her go.

14: CANDLELIGHT

I don't feel better when she's gone. In fact, I'm cold. Filled with regret at her silhouette still pressed into my sheets. I sink beside it, staring at the remnants of the woman I can't hate.

"Mila Taylor? What the hell, Jess?"

I look up as Parker bursts into my room.

"Not now, Park. Please."

"She didn't hurt you enough?"

"It's not like that."

"No? What are you punishing yourself for?"

I grunt and grab my hoodie.

"Where are you going?"

"For a run."

"No, we're talking about this."

"Out of my way, Parker."

He folds his arms and leans against the door. "How the hell did Mila Taylor end up in your bed last night?"

"It's complicated."

"No shit."

"I can't right now."

He shakes his head. "No, this has gone on long enough. We're dealing with it."

"Dealing with what?"

"Everything! Where are we headed next, Jess? Where are *you* going? Grieving period is done, brother."

"Whatever." I reach past him, and he pushes me back.

"The guys and I have been talking."

"Yeah?"

"Yeah. We're taking the deal with Jonas."

My heart slams against my ribs. "What?"

"You want to fuck around in a stupor, fine. But we're getting back up."

Fool me once.

Fool you twice, *Parker.*

"We played 'Jonas' for him. He thinks we can—"

"You what?"

Parker flinches but stands his ground. "He thinks it's elite."

"You had no right!"

"What's that supposed to mean?"

"Fuck you!"

I shove past him and crash through the house to the exit.

Traitor. Promise-breaker.

FUCK!

My fingers clench my hair as I storm down the sidewalk.

"Watch it!"

"Hey!"

I don't see the strangers.

TRAITOR. Fool me twice.

"Shut up, you little fucker!" Another black eye to explain away. Parker? Where's Parker? Thump. Thump. It can't be my body making that sound on the stairs. I feel nothing.

My cheeks are wet. I don't remember crying. Didn't think I was capable of it anymore. This is the shit that happens when you lose Natasha and the security she provides. I should have lied. I could have loved her. I need her. Isn't that the same thing?

I pull out my phone with trembling hands. No answer. Try again. No answer.

Please, Tash. Just one more time!

"Why do you think you're here? No one wants you!"
Thump. Thump. Thump.
I scroll through my contacts and stop at the L's. I hate working with Li but... Luke. My finger rests on Luke Craven.
Darkness. Ghosts of a living corpse on a shag carpet. His eyes are open. Why are his eyes open? Is he dead? 9-1-1... my father is dead!
I press Li instead.

∞∞∞∞

It's dark when I wake up. Cold. My hands are frozen, and I'm afraid I'm stuck to the bench.

Li's stuff is good—and overpriced. Plus, he has a minimum I don't like but this was an emergency. I couldn't go back to the house, so the bench on 14th became my retreat. Jesse Everett, another bum taking an outdoor winter nap.

I pull myself up, vision blurry, limbs stiff. I squint down at my phone to read the list of missed calls and messages.

Why does Parker still give a shit?

I limp along the sidewalk, grabbing lamp posts and tree trunks as necessary. 12th, 10th, 8th. Thanks to Li, I'm even enough to face them again. If they want to work with the devil, they have my blessing. Just, they're not using *my* song. Parker and Reece can write their own shit. Hell, they can keep the band name. What do I care?

My scalp is sore from the pressure of my fists earlier. I notice the half-moons of nail marks in my palms too. At least I don't cut. I tried that line on a caseworker after she confronted me about one of my meltdowns. Got me put on even more restrictions. It never occurred to me to mention the basement.

My steps are little more than a shuffle by the time I reach the house. Even so, I hesitate. The numbness feels damn good. I'm granite from the inside out.

A monument to wasted talent.

I see my bronze image in the Fucked It All Up exhibit of the Hall of Fame. There's Jesse Everett, shit-faced and sprawled out on a park bench. Parker would be pissed that I find this funny.

I'm more messed up than I thought when I try to open the door. My hand won't move. Nothing does and my smile fades into gasps for air. It's… black. Dark. Pain in my head. My shoulder. And…

∞∞∞

Jesse?

My name is somewhere in the distance. A brush of sensation on my hand. I'm flying. In water. Why is there water? No, I'm floating. No. Sinking. A tub? I force my eyes open and squint into an unfamiliar face. Wait.

Unexpected.

"You're awake. Thank god!"

"Where's Parker?" I mumble.

"In the kitchen. I'll go get him."

"No." I scrub at my eyes and manage a full view. "I thought you left."

"I did. Got some stuff from my place in Manhattan and came back."

"Why?"

"Is that not obvious?"

"How is it obvious? You should be anywhere but here."

"Yes, well, I do believe we've established you and I have very different perspectives."

I try for a smile but my lips don't cooperate. I settle on clenching my fists in the water. "What happened?"

"We found you unconscious on the porch."

"How long ago?"

"About ten minutes."

Explains why I'm shaking. I look down at my body beneath a rippling wall. Pale. Stiff.

"Mild hypothermia, probably," she says, scooping a cup of water over my shoulders. I flinch. It feels like lava. "You're shivering again which is a good sign."

"How'd you get stuck with bath duty?"

"I volunteered."

Our eyes meet. It would be a sweet moment if I wasn't shaking so hard. I suck in a breath and grip the edge of the tub. Stop. Shaking. Stop, you idiot. Just—

She loosens my hand and smooths it in hers.

"It's okay."

"What's okay?"

"Everything."

I let out a dry laugh.

"I'm going to add more warm water. Try to relax."

She reaches over and runs the faucet.

"Sure you weren't just trying to get me naked?"

"Well, I suppose I was more eager about that than your brother."

I crack a smile at that. God, I hurt. Everywhere pins and fire ripping through frozen capillaries.

"You'll feel better soon," she says softly. "This might not though." Her fingers brush the right side of my face. "You must have cracked your head on the door when you collapsed."

"You going to post about this tomorrow?"

A legit question. I don't know why she looks hurt.

"No."

"Did you ever do the redemption post you promised?"

She sighs. "No. And I can't now, can I?" Her expression says it all as it moves over me. "I care about you, Jesse, but I can't vouch for you right now. This"—she waves her hand over the tub—"is not talent I can promote."

"So why did you come back?"

I've never seen a person look so conflicted. "Because I can't let go of who you could be."

∞∞∞∞

I feel human again. Warm blood pumping through my brain. Air filtering through my lungs with a steady cadence. My room is safe, normal—except for one thing.

"You brought a suitcase?" I ask Mila, who cuddles closer to me under the blankets on my bed.

"I told you I went back for my things. I don't have to go back to the flat for ten days. I thought I'd take a holiday in Philadelphia."

What? Strange, confusing woman.

Am I actually… happy?

I slide my arm around her, and she settles into me. It feels natural for my fingers to run through silky black hair. "What was it like growing up with George Conway as a father?"

Her body shivers with a chuckle. "Very different to growing up with Jonas Everett, apparently."

"Careful now," I say with a poke. She grins up at me, and I plant a kiss on her nose.

"Seriously though. It's a difficult question to answer. Who wants to be the poor little rich girl? But he wasn't around much. My life was nannies and airports and George

Conway's life. I was *the daughter* at awards shows, dinners, parties... I was never myself."

"And your mother?"

"Lily Hennessy. I almost never saw her until she retired from modeling when I was twelve. Even then, she was gone a lot. That's how I discovered food."

"Traveling so much?"

"Cooking for myself. I used to help our chef. It was nice to have a constant. You know what I mean?" She quiets at my smirk. "Don't you believe me?"

"Oh I believe you. It's just funny how our lives were the same and also polar opposites."

"Tell me about it."

"About what?"

"Your childhood." She lets out a breath at my reaction. Her hand slides up my chest, pressing into suddenly tense muscle.

"It's not something I like to talk about."

"Clearly." She traces a nail over my chin before climbing up to me. The kiss is gentle at first, then deepens. "I want to understand your music on an intimate level," she whispers, tongue bearing witness in its search for mine. I flip her over and push her hands above her head. She gasps when I dig my hips into hers.

"How intimate?" I reach under her shirt to seek out soft curves.

"Fully intimate."

"You want the case file version or the movie version?" My lips come down hard on her breast. Down, down to the now exposed skin of her stomach.

"Documentary version."

"What rating?"

"18."

"Is that like R?"

"No limits."

"None?"

She moans as I find the spot that she likes.

"You sure you want to talk?"

She shakes her head. "I mean yes. I mean... ah!"

I'm not playing fair, but she doesn't know what she's asking. No one wants the unfiltered version of the Everett Story.

Her body arches against my mouth, fingers gripping my sheets.

"*Not bright enough to see my scars...* What scars, Jesse? The ones you showed me or something deeper?"

I ignore her. The words. The darkness.

"*It's all right...* How is it... *ah...* " She jerks. "All right in the..." Again and again and again before sagging against the bed with a sigh. I've spent my life learning how to distract people for their own protection. Her content smile gives me hope that I've succeeded.

"*In the candlelight.* What's the candlelight?" Her voice is still strained as she guides me up and pushes me to my back. She straddles me and locks my wrists at my sides. "Now talk."

"Mila..."

"Talk. Tell me about the candlelight." She taps my cheek. "And look at me when you do it."

"So bossy."

"I need you to see my reactions."

My chest tightens at the compassion already on her face. I can't do this. I know I can't. It's not like I haven't tried before.

"The candlelight?" she insists.

My hypothermia must be lingering. I clench my trembling fists and try to free them. Mila presses her knees together.

"The candlelight, Jesse."

Now I'm just pissed. Bad news for her when my filter goes down. "Yeah? The candlelight, okay. Here's your Hallmark movie. I got labeled as a behavioral problem. Didn't matter what I did, so I stopped giving a shit about the rules. They hated me because I was always one step ahead of them. They'd call me a smartass when they weren't calling me a little fucker or some shit like that. The worst was the crying." I huff a dry laugh. "God, they hated tears. Any kind of tears. If I cried when they…"

Her eyes are glossy, and I swallow. Guilt. Yeah, I still feel it. One of the few emotions I can't block.

"When they what?"

"Let's just—"

"When they *what?*"

I draw in a deep breath. "Beat me. If I cried, they'd throw me into the basement. Literally."

Thump. Thump. Thump.

It's a heavy silence. Her eyes trace my face, my chest, my hands. Anywhere they can reach. I hate what they're saying.

"For how long?"

"I don't know… There was no time down there."

"Oh god. Jesse…"

"Minutes, hours, days—it was just darkness, and the more I cried, the longer it would last so…"

Fuck! *It's all right. It's all right.*

"*It's all right.*" My eyes clench shut. "*It's all right.*"

"In the candlelight."

I nod and force myself to look at her again. "The darkness never went away though. It's still here. All the fucking time, and I…"

The weight in my chest is replaced by the soft pressure of arms. Mila buries her face in my neck.

"I found a lighter one day in the blackness. I felt it first, then… I knew."

"Knew what?"

"As long as I could find one flicker, I'd be okay."

My shoulder is warm and wet but I don't know how to comfort her. I've never figured that part out which is why I do everything I can to protect others from it. Even Parker doesn't know everything.

I start to sing softly.

"Another night in the candlelight
Not bright enough to see my scars, just enough to
Fight, Fight
Burn out
Fade out
Cry out against demon screams
Broken dreams
All that keeps me breathing in the dark
Hold tight tight
Just a spark.
Another night.
It'll be all right.
in the candlelight."

∞∞∞∞

I gasp awake, heart racing, blood pounding. My eyes dart from corner to corner of my room. Where are they? I know the demons are here. They—

I swing my legs to the floor, eyes clenched shut. Leaning forward, my fingers lock in my hair. I can block them. I can...

"Shut up, you little fucker!"

Blood. So much blood.

"Stop crying!"

Thump. Thump. Thump.

"It's all right. It'll be all right." Sweat breaks out over my body as I pound my fists against my head. "It's all right. It's…"

"Jesse?"

"Shut up, you little fucker!"

Thump. Thump. Thump.

I shake my head and cover my ears. They're so damn loud tonight!

I jump up and fumble through piles in search of my hoodie.

He's dead! Why are his eyes open? Don't look at me if you're fucking dead!

Air rushes through my lungs in short, violent breaths. Where the fuck is it?

"Jesse, you okay?"

Here. My hands shake as I pull the bag from the pocket. Thank god for Li's minimum.

I move to the door and stumble toward the bathroom.

Pain radiates up my arm. My wrist this time. Broken? Sprained? I cradle it as I inch back toward the wall. So cold tonight.

Thump. Thump. Thump.

The bathroom light roars on. The demon is me, staring back through bloodshot eyes.

No one wants you.

"Jesse?"

The bag is pulled from my hand and tossed in the toilet. Warm hands slip around my waist. Soft hair tickles my back.

Air starts to flow again. Steady. 1-2… 3. I close my eyes. 1-2… 3. It's all right.

It's all right.

Gentle fingers move over my skin, slowing my heartrate.

"It's all right," she whispers.

∞∞∞∞

Parker is polite when we emerge the following morning. Even says hi from his old man chair at the head of the kitchen table. Mila doesn't say anything as I swallow a couple of pain relievers and pour us coffee.

"Jess, I'm working on the spring schedule. When's the *you-know-what* in Toronto?" He casts a look at Mila, and I snicker into my mug.

"The stadium tour to celebrate our Grammy nomination?"

Mila snorts a laugh, and we exchange an amused look.

"I hear nothing when I'm in this house. I swear it," she says to Parker.

He gives me a hard look. "Fine. When's the Alton Wedding?"

"I'll check with Wes and let you know."

"Wes Alton?"

I narrow my eyes at Mila. "You hear nothing, remember?"

She holds up her hands. "Not a word. But... Wes Alton?"

"We're playing his sister's wedding."

"Ah. So you're in touch with him?"

My smile turns mischievous. "Yep. He hates you too."

"He digs his own graves."

Can't exactly argue with that. "Maybe. You should hear their new record though. It's pretty epic."

"'Swan Song?' Their label sent it over but I haven't given it a listen."

"Really." I cross my arms. "Ms. Open-minded Music Expert hasn't touched this month's most controversial release?"

She scrunches her nose in defense, and I crowd her against the island. "I don't think you're getting breakfast until you check it out."

"Oh, you're extorting me now?" She wraps her arms around my waist and flat-out owns me with a firm grip on my ass.

"Maybe." Her lips are so damn perfect. Just a small taste.

Parker slams his laptop shut. "Well, I'll leave you two at it."

I bite my tongue to keep from laughing as he stomps off.

"He's not a fan of us, is he?"

"Can you blame him?"

"No. I suppose not." Her smile widens. "But to make sure *you* are, I'll give your Tracing Holland friends a listen."

∞∞∞∞

"Jane is Mila Taylor? No way. No fucking *way!*" Derrick bites down on his fist as he jumps around his kit.

I throw a look his way and tighten my strap. "Just thought you should know since she'll be around for a few days."

"Holy shit! And she ate our eggs!"

Parker grunts as he leans over his amp. "Stupid thing is flaking out again."

"I thought you were trading that piece of crap in for the Matchless?" I call over.

"I was. I am."

"Wait, she uses our bathroom! Our toilet paper!" Is Derrick clapping?

"Just use the Fender for now." I return my guitar to its stand and drag our spare amp from the corner.

"Who knew she was so freaking hot, though? Like way out of your league, man."

I glare back at him. "Dude, just. Stop." Guy's a walking headache I don't need right now.

"We should pick our set for Friday," Reece says, tuning his bass.

Parker nods and zeroes in on me. "I'm guessing Mila's coming?"

"Probably."

"So are you two a thing now?" Reece.

I shrug. "Just hanging out."

"You trust her?" Parker asks.

"I don't know. More than I trust Jonas."

"Whoa. Burn!" Fucking Derrick.

I sling my guitar back on. "We doing this or what?"

15: THE TUNNEL

The Tunnel is one of our favorite houses to play. It's small but solid. Good energy, great layout for an intimate experience with the crowd. It was rocking this stage three years ago when our dream started to feel real.

"Aw, club's cute," Mila says as she joins us at the trailer. I send her a look which she returns with a shy smile. "What? I had a look. It's cute."

"Can you grab that case? It's just a few stands."

I hoist Reece's amp and lug it through the loading dock door. Derrick and Reece are arguing about something related to the in-ears, and Parker... I'm not sure. Probably making love to the Matchless he picked up two days ago. Dude's enamored.

"Are you going to let me watch from backstage?" she asks.

"Depends. You here as my arm candy or my critic?"

"Can't I be both?"

I drop the amp once we're inside and wipe my face with my shirt. "I have a feeling you will be regardless of my answer."

She reaches up for a quick kiss. "You know me so well already."

"You need to earn it then. What do you know about unloading and setup?"

"I'm George Conway's daughter."
"Is there anything you don't do?"

∞∞∞

The crowd is electric tonight. The band is locked in, and my blood pounds to the rhythm of drums and bass. I grab the mic, bending it to my will because I fucking own this.

"My reaction time is lacking
No backtracking now that you've got me on the prowl
Hey hey

I'm looking at you, traitor, faker, promise-breaker,
Re-arranger of the lies we've tried to bury
Hey hey"

I shoot a smile to the gorgeous woman on stage left.

"I'm looking at you, pretender, mender, truth-blender
Defender of the game I thought we ended
Yeah, yeah, I'm looking at you"

I spin away from the mic and unleash. No demons. No basement. No Label or Jonas, just me and the music calling a truce now that I've given it life. Yeah it's a curse, but it makes the reward so sweet.

"That knife you hold is so damn pretty.
How's it look in my back? Hey hey"

The place is on fire. I want to live this moment offstage too.

"Yeah, yeah, I'm looking at you."

∞∞∞∞

"Fucking yeah!" Derrick shrieks as we stalk into the green room.

Mila wasn't there when we wrapped so I assume she's waiting inside. I look around and find her seated in the far corner, nursing a glass of wine. She barely reacts when we enter, doesn't smile, just runs her gaze solemnly over me. The others quiet when they see her, and Parker clears his throat.

"Uh, I'm gonna go check on Jay and see if he needs anything."

"I'll come with you," Reece says.

"You guys don't want to chill?" Derrick. Idiot.

Reece slings an arm around his neck. "Later, dude. Come on."

I take the seat across from Mila. "You didn't like the show?"

She bites her lip. Are those tears? Can't be.

"I'm sorry." Her voice is so soft. Fuck.

I rub my face. "No, it's okay. I mean, it's not like it's a secret."

She shakes her head and sets down her glass. "Not that." Her eyes trace me until I'm raw. "You…"

Her lips crash against mine, hands threading into my hair. "I'm sorry. I didn't know." She pulls away and forces my gaze into hers. "I'm so sorry."

My smile slips out slowly. "Wait. You liked it?"

"You're… I've never seen anything like it. Don't you understand what you have?"

She rocks my head with each word, and now I'm full-on grinning.

"Wait, are you pissed or excited right now?"

"Both. Bloody hell, Jesse!" She leans back and squeezes my shoulders. "Promise you'll—"

"Don't go in!"

We both straighten at Parker's shout and turn toward the door.

No. *No!*

"Just hear me out. Hear—" an intruder says.

"Who the fuck let you in?" I jump to my feet. The guys rush in after him and stop cold. "Did you invite him?" I shoot at Parker.

"I told you we want to work with him. I thought—"

I clasp my hands on my head.

It's all right. It's all right.

Not tonight! It's the wrong night for candlelight!

My pacing stops. My arm is moving down and the other drops with it. Mila locks my hand in hers and walks us forward.

"I'm Mila. Who are you?"

The Devil clears his throat. "Jonas. Jesse's father."

Her hand tightens around mine. "Oh right." She looks to Parker. "Are you planning to work with this man?"

He shrinks a bit and nods. "He's going to help us get back on our feet."

Jonas takes a step forward. "I screwed up, but I'm clean now and I have contacts that can help the kids. I want to make it up to them," he says—he *lies* because that's what he does.

"Ah." She turns to me and squeezes my hand again. "Love, do you mind if I hear him out for you? Go for a walk or something?"

I stare at her. What planet is this? But fuck if I'm going to listen to any more bullshit from that man. I glare at Parker on my way out.

The halls are infested after the show. I do my best to navigate the hives as seamlessly as possible and finally find a quiet retreat in a storage area. I sink down behind a stack of chairs and rest my head in my hands.

Fuck!

I kick a stool and watch it crash into a pile of risers.

I pull out my phone when it buzzes. More messages from Natasha. I delete them. What was I thinking reaching out to her again? I don't think—can't—when the demons take over. And now?

As I push it back in my pocket, it starts vibrating again. Dang, she's relentless. I go to "ignore call" when my finger freezes.

Luke Craven.

Shit.

"Hey, man," I say.

"Hey." He's too quiet. "You okay?"

"Fine, why?"

Still quiet. Does he seriously have a mini ghost following me around?

"You don't sound good."

"Yeah? Well, I'm fucking great."

He huffs a laugh. "Right."

"Sorry." I clench my eyes shut. "Okay, no, shit is messed up right now."

"Yeah?"

"I don't know, dude."

"We'll be passing through on Sunday. Want to grab a bite?"

No. "Yeah. Sounds good. Text me when you're here."

The universe is not on my side.

ooooo

Jonas is gone, and it's safe to return her message says.

Safe. What a stupid, subjective word.

The guys are quiet when I enter, staring at me like they do when they're not sure which stage of breakdown-recovery I'm in. Mila doesn't know enough to be afraid. She pushes a bottle of water into my hand.

"So we listened to what he had to say," she begins.

I lean against the refreshment table. "Yeah? You sign?" I ask Parker.

He glares at me. "It was a good offer."

I focus on Mila. "That what you think too?"

She leans back in her chair and scans the four of us. Interesting how I'm not the only one hanging on her response.

"Honestly, boys, I'd turn it down if I were you."

Exhales and grumbles lift from the circle.

"Of course you would. You're on Jesse's side," Parker mutters.

"My opinion is my opinion. Jesse can vouch for that." She sends me a smile before leaning forward to face them. "Look, it's a good offer—for a different band."

"Seamless is a huge label," Reece says.

"Yeah, and they also cater to pop artists and mainstream markets. If what I saw tonight is any indication, you're headed in a much fresher direction. Your stuff is innovative and new. You need a label that will embrace your creativity, not try to shove you into a mold. Seamless is even more hesitant to take risks than SauerStreet. They know what formula works for them and it would be up to you to conform. You'd have zero leverage."

Parker crosses his arms. "Jonas worked with them for years."

"Exactly." Mila says. "Look, I've seen it all. You guys are special. It's so rare to find *different* done with such passion and expertise." She draws in a deep breath, eyes serious. "I'm not blowing sunshine up your arse, here. You guys have the potential to be genre-busters."

Derrick snorts a laugh, but Mila's stare cools and freezes on him.

His smile fades. "You're joking."

"I'm not."

Parker shakes his head. "Thank you for the support, but how the hell are we supposed to *bust genres* without a label? I get that Seamless isn't ideal, but if we can just—"

"You don't need a label."

Parker throws up his hands. "Right. Because that's been going so well for us."

"We play bowling alleys and dive bars," Reece adds.

She shrugs and leans back. "Then you're doing it wrong."

Parker pushes himself to his feet. "Okay, if no one else is going to say it, I will. Why the hell do you even get a say? I don't know why Jesse's forgiven you for fucking him over, but I haven't. I get that you know this industry, but thanks to you and your bullshit no one will work with us anymore. So if fucking Seamless Records is willing to give us a shot, then we fucking take it."

He shoves his chair against the table and storms off.

Mila clears her throat. "Is that how the rest of you feel?"

"I think you're both right," I say. All eyes turn to me, and I take Parker's empty seat. "Maybe you don't realize the damage you did to us, but Parker's not exaggerating. You made things impossible for us, Mila. Our own manager dropped us. Promoters, venues, he's not kidding that we get bowling alleys now. Tonight's show at the Tunnel is one of our biggest bookings for the entire year. The Alton wedding? Probably number two. We went from stadiums to fucking dive bars. I get what you're saying, and maybe that would have worked before you wrecked us, but we're kinda screwed now."

She nods slowly.

"We still love you though," Derrick blurts out, and I release a laugh.

"Yeah. Fuck you and we love you."

She returns my crooked smile with a weak one. "Nope, I know what you're saying. I do. I've already apologized to Jesse for reading you lot wrong, and it's long overdue that I do it for you too. I'm sorry. I made a mistake." She studies us carefully.

"Listen. I believe in you so much that I can't stomach the thought of seeing your music corrupted by Seamless. Will you give me a couple of months to help you get back up? If after a trial you're not happy with the direction, you can sign with Seamless. I have enough connections to make that happen for you if you want it."

Holy shit.

I exchange a glance with Reece and Derrick. They're just as stunned as I am.

"You want to help us?" Derrick asks. "Mila Taylor wants to help us," he directs to Reece and me. He looks back at her. "You have like a billion followers."

She laughs. "Considerably less, but I have some influence, yes."

"What exactly are you proposing?" I ask.

She meets my gaze across the table. "You said you're currently looking for a manager?"

∞∞∞

"No fucking way."

Our server and a few bleary-eyed patrons are the only witnesses to our impromptu after-show band meeting at an all-night diner. Still too many eyes if a fist-fight breaks out.

"She has an extensive platform, Park. We should at least think about it," I say.

"Let me get this straight. You won't even *hear the pitch* of our own father, but you're willing to give control of our career to the woman who blew it up?"

"Our father? How can you call him that?"

"You know what I mean."

"No. Wake up, Parker! We've tried that door already, remember? Mila may have hurt us, but she didn't betray us."

"I'm telling you, he's different now. If you just—"

"Whatever. Besides, Mila also admitted she was wrong. Even apologized to me and the band."

"She did." Parker and I glance over at Derrick who shrugs. "What? She did."

Parker focuses back on me. "Really. If all of that's true, why hasn't she used her 'extensive platform' to prove it and tell the world?"

I swallow ice water to soothe the burn in my throat. "She was going to."

Three surprised gazes lock on me.

"What?"

More water. Still not enough, and I have to force the rest out. "She was ready to put her name on the line for us. She planned to post a retraction the day I almost froze to death on a park bench."

Congratulations, Mr. Everett. You win this round.

The table stills as I successfully transfer villain status to myself. Worst part? There's no surprise. No need for clarification. No effort to hang me—I brought my own rope.

"Give me a chance to fix things for once," I say, unable to look at them. Who's the traitor again? "It's only a couple of months. Let me prove to her—and you—that I can do this."

∞∞∞

After a good sleep and apology breakfast, the guys at least agree to a trial period with Mila.

Here we are at our kitchen table: our first band meeting with our new manager.

"Okay, let's start with the basics. Who is your audience?"

We stare at her.

"The demographic for your music?"

We stare at each other.

She sighs. "All right, then we start with that. In my opinion we should be focusing on the university market. They'll connect with your story and innovative style."

"They love us at Temple," Reece says.

"Perfect. We'll get you on the college radio scene right away. I also know a guy who runs a great club that caters to the university demographic. I'll give him a ring and see if we can set something up. It will be a good showcase for us."

Parker lets out his breath. "You really think one show is going to turn things around for us?"

"It will if I'm in the crowd and post about it."

My smug smile fades when her eyes lock on me. "Before that happens, however, you and I need to talk."

I shrug. "Okay?"

"In private."

"Ooh!" Derrick snickers. "You're in trouble!"

"Shut up, D." I nod toward the hall, and Mila follows me to my room. "What's up?"

Yeah, this isn't going to be good news.

"You know how much I care about you," she says, eyes heavy with our immanent conflict.

"Yeah..."

"I will commit to you. I will endorse your career, but only if you commit to yourself."

I cross my arms. "Meaning?"

"Meaning, you get your addiction under control. If not, you can't reach your potential as an artist. I'm committing to the person I believe in, but you still have work to do."

I huff a laugh. "Whatever."

"This isn't a joke, Jesse. I care about you, but I'm not staking my reputation on a bloke who ends up passed out on pavements every time he can't handle his demons."

Fire ignites. "I'm not a junkie."

"I didn't say that, but you clearly have a problem."

"Bullshit!"

"Jess—"

I back away from her. "You don't even know me."

"I know enough to see where this is headed if someone doesn't stop it."

"I'm not a *project*."

She grabs my arm, and I'm about to fire again when I see the glisten in her eyes.

"Don't you get it? You're—"

I yank my arm away. "No. And you don't either."

∞∞∞∞

I feel like shit. Like I lost a lung.

My fingers wrap around the railing of our stoop. Cold iron melts into my skin as I work to inhale enough air.

Overrated. Garage band wasted.

Talent-jaded. Faded. Hated.

Wasted. Wasted. Overrated.

Failure sated, grated, inflated.
FAILURE. FAILURE. FAILURE.
"STOP CRYING, YOU LITTLE SHIT!"

But I can't. No, because *thump, thump, thump* down dirty wooden stairs. *Crash* onto harsh floors. *No one wants you.* Open dead eyes. *NO ONE WANTS YOU!*

I drop to my knees, concrete slicing through rips in my jeans. Blood, god I hope there's blood because I need something to erase the tears searing down my cheeks.

"Jesse?"

I shake my head. Not now. *Not now!*

She wraps her arms around me. My forehead finds metal as my grip tightens on the cage.

Stop crying. Stop...

Her hands lock around my chest. Her head presses into my back. Is she crying too? Are we all just a bunch of sobbing little shits? My disaster is addictive.

"I'm an infection."

Nails rip through my veins when I hear the demon shriek through the air around us.

Infection! Infection!

Mila squeezes harder, and I know she heard it too.

"You're not."

She's a liar. She's...

No one wants you! NO ONE!

My head is moving again. Violent jerks from left to right.

NO ONE.

NO ONE.

NO. ONE.

"Jesse, please."

"Go away!"

"I can't."

"I'm not your problem."

"Just—"

"You can't save me!

"I don't want to—"

"Then what do you want!"

"You!"

Air freezes in my lungs.

"Just you." Her voice is a whisper as she frames her palms on my cheeks. Her gaze digs into mine, picking through the sludge and monsters crowding the recesses of my head.

No one does.

Someone does?

I don't have a response for that. Maybe it's a lie. Another trick to get a treat. That's what I'm good for, right? A means to other people's ends? Currency or waste to be tossed from one dump to the next.

So what's the end game for a woman who owns the world but inserts herself into my nightmare?

"Will you just come back inside? It's freezing out here."

"Give me a minute," I say, voice monotone. My tears freeze into something darker, harder, as I squint through the bars toward the street.

Another night in the candlelight

Not bright enough to see my scars, just enough to

Fight, fight

I'm Jesse Fucking Everett. Tormented, broken, and gifted beyond reason. I'm on stolen year twenty-three. Twenty-three years of Life trying to beat my ass six-feet into the ground. But I'm breathing. Why?

Fool me once.

Even Mila Taylor can't fool me twice.

ꝏꝏꝏ

I go back inside. Calm, resolved, and cold from more than a Philadelphia winter. The kitchen quiets when I enter. Eyes shift in nervous patterns.

I stalk past Reece and grab a beer from the fridge. Bottle caps are damn loud in exotic silences.

"Okay, so tell us more about this club," I say to Mila.

She's listening for all the words I don't say, but it's time for her to see how I survive.

Her eyes search mine for a message she won't find, and she finally clears her throat. "Well, Smother isn't a huge venue, but it's a university crowd, and they're dedicated. The club doesn't do a lot of live shows but are famous for their signature theme nights. It's a perfect fit for what we want to do. We can propose a band night, and if they're in, they'll do it right. Leon Stonewell knows how to draw and manipulate a crowd."

The guys bounce their heads in thoughtful agreement, and I'm happy for them. Heaven knows they deserve a flirtatious brush with Hope. Mila leaves out the part where she and I still haven't figured out our shit.

The glint in her eyes, the clench of her fists as she leans into her scheme, this woman wants to *make* us as much as she wanted to break us a couple months ago. Our "potential" is crack to talent junkies like record execs. Managers. Promoters. Fans who all want to believe that we can achieve their dreams. Like Mila. She'll see the truth soon enough.

"When are you thinking we'd do this?" Parker is building spreadsheets and booking equipment rentals in his head.

"I'm going to propose early May. That gives us plenty of time to construct our vision and put together a show worthy of the hype."

"What hype?" Derrick's head jerks like he just woke up.

Mila's smile makes me wonder how deep her reservoir of sass runs. "Did I forget to mention the publicity portion of the plan? You work your magic. I'll work mine."

The guys are too busy exchanging *hell-yeah* smiles to notice her warning look to me.

∞∞∞

The way her eyes trace my body when I pull my shirt off accentuates the tense lock of her shoulders.

I grip the button on my jeans and watch her chest inflate with a quick breath.

"We need to talk," she says finally. Her eyes, though. They don't want to talk. They caress my skin until my zipper becomes painful.

"Can it wait until after my shower?"

I don't wait for her to answer. Well, my *body* doesn't. It's hard and ready and pretending to search for a towel as it shrugs off the jeans. Mila's breath catches at my boxer-briefs' effort to hide my arousal. Her eyes must have forgotten she wants to talk.

"What is it?"

"We…"

Damn, she's easily distracted. I allow my amusement to play on my lips as I approach. Is it fair? No. Like everyone else she believes she knows what's best for me. I should let her comfort herself with the fight for my future, but I'm bored with it.

Those curves, though? Her hair? The wit that slices and knocks me down? I'm so not tired of that.

She can talk all she wants while I interact with the skin on her neck.

"You were saying?" She tastes like raspberries today.

"Jesse…"

Maybe she's pissed but not enough to fight me. No, her hands are just as guilty as they grip my ass and force my hips into hers. I back her against the closet door.

"I'm serious about rehab. You need…"

"I need what?" I breathe through raspberry mist.

"Help," she gasps out.

"Hmm." Maybe, but not with this part.

∞∞∞

She's quiet when we finish. Quiet while we clean up. Quiet as we get dressed after our shower.

Shit.

"I hate how you do that."

"Do what?" I scrub a towel over my hair, search for a shirt, any damn thing to avoid *Real Talk.*

"Use sex to distract from what's going on inside."

"You hate sex with me?" I almost wink to complete the total asshole ensemble.

Her groan would be adorable if it didn't mean she's committed. "That's exactly what I'm talking about. The sex, the jokes. You're hiding, and now that I know how much, it kills me!"

Hiding. No. Protecting maybe.

Surviving.

I glance at my phone and curse. "I'm late for rehearsal. The guys are waiting. Rain check?"

Glacial eyes turn to razor-ice but my defense is too legit.

"Fine. I have work to do anyway."

16: REUNIONS

I suggest Estates, but one of the things I always loved about the NSB guys is their denial of god status. They'd rather do Benson's. Pitchers of pedestrian beer and uninspired bar food. I've seen Casey Barrett eat fries I wouldn't have touched when I was a starving ward of the state. Dude is an inspiration.

I also don't tell Mila that "hanging with the guys" would be a music blogger's Olympus. She had no problem curling up on my bed with her laptop while I have my secret *chinwag*.

I secure us a table in the most secluded part of the bar and watch for "The guys." They're easy to spot when they enter and knock Benson's off its axis. Until this moment, I was the biggest celebrity in here. This shitty dive has no clue what to do with icons like Luke and Casey, and I wave them over to our table.

"Dude," Casey says with a grin. He adds an awkward hop to his step to maximize the volume of squashed peanut casings. They scream with each stomp, and I laugh at his enthusiasm. God, I've missed these guys.

"'Sup," I say, rising from my chair.

"Hey, man. Good to see you." Luke tugs my hand for a yank to his chest and firm arm on my back. Casey shoves my shoulder like I'm his little brother or something.

"Glad you could make it. Thanks for coming by."

"Of course," Luke says. "Like I said, we're passing through."

"You headed up north?" I ask.

"Nah, south actually. Baltimore, baby!" Casey demonstrates the "Baltimore" dance, which looks more like an uncommitted stripper routine. His smile, though. It's contagious, and I realize my lips still haven't flattened into their usual scowl. Did I mention I missed these guys?

"What's in Baltimore?"

"Wedding shit," Casey sings with a Baltimore Dance reprise.

I laugh as Luke smacks him.

"You're lucky Callie isn't here," he says.

Casey smirks and reaches over him for a handful of peanuts. "She hates this shit as much as I do."

Crunch.

"You finally picked a date?" I ask.

"Yes, sir," Casey says through a mouthful of peanut. "September fourth."

"Awesome! Congrats, man."

He pops another nut in his mouth. "Thanks. I wanted to do the judge thing, but you know Cal. Has to do the whole dress-frilly shit to make everyone else happy."

Luke shakes his head. "You'll be glad you did, Case. Especially when you see what Callie has planned."

Casey rolls his eyes. "Those two."

I laugh. "What?"

"Luke couldn't be my best man because he's Callie's maid of honor."

Luke snorts and shoves him. "Shut up, loser."

"Is she making you wear that tutu shit?"

"You mean tulle?"

"Why the hell do you even know that?" Casey picks up a menu and focuses on me. "What's good here?"

"Nothing really," I say with a smile. "But the wings won't make you puke. Plus, they're cheap."

"Perfect."

I signal the server who takes our orders. She gives Luke and Casey an extra-long opportunity to add to it as she hovers, eyes wide. Izzy can't believe that:

1. He's here. At her table.
2. And he's here. Also at her table.
3. And we want wings and three seltzers.

I'd forgotten Luke doesn't drink. Right, he's the one who fought his demons and won.

"So how's life on the rocks?" Luke was never one to play things subtle.

I shrug. "Fucking sucks, but we're working on it."

"Yeah? How so?"

Mila Taylor has moved in and adopted me as her pet.

"We have a few ideas to get back up."

"Like?"

"We're..." *Doing a huge favor for your arch enemy.* "Working on a new track. It's had a good response the couple of times we played it live."

"Yeah? Sweet. You have a sample?"

I pull out my phone and queue our latest mix. It's by no means a pro job, but it's better than the shitty work tape I showed the guys.

Luke holds it to his ear, and Casey leans in.

I try to temper my grin at their reactions.

"Dude! That bass line," Casey says.

I nod.

"Four on the floor, baby! Hot damn."

Now I can't contain my joy. Of course Casey would pick up on the EDM influence.

"Shit, and trap? Fuck, what is this monstrosity?"

I laugh. "Thanks."

"And by that he means masterpiece. This is sick, dude." Luke hands my phone back. "You've got to get that out there."

"Like I said, we're working on it."

He nods, and we quiet as Izzy distributes our seltzers. Also a bowl of unrequested limes... because only the best for Benson's clientele. I wonder what we'll get next courtesy of star-struck bar staff. Maybe ranch *and* bleu cheese? A guy can dream.

"So what about in the *lady department*?" Casey's question comes with mischievous big brother brows and excessive innuendo.

"Nothing too exciting."

"Well, you're young. Best to play the field while you can." He'd probably pat my cheek too if he could reach me. Casey's all of two years older than me and is the only person I know whose version of *asshole* is everyone else's *charming*. I swear the guy could make a cockroach crack a smile. Do roaches have lips? The stuff Casey Barret makes you think.

Izzy's back. "Your wings will be out in a few minutes."

"Thanks," I say.

She visually measures each millimeter of water in our glasses to be sure we're properly hydrated. The pile of limes we didn't order is still untouched. We're also good on the utensils we don't need.

"You sure you don't want something from the bar? Can I get you any ketchup?"

"Thanks, Izzy. All good."

She nods even as she's hesitant to accept this.

"Hard to believe *the* Jesse Everett's at your table, huh?" Casey says, eyes wide with wonder.

Her lips turn up slowly, then break into an open grin. "Sorry. Yeah. I mean. You're… and you're…" She clears her throat. "I'll go check on those wings."

"You're welcome." He grins to me after she leaves.

I shake my head. "You're a dick, you know that?"

His hand flies to his heart. "After I just wrote you a blank check with that chick?"

"Ha. Whatever, dude." I drain my water. Where the hell is our server when you need her?

"Wait!" Casey smacks Luke's arm. "You see that? Our little guy was lying. Oh my god, did you" — he looks around and leans close — "lose the *V-card*," he whispers.

"Fuck off!" I laugh, shoving him back to his side of the table.

He gasps. "Language!"

"Okay," Luke mutters, smirking too. His expression stills. "So, how's everything? You keeping your shit together?"

"Sure," I lie. Am I lying? What's with all the subjective questions anyway? "I'm doing okay."

"Two days ago you sounded ready to jump."

I shrug. "Yeah, well, Jonas will do that to a guy."

"Your father?" Luke's face always pinches into unrest at the mention of family. He has his own ghosts, which makes it hard to ignore him.

"Yep. The bastard's back."

"Shit."

"Yeah." My glass is still empty so I pretend to want a lime. I pick one out of the bowl… and have no clue what to do with it.

"You into limes now too? Heard it's a big thing on the East Coast," Casey snickers.

I shove it in my mouth. Hell, Jonas already left a sour taste anyway.

I add a lip smack at the end for style points and drop the peel on the table.

Izzy approaches with two large plates of wings. Ranch, bleu cheese, *and* a mystery sauce.

"Dinner's served, boys. I had the chef throw in his special garlic sauce for you."

She legit winks, I guess because that's what you do when you deliver extra garlic sauce to rock icons.

"Thanks, Izzy."

"You need more water, hon?"

I have to block Casey who raises a fist to his mouth to cover his laugh.

"Please."

"You got it, sweetie."

She's never called me sweetie. Ev. Er.

"I was wrong," Casey wheezes out. "She might not sleep with you, but I bet she'd babysit."

∞∞∞∞

Dinner improves from there. Izzy eventually leaves us alone, and Casey gets wrapped up in pursuit of tiny chicken parts. Yeah, this afternoon is borderline fun, which is exactly why I'm not at all surprised when three almost-rock stars thunder to our table.

"No fucking way!"

We hear Derrick before we see him. Everyone hears Derrick.

"Dude! You held out on us," he barks at me.

I shrug. "Hey, guys. Luke and Casey are in town."

"No shit!"

Hope Luke was ready to be tackled by a six-foot-two drummer. Parker is more civil with a normal handshake, and

Reece nods. Kind of. He never got used to sharing air with his idols.

Derrick, though?

"Oh, wings? Ah yeah!" He helps himself to a handful—a handful!—and drops to the empty chair beside me. Parker and Reece pull up chairs from a neighboring table.

"Wha're ya doim im hilly?" Derrick pushes through a mouthful of chicken.

"Just passing through," Luke says. "Wanted to say hi quick."

Derrick nods, swallows, and grabs Luke's glass. "Right on." He reaches for my napkin next. You know, so as to wipe hot sauce off his face in a gentlemanly manner. "How long you in town? You have to run?"

Casey shrugs. "Not really."

"Hell yeah! You have to come by our place then. It's right down the street. You probably passed it."

Fuck!

"Uh, I'm sure they don't want to see our shitty little place," I say. Except my voice is more strained than playful. Luke is too smart to miss that.

"Is this the band house you always talked about? We'd love to stop by."

The other guys look ready to shit their pants. Especially when he says, "Actually, Jesse played your new track for us. Mind if we discuss it a bit?"

"Seriously?" Parker's voice cracks, and I know I'm screwed.

The exchange from hell continues on in a distant plane around me as I pull out my phone. How to get rid of Mila... We need groceries? Not long enough. Spontaneous fumigation appointment? FML.

"You okay, dude?"

Someone says that. To someone. Me? I look up. Five sets of eyes watch me slowly tuck my useless phone back in my pocket.

"Just checking my messages."

"Oh to see if—ouch!" Derrick reaches down to rub his shin.

"We should hit the rehearsal room first."

∞∞∞∞

No. Everyone agrees first is the rowhome tour of hell. Damn, the devil will be so bored with me when I finally get there for real.

I push through the crowd to reach the door first. "I need to grab something from my room quick." If I can at least give her—

"Hey, Jess." Her smile fades as the foyer fills with former targets. Victims. Enemies.

"Mila Taylor?" I've never seen Luke flustered. Never. But that's my specialty: turning normal shit into documentary fodder.

I clear my throat. "Yeah. We've kind of become friends."

Now I've pissed her off too. I'm on a roll.

"Friends? Right. Friends." She forces a smile and offers her hand. Luke takes it with robotic grace.

"Wow. Been a while," he says.

I've also never seen Casey look ready to punch a girl before. "What brings you above ground? Lucifer give you vacation days or something?"

The guys snort behind us.

"Right. Well, clearly you have plans I didn't know about, so I'll leave you to it." Her lips are so tight, it's amazing words even escape through them. Oh I'm in a shitload of trouble.

"Wait, you all know each other?" By his grin, Derrick didn't catch the tone or any of the previous exchanges.

"We go way back," Casey says.

"Really? Wow! How…" We can see the moment when Derrick joins the rest of us in the present awkwardness. "Ohhh. She talked shit about you too, huh?" At least it shuts him up. Or not, when the silence turns from awkward to unbearable.

I clear my throat. "So how about heading over to the studio?"

Bodies are already moving toward the door before the matching chorus of *yeps, sounds good,* and *okays* joins in.

"I'll catch up with you," I call after them. Except it's Mila I have to catch when I turn around. I follow the sound of dishes banging in the kitchen. Back straight and fist clenched around a spatula, she's prepared for battle—or murder. Death by pancake-flipper. I dunno…

I've never been great at hiding my amusement.

"What's so funny?" she snaps.

"Just calculating how long it will take you to kill me with that."

She glances down at the weapon, and her shoulders relax with the twist of her lips. "Quite a long time, I reckon."

"Bet you'd get bored."

"Bet you'd stop me first."

"You'll just have to tie me down then." I reach from behind and close my hand over hers. Air releases from her lungs as she lets go of the utensil to lace her fingers with mine instead.

"Friends, eh? Is that what we are?" she says, leaning into my chest. I cross our arms around us to force us closer.

"I don't know what we are. It's just—"

"No." Her hair brushes against my lips as she shakes her head. "You don't need to explain. It's the nature of what I do, what I've done. I guess... It's just never hurt before."

Her voice is soft. "Where did you come from? You've made things very complicated for me," she mutters, and see, that's funny.

"I've made things complicated for *you*?"

I feel her smile when she burrows in my arms. "I suppose I can appreciate the challenge you face as well."

"Oh, is that what you *suppose*?" I turn her around to align our bodies in a completely different pitch. The biology of my reaction is basic science, and she groans.

"Don't you have to go meet your friends?" Her warning doesn't match the way her hands slide down to lock our hips together.

"*You're* my friend, aren't you?" I move enough to elicit a gasp.

"You need to go before your *other* friends get concerned." There's no conviction in her counsel.

More in her arousal, so doubtful, my damsel with a hammer to all resolve. This assault on conviction, her mission to make me lose my mind...

"Jess?"

I drop my gaze to hers. "Yeah?"

She runs her fingers down my cheek, along my jaw. "Where do you go?"

"What?"

Her eyes narrow in search of something behind mine. "Sometimes you're... not here."

A shrug is a great way to pretend to be confused. A kiss for goodbye.

"I should head over to the practice room. See you later?"

Mila Taylor reads me like a flashcard. And I know her nod is also a lie.

∞∞∞

Luke Craven and Casey Barrett own Grammys. Oh, and an Oscar for the song in that motorcycle movie. So when the NSB superstars tell you your shit is good, it's probably okay that your brain explodes. I'm still grinning when Luke and I lean against the brick exterior of our practice building.

"So Mila Taylor, huh?" His lips curl into a smirk as he squints at traffic on the cross street.

My shoe scrapes at an imperfection in the sidewalk. "Shit. I know, dude, okay?"

"You know what?"

"How fucked up it is. It's just—"

"Did I say that?"

My gaze flickers over to find humor in lieu of critique.

"Would I shack up with Mila Taylor? Hell no, but I'll tell you one thing, love her or hate her, the chick has zero tolerance for bullshit."

I release a breath. "Ha. No kidding."

"What I mean is, her presence says a lot about you. I couldn't imagine any guy being good enough to attract that dragon."

I laugh and shake my head. "Awesome. Thanks, man."

He grins and crosses his arms. "Seriously, dude. I'm not surprised it's you. You're the real deal, and if Mila Taylor thinks so, then it's only a matter of time before the world knows."

I grunt and drop to a step. "Yeah well, it's not that simple."

Luke lowers himself beside me. "It rarely is."

I rest my elbows on my knees, staring out over the street. "How did you do it, man?" My voice shakes as blood starts pounding through my body.

"Do what?"

I glance over, hoping he's distracted enough for me to retract the question. His fixed stare allows no chance of that.

"Recover."

His sigh is hard to read. "You think I've recovered?"

"It sure looks like you've got your shit together."

"Yeah? Well, it's not about recovery. It's about finding something worth fighting your ass off to keep."

"Holland?"

"Holland, music, Casey, Callie. You keep adding to that list until the thought of losing it is unbearable."

"That simple, huh." It wasn't meant for him, but he laughs.

"Simple? Fuck no. It's the hardest thing I've ever done. I needed counseling, rehab, meds, and a ton of support to get here, and it never goes away. You don't *recover*. I'm still fighting. Every day. Every damn minute, I fight."

I let out a nod. Shoulder Luke is hard to ignore. Real Luke makes it impossible.

"What if I can't?"

"Can't what?"

"Fight."

"Everyone can fight."

I shake my head against the sudden burn of tears.

Just enough to fight, fight. Hold tight.

Thump. Thump. Thump.

Overrated. Garage band wasted.

Dead eyes, swirling flies, so many lies.

Lies. Lies. Lies.

Thump. Thump. Thump.

I crush my eyelids with my palms. No... Please no. Not now. Not in front of Luke!

Breathe. Just—

Thump. Thump. Thump.

"Stop crying!"

Thump, thump, thump.

"Why do you think you're here? No one wants you!"

Breathe!

"Shut up, you little fucker!"

"Jesse, hey."

My shoulder moves, pressure on my back.

"Hey, man!"

I blink. Why is it so dark? Where's Parker? Parker!

No!

No, no, no!

I jump up.

They're screaming upstairs. I cover my ears because no matter how many times you hear them, the words don't lose their power. The left side of my face throbs. I count the heartbeats in my cheek. One-two-three-four. There's a cadence, so poetic this pulse. One-two-three-four. One-two-three-four. I press my fingers against the heat and find the slick sensation of blood. I hold out my hand out but there's no proof in the darkness.

Breathe. Don't cry. Don't cry.

I won't. Not today.

The padlock rattles outside, and panic rushes into the song. One-two-three-four. The lock siphons all air from the basement. Breathe. One-two-three-four.

Jesse!

Jesse!

Who's that? They never call me by my name.

They're here, the demons, and I jerk away when one grabs my arm. Another. How many hide in this basement?

One-two-three-four.

Jesse!

Call 9-1-1.

Just give him a sec. He's having a flashback.

Parker? Parker!

"I'm right here, brother."

I clench my eyes shut.

"Does this happen a lot?"

"Not anymore. Not like this anyway."

I shake my head.

"Where are you? I can't see you!"

"Right here." His voice is soft. Too soft to be coming from upstairs. I force my eyes open, and...

"Parker." His name shatters on my tongue, and he pulls me into him. Tears of hatred, relief, terror explode from my eyes onto his shoulder. His arms tighten around me.

"We're here, brother. We're here."

I nod but can't let go. He might not be there if I do.

People leave.

"Jess?" This voice is strong and full of fear. It's close, and Parker starts to pull away to let it in.

The air thins, one-two, one, three—I shake my head and reach for him, but he's gone—They leave. The darkness steals them all.

"Jesse." Gentle hands rest on my cheeks, force my gaze into glacial crystals.

"Mila."

She nods, and I recognize the look of relief that so often accompanies my journey back to consciousness.

Her arms constrict around me, replacing Parker's warmth.

"You go back there, don't you?" she whispers so only I can hear.

There'd be too much to say, so I close my eyes and refill my lungs.

"We should get him back to the house."

∞∞∞∞

Overrated, garage-band wasted, talent-jaded
  They said

My eyes snap open. Air shoots into my lungs.

Destined for rejection, binding imperfections, nothing but
objections
  They said, they said

I roll out of bed and fumble for my notebook. A pen, my guitar, and I'm in the dim lamplight of the living room.

Attractive fraud, where's your army now to defend the legend
that only exists in
  Could have beens
  Would have beens
  Should have been vapors afraid to face the wind

"Jesse?"
Bm. A. Passing G to Em? No, two beats. Two. I play the progression again.

Attractive fraud, where's your army now?

There are other words in the room now but I can't hear them over the ones screaming in my head.

Could have been,
Would have been,
Should, should, should have been
Too hazy for a spotlight
  They said

"He's okay."

"But look at him! It's like he's not even here."

"Yeah, he got the music."

"The what?"

"This is what happens when the music comes. He's writing."

"This is normal?"

"Nothing about my brother is normal."

Couldn't be
Shouldn't be
Wouldn't be if not for helping hands that cower under streetlights

"So what, we just leave him like this?"

"Basically. You can't stop it."

"For how long?"

"I don't know. Hours? Days?"

"Days?"

"He left us for three to write 'Jonas.'"

You're special
She said
A fucking god beneath the fraud
She said

Could be
Should be
Won't be
Unless she collects
the lies she tells

"He needs help, Parker."

"It's who he is."

"Is it? Or is it who you need him to be?"

"Fuck you, Mila. You exploit him as much as everyone else. How much was the paycheck for ripping him apart?"

I'm no god, just a piece of hell
Here to tell you how it is

∞∞∞∞

Voices drift from the kitchen. This house is great at turning private conversations into murky public broadcasts. I listen for clues, but only get enough to know I'm not supposed to hear.

I don't have to. I know this conversation by heart.

Mila is sorry but this isn't what she signed up for. I'm too fucked up to fake a career, and she's not equipped to deal with it. She wishes us the best. Maybe call her if I get my shit together. Until then, we should concentrate on getting me help. Do they know how to stage an intervention? She knows all kinds of random shit. Bet she knows how to do interventions too.

My chest tightens as I trace the indent of the woman I'm starting to need. It's a vacuum, painful as it sucks my heart back into the shadows. That's the problem with secrets. Once they're exposed, they become connections. Connections that rip out a chunk of your soul when they snap. It's why my heart tucked itself safely into the depths of me, beyond reach, further protected by substance clouds and casual encounters. Connections bleed. Connections hurt.

Vague memories of last night filter through my head. The music has finally let me go, as evidenced by how I'm awake in my bed. There were witnesses with me, watching, judging, but I can't remember more than that. I have to assume Mila was one of them.

Footsteps tap toward me from the kitchen. By their delicate gait, I know what's coming. My heart, that beating defector that crept into view against my will is about to pay for its betrayal. Ripped out. Shredded. Grated into a pulp that will watch as its connection packs her suitcase and delivers the sentence it deserves.

This is the problem with secrets.

Her eyes are heavy when she opens the door. Apologetic. I can't look anymore and squeeze mine shut.

"Don't."

"Jesse—"

"I'm serious, Mila. Don't soften the blow. Just go."

"What?"

"I don't hate you for it. I don't even blame you." My voice breaks, and self-hatred fills my throat with bile. "People leave." Everyone. Everyone.

No one wants you.

Why do you think you're here?

No one wants you.

No. One.

Except the sounds move in the wrong direction. Closer?

Everyone leaves.

My bed creaks from unexpected weight.

Everyone! Everyone, everyone.

The indent beside me fills with a heartbeat. A warm hand. A soft breath against my ear.

"Not everyone," she whispers.

17: GINA

We pretend the incident outside the practice room didn't happen. At least, the guys and I do. They're used to my crazy. Mila, though? She's just being patient. I see the questions swirling in her head, the pleas she's fighting to suppress. She does, and as the days pass with a distinct vibe of "normal," the urgency of her silent protests subsides.

"I have to go back to New York tomorrow."

The blankets on my bed can't block the sudden chill. She traces the tattoo on my chest as I tighten my arm around her. It didn't take long to need her warmth to sleep at night.

"Does that mean..." God, I can't even say it.

Her eyes widen. "No, of course not! I have a few things I need to sort, then I'll be back."

Air rushes into my chest as her hand spreads over my cheek to turn my gaze on her.

"You promised me a couple of months, remember?"

"I know, but—"

"I want my time."

Her lips are warm, flames that scorch a new message into my brain.

Reasons to Fight:
1. *Parker*
2. *Mila*

ꝏꝏꝏ

My plan to spend the day brooding alone falls apart when I wander from my room to find the Feather Duster King raging through our house.

I join another witness in the kitchen and lean beside him with my own cup of coffee.

"So?"

Parker takes a sip and studies the path of Hurricane Reece through our living area.

"Gina's coming."

I almost choke on my drink. "*The* Gina?"

He shrugs. "He's cooking too. Says we better have our asses at the table at seven-thirty sharp."

"Cooking? What the hell does he cook?"

"My guess? Esposito's takeout."

I suck back a snicker when our entertainment starts shoving his way through the kitchen with a vacuum. His wrath for messes shows no mercy. Parker and I watch him attack the crushed cereal by Derrick's chair for a good forty seconds before I pull out my phone.

Should we tell him about the hard floor setting?

A grin slides over Parker's lips as he reads my message.

Nah. It's his own fault for never using the damn thing before.

It's not Reece, but my concern for the floor, that finally leads me to halt his efforts and pull the attachment arm.

"Just a suggestion," I shout, handing it back to him.

His gaze narrows in suspicion. I guess not everyone is blessed with the domestic training provided by the fine folks of the NEC.

Good deed done, I prepare to spend the rest of the day in seclusion. It was a nice thought until dark puppy-dog eyes follow my retreat, plea for help.

Ah, shit.

I sigh, retrace my steps, and turn off the vacuum.

"What do you need?" I ask.

His gaze moves to the stove as he swallows. "Gina's coming."

"I heard."

"I told her I'd cook."

"I heard."

"I can't cook."

"I know." He bites his lip, and I grunt. "Fucking hell. What am I making?"

∞∞∞

I'm not surprised the menu includes no items actually in our kitchen. She loves Thai food. Who doesn't, but that's not happening on such short notice; of course a house that can't stock bread doesn't have lemongrass and coconut milk. We settle on Italian instead thanks to my current fixation on Esposito's shrimp fra diavolo.

I send Parker and Reece to Weavers Way for supplies and assign Derrick to the remaining bachelor offenses in the house. He groans at the state of the bathroom, but it's mostly his shit anyway.

"Zero sympathy, dude!" I call out from the kitchen at the muttered curses and haphazard banging drifting down the hallway.

"Where's the suction thingy?" he shouts.

Crap. "The plunger?"

"Yeah!"

"You shouldn't need that to scrub a toilet."

"Then how do you get the paper towels out?"

Aw, fuck.

I dry my hands on a dishtowel and march toward the bathroom. Sure enough, there's Derrick, knee-deep in heaven knows what.

"How the hell..." I shake my head. "Forget it. Don't want to know."

I grab the plunger from under the sink and transfer my frustration to whatever monstrosity our drummer tried to flush.

"Toilet paper," I growl when the drain finally wheezes and gurgles itself empty. "The only thing that goes down that hole."

"But the paper towels..."

I point to the wastebasket after washing my hands. "Only toilet paper in the toilet."

Seriously. And I'm the dysfunctional one?

Head pounding and patience wearing thing, I press my palms against my eyes. I need a break, just a little something to take the edge off, and make a detour to my room. Ice spreads through my limbs when I pull open my drawer. Shit. I forgot that other things do get flushed as well.

Fuck!

∞∞∞

I'm in a terrible mood when the guys return with our groceries. They sense it and give me a wide berth while I yank ingredients from bags and utensils from drawers. The kitchen is a ghost town when the knives come out.

Someone must have something.

"Yo, D!"

Derrick's face peeks around the corner. "'Sup, man? I finished the bathroom, I swear."

"Great. You have any weed?"

"Nah, man. All out."

Shit.

He salutes and disappears. I go for the tequila instead. Not ideal, but two shots and the burn puts me back on track.

Peeling shrimp ain't child's play.

"Need help?"

Nice of Reece to offer since it's *his* date.

"You know how to devein shrimp?"

"I don't even know what that means."

Figures. "Then, how about you open those cans of tomatoes."

"How many?"

"Three. You got the basil?"

"I think so?"

He holds up a plant wrapped in a bag. "Good. Start chopping that too."

"Okay..."

I sigh and point to the knife block. "Use the one on the top left. Were you able to find fresh bucatini?"

"Um..."

I don't have time for this shit. "Parker!"

"What's up?"

Even Parker doesn't take more than a half-step into my lair. "Did you get bucatini?"

"We couldn't find any fresh so we grabbed linguine instead."

I nod. "You should start chilling whatever wine you got," I direct to Reece.

Did I just ask him to recite the Japanese alphabet? "Dammit, man, seriously? Have you never dated a girl before? Like, ever?"

"How am I supposed to know all this shit?"

"Common sense, dude." I let out a breath. Those poor shrimp need me to keep it together. "I'm good here. Go to the state store and pick up a few bottles. And not the cheap shit."

"Red or white?" he calls back. The guy has never looked so afraid. "Red. Sorry. Probably red."

"I'll go with him," Parker mutters.

∞∞∞∞

Nothing improves from there. Within seconds of their departure I lose my favorite shirt to Reece's terrible can-opening skills. I curse and toss it in the hallway. This kitchen is a thousand degrees anyway.

I grab another can and call Derrick to clean up the tomato explosion. His eyes ignite with amusement when he sees me half-naked in front of the stove.

"Not a word," I warn.

His mouth closes abruptly. My glare has that effect.

"Just set the table for five, okay?"

"Only five?"

We both glance toward the unexpected voice, and my sour cloud slips away.

"Mila?"

She smiles. "I finished my meetings and thought whatever was going on here had to be more interesting than a night in my flat. I see I was right. Should I be jealous?"

She slinks forward and slides her arms around my waist. Only one thing can distract me from the prospect of overcooked shrimp, and those lips have no mercy.

"Daaaayuuum."

We pull back and exchange a smile at Derrick's feedback.

"Teach me how to cook?" By the way his eyes flicker between Mila and me, he might be serious.

I smirk and turn back to my shrimp. It feels damn good when Mila settles in against my back, fingers tracing the ridges of my abs. I'm more than ready to skip dinner.

"And he cooks," she says against my shoulder. Words become lips which become a scorching distraction on my skin.

"He's an amazing cook," Derrick interrupts. "When he actually does it. Remember that prime rib you made that one time?"

I pull in a breath. "I remember."

"Oh! And the Tahiti chicken! That was epic."

"Tandoori chicken."

"Yeah! That one. I could eat those pita thingies with anything."

"Naan bread."

"No, they were definitely bread. Not normal bread, mind you, but..." Derrick gets sidetracked trying to remember everything I've ever made, and I suck in a breath at the sudden pressure on my zipper.

"I've missed you." That voice goes straight to my groin. Every. Damn. Time.

"I missed you too."

Shrimp. Pasta. Boil water.

The button releases, and her hand slips into my jeans, forcing the zipper down. I brace against the counter. *Shit.*

"Hey, D. You know how to boil water?" I call over, somehow keeping my voice steady.

He pauses. "Um... do we have a water-boiler?"

I groan, and Mila giggles. She gives me a hard squeeze before letting go. "Oh well, maybe for pud," she whispers.

With her seduction officially thwarted, Mila retrieves a clean shirt for me instead. I'm still buttoning it when three more bodies cram into our kitchen.

"Look what we picked up while we were out." Reece beams as he presents a curvy blonde woman five times out of his league.

"You must be Gina," I say since Reece clearly hasn't mastered introductions yet either.

She smiles and nods. "And you're... Jesse?"

"I am."

"The hair," she says, tugging her own. "Which means, you're Derrick."

"She's a genius," Derrick whispers to the rest of us. It would be offensive if he were joking.

She only laughs. "Okay, got it. And you're...?"

"Mila," my girl says with a smile.

Gina returns it. "You're with Jesse?"

I love how she tucks her arm around my waist. Possessive. Gina's not even a threat. This message is for me.

"Yes," I say. She looks up, and I'd say it a hundred more times to see that shine in her eyes.

"Well, the food smells delicious. Did you make it?" Gina asks me. Uh-oh. "I helped Reece a little."

He tosses me a grateful smile, and Mila gives me a squeeze. Note to self: teach the boy how to cook for real if he wants to keep that woman.

ooooo

Verdict is in: Gina's real.

By the time dinner ends, she's confirmed almost all the lies Reece fed us for the last six months. She *is* in fact a grad student who was studying abroad. She *is* a classically trained violinist. She *does* speak two other languages fluently.

Reece glows the entire time we quiz her for a flaw.

"Way to go," I whisper as we take a load of dishes to the sink.

He's a man in the clouds. "She has a place in center city. We're heading there in a minute."

"Center city?"

He cringes. "Yeah, her family owns a brownstone in Rittenhouse Square."

I snort a laugh. "Of course they do. Gonna meet the parents?"

"Nah, nothing like that. They're in Europe or something. We'll have the place to ourselves."

I slap his arm. Is he blushing? "You know what to do, right? You have protection?"

"Fuck off," he grunts, but a smile peeks out as he glances back toward the dining area.

"Go, man. I'll clean up."

"You sure?"

"Of course." I step back. "Just don't kiss me, geez."

He shoves me instead. "Seriously, though. Thanks, man. I owe you."

"No you don't. Just don't screw things up with that one."

"Hell no!"

∞∞∞∞

The happy couple is off to their center city honeymoon. Derrick and Parker head out to play, which leaves Mila and me alone with the dishes.

"You don't have to do that," I say as she struggles with a pot in the sink. I drop my stack on the counter and reach for it.

She swats me away. "I can wash a pan."

"Really." I lean against the fridge and cross my arms.

"What? The spoiled rich girl can't clean a dish?"

I shrug, mostly to earn an adorable scrunch of her nose.

"I'll have you know, I volunteered in a soup kitchen for an entire term in senior school."

"An *entire* term, huh?"

That gets me a soapy sponge in the chest. I laugh and toss it back at her.

She shrieks when it lands in her hair. "How dare you!"

I wrap my arms around her from behind, suppressing whatever plans for revenge are ripening in that brain. "I don't think you're a spoiled rich girl."

"I can see why you'd think that."

I kiss her head, inhaling her intoxicating blend of flowers and fruit.

"Did you mean what you said to Gina?" Her voice is porous with hope.

Ah. The public confession. "Do you want me to?"

Her weight settles against me. "I do..."

My heart hammers at the hesitation. "But?" I tighten my arms around her.

"Not a but, just"—she twists back to face me—"we don't have a future. We won't until *you* do."

I tense at the familiar warning. "I haven't even used since you got back."

"No, and you haven't dealt with any of the underlying issues either."

This argument feels familiar, and I swallow the instinctive protests. Been there, lost that, not interested.

"So how was New York?"

She blasts me with another look, before channeling her frustration into sauce stains instead.

"Fine."

"Your book thing?"

"Fine."

"Your apartment?"

"Fine."

"Wow. What a *fine* day you had."

Her glare softens into a sigh.

"Not even an *acceptable* or an *okay* or an *adequate* or a *satisfactory* in there?"

There's that pretty tug of her lips. "Shut it."

I rest my chin on her shoulder from behind. "I would, but your story-telling is captivating. When you say *fine*, are—"

A sponge to the face shoves me back a step.

"Oops," she laughs, not looking remotely sorry. I wipe my face with my shirt, and she softens further. "I spoke to your friend."

"Which friend?"

"Your arsehole pal. His people reached out for a *chinwag* so he could tell his side of the story."

"Wait, you're talking about Wes?" Now she has my attention. "Does that mean you listened to their album? What did he say?"

"So many questions. You'll just have to read my post tomorrow."

"Seriously?"

"Seriously. I also spoke to my contact at Smother. Leon is definitely interested in the idea of a live band night and happens to be familiar with your music. He's going to discuss it with his wife who runs the special events at the club and get back to us. No promises, but I'm fairly certain we should start talking strategy."

18: A Piece of Hell

Manager Mila has a lot of ideas for the Alton Wedding. Tons, and her presence has certainly changed the dynamic of rowhome kitchen table band meetings.

"Instead of covering contemporary music for the prelude, why not cover classical songs? You have time to arrange a couple, right?"

Whoa. Interesting. Could be fun.

"Classical?" Derrick asks.

"Sure. Maybe Pachelbel's 'Canon in D' or Bach's 'Jesu, Joy of Man's Desiring?'"

"Pockmark what?"

"Johann Pachelbel?" Mila says.

Derrick shrugs.

"Pachelbel's Canon. Really?"

"Assuming that's some kind of army song?"

"Oh my god. Have you never been to a wedding?"

"Yeah, but—"

"Johann Pachelbel is a classic German composer!"

I snicker watching Derrick's brain explode.

"Ah... But Jesse doesn't speak German."

I bite my lip at Mila's exasperation. Time for our manager to manage.

"They're classical songs, Derrick. Typically played without words."

"Wait, so like, we'd do an instrumental version?"

"Canon in D is always instrumental! It's..." She pulls in a deep breath. "Hold on." After a quick phone search, she holds it out to us.

Derrick's face brightens. "Okay, sweet! I'm diggin' it. But none of us plays the harp."

∞∞∞

I laugh as Mila grasps her head and drops to my bed.

"He's an amazing drummer and has a good heart," I say.

"I know. But seriously. Please tell me *you* know Pachelbel."

With a faint smile, I grab my guitar and start picking out the iconic riff of his famous Canon.

She lets out a relieved sigh. "Thank god. Eh, that's pretty good. Where'd you learn that?"

"June and Toby," I lower myself beside her and continue working my way through more lines of history.

"June and Toby?"

"Foster parents. I lived with them for eight months. Best eight months of my childhood. They were musicians and let me fool around in their home studio."

"Really, wow."

"Yeah, it's where I learned that music doesn't have to equal pain and drugs. They're the reason I'm here and not strung out under a bridge somewhere."

"What happened to them?"

"Nothing," I say with a shrug. "They're still around. We do dinner every so often. They've even come to a couple of our shows."

"They sound ace."

"They are. I did really well with them."

"Then why did you leave?"

My fingers stall on the strings. I lose the rest. "Jonas came back."

Her reaction is in the silence. Jonas has that effect.

"Anyway…" I push myself up and return the guitar to its stand. A knock rescues me from more awkward seconds courtesy of Jonas Everett.

"Jess, can you come out here?"

The urgency in Parker's voice makes my stomach knot. "Be back in a minute?" I say to Mila, on my way to the door. I pull it open, and Parker yanks me into the hall.

"She's here," he hisses.

"Who?"

"Natasha! I thought you said you were done with her."

"I *am*."

"Well…" He waves his arms to emphasize how wrong I am.

"Where is she?"

"On the porch."

He glances at my closed door. "Want me to distract Mila?"

"Thanks, man. I'll get rid of her."

I take off for the entrance before Parker can unload any of his *told-you-sos*.

Derrick offers a slap on the arm as I pass through the kitchen.

Natasha waits with arms crossed, mascara smudges etched into the creases around her eyes. I can't tell if the makeup is exaggerating or dulling her death stare.

"Hey," I say, stepping onto the stoop and closing the door. A biting March wind cuts through my thin t-shirt, and I cross my arms.

"Why haven't you responded to my texts?"

"Why are you still texting me?"

"Excuse me?"

"I thought we resolved everything. I got your messages, but I don't have anything else to say."

"So I tell you I still love you. That I want to see you, and you just ignore me?"

My fists clench. "You don't love me. We already talked about this."

"Don't tell me how I feel!"

I cringe and glance around. I know how well voices carry through the glass to my room. "Can you keep your voice down?"

"Why? Don't want the world to know what an asshole you are?"

"Natasha..."

"Or do you have another girl here? That's it, isn't it? Found yourself a new dealer?" She leans toward my closed window. "Hey, new slut! He's only using you!"

"I'm going back inside," I mutter and reach for the door.

She smacks my hand away. "You've always thought you were too good for me."

"Tash, please—"

"Don't call me that! You're a junkie, Jesse Everett. Just like all the other shitty lowlifes who pound on my door."

"I'm not a junkie."

"No? Because I seem to remember a desperate loser begging—yes, *begging*—at my door for a hit. You were so wrecked you let Trav drug and assault you just for a taste."

"Fuck you, Natasha. I haven't even used in weeks."

"Ha! Well, congratulations. You want a trophy? You'll be back. You always come back, and when you do, guess what? I'm gonna say 'fuck you, too.'"

"I won't be back."

I won't.

Just enough to fight, fight.

"You're weak, Jesse. You can't change what you are." Her face twists into an evil I haven't seen before on her. "Good luck, *boy scout.*"

She throws a small plastic bag at me and storms off.

Four white pills. My hand shakes as I pick it up. Blood pulses through my chest in a painful rhythm.

Just enough…

Just enough.

∞○○∞

I shove the bag in my pocket before going back inside. If ever I needed a moment alone to figure shit out it's…

Fuck.

The entire house is waiting for me in the foyer—Mila front and center. I close the door slowly behind me and brace for war.

"I'm guessing you heard all that."

"Is it true?" Parker asks, stepping forward.

"Which part?"

"The *mugging* a month ago? Was that an assault by a dealer?"

"I don't want to talk about it," I say, trying to push through them.

Parker grabs my arm and yanks me back. "I asked you point blank and you lied to me! And what did she mean by letting Trav drug you? What else happened that day, Jess?"

"It's none of your business."

"Of course it's my business!"

"I'm not a kid anymore. Stop acting like my parent."

I flinch as he slams me into the wall. The jolt is enough to ignite an older burn in my ribs, and I double over to catch my breath.

The small plastic bag falls from my pocket.

"What the—"

He swipes it off the floor, eyes burning. The room goes dark.

"You fucking liar!"

"I didn't ask her for it."

"But you were going to keep it, weren't you? Dammit, I'm so sick of this!"

Parker storms toward my room, and I rush after him.

"What are you doing?"

"How much is there?"

"What? There's nothing in my room!"

"Stop lying! What else are you hiding?"

"Nothing!"

He rips through the contents of my desk, scattering papers and supplies. Frustrated, he shoves it away from the wall, burying my notebook in a grave of debris.

"Stop it, Parker! You have no right to touch my stuff."

"No?" he shouts back. "Then who's supposed to keep you alive?"

On to my dresser. The pile of clothes on top hurtles to the floor. Another wave crashes from the first drawer. Then the next.

"Parker!"

I lunge and grab his arm, but he sends me staggering to the floor. My dresser is a skeleton when I look up, empty drawers hanging like broken limbs.

When he goes for my closet, I've had enough. I charge him, and he lands against the wall with a thud. A second later, my own face explodes with pain from a hard fist. I fall back, and he's on me, angrier than I've ever seen him. I block the first blow but can't bring myself to fight anymore. It's Parker. It's.

Another strike. And another. And—

I cough painful air from my lungs, and the weight suddenly lifts.

Parker's expression shatters as he stands over me, gaze scouring my bloody face.

"Shit, Jess."

He reaches down to help me up, but I push his hand away.

"Just get out of my room."

My arms tremble as I brace them against the floor.

"Jess…"

"Leave!"

His eyes make one last pass at the damage before he stalks away. By the time I push myself up, only Mila remains.

Only disappointment. Fear. Regret. Pity.

"He had no right," I say quietly. *He had no right.*

She shakes her head, eyes dark. "You promised."

"I'm no god, just a piece of hell. Here to tell you how it is." My throat closes around the lyrics as they seep out.

Tears veil her eyes. "I hate your choice, Jesse. I hate it."

My chest throbs from more than a misplaced strike when she backs away. Footsteps down a hall can hurt just as much as a fist.

This is why no one wants you, you little shit.

Nausea sweeps over me when I stare at what's left of my room. Is it even worth piecing back together? I drop to the floor by my closet and rest my head on my knees. My closet. Inviting images flash through my brain. Hiding. Safety. Just—

I burst to my feet and pull open the door. Hazy memories return. A shelf. A strip of tape. I tear through clothes and old shoeboxes.

Peace. It's right here. I know it, sense it, even if I can't remember.

My fingers slide over edges and cracks.

Where is it? Think.

There! I rip the bag from its hiding place and soak in the contents. Six pills in this one.

Just enough.

∞∞∞∞

I wake to a dark, empty house. It takes a moment for the swirling to steady enough to navigate the switch on the lamp by the couch where I finally passed out. Light breathes life into the room, and I squint at the shadows. The demon screams are muddled, giving me the freedom to swing my legs to the floor and pull out my phone. Eleven twenty. Maybe everyone's in bed? Parker, D, Reece—Mila!

No no no. Please no.

My pulse picks up as I force my knees to straighten. The walls continue to shake, and I stumble toward the French doors separating the living room from the kitchen. After a few seconds of forced breathing against the frame, I inch along the wall, through the kitchen, and into the hallway toward my room.

There are no sounds from upstairs so the guys are either sleeping or out somewhere. I wonder if Parker ever came back. I check my phone again, but there are no messages from my brother. Funny how you come to miss the things you hate when they disappear.

The air thins the closer I get to my door. What if she's there? Oh god, what if she's not?

It's all right in the—

No. Because there's no candlelight if she's gone.

Pain sears along my chest, and I can't tell if it's just my bruised ribs.

"Please be here. Please be here." Even in the croak of a whisper I hear the naked fear.

You're Zeropower Jesse Everett.

A slave.

A joke.

An assassin.

Thump. Thump. Thump.

My eyes burn. The mass in my chest becomes a pulsating tumor, pushing up, up until I can't breathe. I press my fingertips into the wallpaper.

Please be here. I'm sorry. I'm sorry.

Everyone's sorry. No one's really sorry. Sorry is a tool.

No! I am, I am.

"I am. Mila, please. I'm sorry. I need you. I need help. Please be here. Don't leave—"

I stagger through the open door, and...

Everyone leaves.

No one wants you.

Everyone leaves because you're a piece of shit failure not worth the air in their lungs.

*Everyone leaves because **you're** the traitor, faker.*

A fucking promise-breaker.

I collapse against the wall, hug my arms around my knees, and let the demons have me.

∞∞∞

They howl in the darkness. Old memories, new accusations. They show no discretion in their attack. I cover my ears—a useless habit I picked up in a basement ten years ago. Pain works better. Bloody fingernail arcs in palms or scalp-tearing grips on hair.

I'm not a pushover. I fight. I endure. I even have enough strength to open the message from Mila on my phone. It's only when I can't take anymore that I shove the rest of my secret stash in my mouth.

Four pills. Just enough. Not enough. Too much. I just need the screaming to stop.

I curl up on the wood floor, drifting in and out of my cloud. It's peaceful there. Serene and hopeful, until I'm jerked back to the chaos. Screams and pain. Then, the cloud. Then hell. Then cloud. Then.

Then.

∞∞∞∞

This time I wake to familiar and strange.

Familiar: my ceiling, my sheets, the rustic smell of our 19th century surroundings.

Strange: the face leaning over me, the restrictive pressure on my arm, the light that penetrates still-foggy pupils.

"Vitals look good. He should come out of it, but…" The stranger transfers her focus to someone else.

"We know. Thanks for your help, Meg. We owe you."

That voice. I know that voice. My stomach churns from another *familiar*.

"You're welcome, but I'm not doing it again. Next time, he gets admitted. Get him help. Got it?"

"Got it." And *that* familiar voice settles my nerves.

"Parker?"

"I'm here, brother." A second later he is, his face hovering close, his hand warm around mine. "You scared the shit out of us."

I look past him toward the familiar intruder. Every muscle in my body tightens.

Parker follows my gaze. "You have him to thank for the fact that you're alive and out of the tabloids with a hope of a career. Meg is *his* doctor friend."

"Former doctor friend if you ever call me like this again," she warns.

The intruder nods. "I understand. Thanks again."

She stops for a hard look as she passes him. "You of all people know where this road leads if you don't get him help. He was lucky. This time."

Now the familiar man turns strange. I don't recognize him with that expression. Afraid? Conflicted? Guilty?

"Get him help, Jonas. At least get him to group with you. Introduce him to Chris."

He must have lied to her about who I am. She probably thinks I'm his son. That he cares, that I listen to him.

"We'll do our best. Thanks, Meg."

Parker's assurance is harder to shrug off.

"Your best may not be good enough," she says, eyes resting on me as if for the last time. She knows the difference between temporary and permanent goodbyes. I don't know which kind I want this to be.

Her exit brings no relief.

"I thought you weren't using anymore," Parker says.

"I wasn't. I'm not."

He drops next to me. "Really? Then how'd you fuck yourself up to the point of needing a doctor?"

"It's complicated." My voice is weak.

"Complicated? No, Jess, it's not. You're an addict and you need help. You're going to kill yourself one of these days, and—"

"Parker?" The intruder's voice is calm. A hand reaches out and compresses on my brother's shoulder. A strange hand. "Why don't you go grab us some coffee or something?"

Parker glares at the man. Then me.

The silence after Parker leaves is eclipsed by the sound of a desk chair dragging along the floor to my bed. The man lowers himself into it and studies me.

"I don't care what Parker says. I'm not thanking you." My voice is starting to come back.

"I don't expect it."

"This changes nothing."

"I don't expect that either."

"And don't think for a second I'll ever—"

"Jesse, please." That unfamiliar hand now rests on my bed, and even stranger, I don't smack it away. "That's what I've been trying to tell you since the beginning. I'm not here for forgiveness. You owe me nothing, and I wouldn't accept it even if you tried. I failed you, son. I failed in every way a father can fail. I'm only here to do everything in my power to make sure you don't end up as the same pile of garbage I was. I want you to have the future you deserve, not the one I forced on you."

Strange.

So fucking strange this scene.

I close my eyes and pretend it's not.

∞∞∞

I keep my eyes closed until I hear the creak of a chair and click of a door. When I look up my room is empty but not dark. Sunlight streams in through the window, and I pull out my phone. That change makes me less afraid to face Mila's messages. There are two.

I start with re-reading the first.

Jesse,

What can I say that will make me walking all right? It rips my heart out to leave you, but I can't stay. You think I don't understand, but I do. I've seen the pain, the battles you fight, and although I may not suffer the same pain, I've suffered its effects. When I was seventeen I attended a charity dinner with my dad. Within five years, four of those in attendance had died of an overdose and two died by suicide. When I saw you passed out on the couch again, I saw your choice. I've seen the path you're on too many times. I was willing to fight with you to change course, but I won't stand by as an escort. You can't afford an accomplice, and I deserve better. You will hate me for this, but I care about you too much to leave without a last fight. I had a long talk with your father before I left. Jesse, I believe him. All he wants is a better future for you. Let him help you.

Yours,
Mila

There's another waiting for me, sent after the first. Bold and bright it warns me of coming pain. Warns and entices. It's Mila. Her words. Her link to my shattered heart, and I have to open it. It's Mila.

Jesse,

I still haven't heard from you. Parker told me you OD'd. God, I'm scared. Please at least let me know you're okay. Ring me?

Mila

My heart races. *Ring me.* Call her and what? Tell her I'm okay? But I'm not. So call her and lie? That's the right thing to do.

I message her back.

Mila,

Got your messages. I'm fine. Don't worry about me. I understand why you left. Good luck with everything.

Jesse

It might be the biggest lie I've ever told.
The first thing I do after pushing send is find my notebook.

Overrated, garage-band wasted, talent-jaded
They said

Destined for rejection, binding imperfections, nothing but objections
They said, they said

Attractive fraud, where's your army now to defend the legend that only exists in
Could have beens
Would have beens
Should have been vapors assaulted by the wind

Attractive fraud, where's your army now?

Could have been,
Would have been,
Should, should, should have been
Too hazy for a spotlight
They said

Couldn't be
Shouldn't be
Would, would, wouldn't be if not for helping hands that cower under streetlights

You're special she said

A fucking god beneath the fraud she said

Could be
Should be
Won't be
Unless she collects
the lies she tells

I'm no god, just a piece of hell
Here to tell you how it is

I grab my guitar and start strumming through the progression. The melody crawls through my brain, the lyrics scratching against the sides now that Mila's gone. Still, I play, gaining confidence in my creation with each pass. Somehow it brings her back.

Parker pushes through the door, eyes wide.

"Is this the Sunday song?"

I flinch, startled. "Yeah."

"Play it again?"

The look in his eyes. I can't say no. But Jonas hovers behind him. I blink and stare at my notebook. My fingers start moving on the frets. Lyrics pour out, and Jonas moves into the room.

The music ignores him, tells him he's not important enough to destroy it. It tells Parker I'm a disaster, but I'm worth the pain. It tells me there's a future I didn't see until this moment. That the only person I need to hear my song has fled to Manhattan.

It tells me I'm blowing it and it's time to fight back.

I'm no god, just a piece of hell
Here to tell you how it is

It's good but not finished. I fish a pencil from the pile on my floor.

I'm no god, just a piece of hell
Here to tell you how it is

That I could be, should be.
And I will.

∞∞∞

People like to say stuff like, *if you'd told me when I was fifteen that I'd one day be having coffee with Jonas Everett I would have...* But I never played that game. No, my only future with Jonas Everett was as a reluctant guest at his funeral. Unless he was a guest at mine. Our lives were on a race to self-destruction.

I don't know the man who's sitting at our table, sucking the edge of a steaming mug. I certainly don't know the appropriate response, so I watch him navigate Parker's terrible grasp of beans-to-water ratio.

I ask the only safe question for this scenario. "Where are the guys?"

"Reece is with Gina. Not sure about Derrick. The gym maybe?"

I nod and sip my own steaming cup of sludge. God, it's awful. I put it down and take pleasure in Jonas' gallant attempt to prove himself. If he survives Parker's coffee, I'll have no choice but to hear him out.

"Who's Chris?" I ask next. Jonas nearly chokes, whether from my question or the liquid mud, I don't know.

"You mean, the Chris that Meg referenced?"

I nod. Parker stops fussing with creamer and looks at me like I just proposed a father-son camping trip.

Jonas plays it cool. "The leader of my support group. Chris fronts a band called E-Z Kings."

"A musician."

"The entire group is made up of musicians."

Interesting. "How long have you been clean?"

"Two years, seventy-three days." He looks at his watch. "Six hours."

"What have you been doing that whole time?"

"Getting stable."

"When did you and Parker start communicating?"

They exchange a look, and I wait.

"I contacted him six months ago. I wanted to contact you too, but figured you wouldn't accept that."

"You figured right."

He pushes a folder across the table.

"What's this?" I try to keep the alarm from my voice.

"My plan."

I cross my arms and lean back. "We already told you, we're not interested in any more of your *plans*."

He shakes his head. "Not for that. My plan for how I'm going to pay back what I stole from you and get you and Parker back to where you should be. At least financially."

More strange words from the strange man. I open the folder and stare at its contents. Spreadsheets. Graphs. Official-looking documents and business cards.

"My financial manager thinks we can have you restored within two years. I have the first payment set aside and ready for you as soon as I get your account information for an EFT."

"I'll get you that," Parker says. Glad one of us can still form words.

"Great. It's small. I'm sorry. I'm still selling assets and moving things around, but hopefully it will help you with your new direction. Parker said Mila Taylor has agreed to represent you?"

My heart twists at the name. "Well—"

"She is," Parker interjects. I glance over at him, and he gives me a nod. "She had to return to New York, but she's working on our strategy from there. She's setting up a showcase at a club in the south."

Another thing I've never seen: a genuine Jonas Everett smile.

"She's a golden ticket, boys. I've never heard of her representing talent before. She's mostly known for shooting it down."

I still don't have words for this, and Jonas clears his throat.

"Anyway, I should get going, but send me that account info. I'll have Brian transfer the twenty-six thousand as soon as I get it."

Parker and I both choke.

"What?" Parker spits out.

"I know. It's not much, but it's something, right? I'll get you the rest as soon as I can."

I stare at the pile of paper in the folder again.

Then at the stranger across the table. He holds out his hand as he passes. For the first time in twenty-three years, I take it.

∞∞∞

We sift through the file after Jonas leaves. Although we don't understand a lot of the numbers and calculations, one thing is clear: Jonas stole a lot more from us than we thought. He also has an aggressive plan to make us very comfortable in the near future.

"We have to tell Mila," Parker says.

"Why? This is the past."

"This is our entire future! She's our manager. She has to see these."

"Oh?"

He glares at me. "Save the *I-told-you-sos*. I already admitted she knows her shit."

I let out a breath. "Fine. Go ahead and call her."

"Uh, pretty sure you should be the one to call her."

"I can't."

"She's worried sick about you."

"I e-mailed her and told her I'm fine."

"Exactly."

I shut the folder and push to my feet. "We should talk to Reece and Derrick. This is their money too."

"Agreed, but that doesn't get you off the hook with Mila." He sighs. "She cares about you, man."

"Yeah? Not enough to be here."

"You didn't give her a choice."

I know. Doesn't help me now. "Please, brother? Just call her for me?"

Parker's forehead creases in protest, but I sat through coffee with Jonas. Listened to his pitch. Shook his fucking hand. Parker loses by a landslide, and he knows it.

"Fine. I'll call her. *This* time. But you can't avoid her forever."

Actually, I'm the Prince of Avoidance. "Thanks, dude. I'm gonna go work on the new song."

19: RUNNING

Jonas thought it would be best if I met Chris for coffee on my own. Given my aversion to all things Jonas, I can't argue.

I search the coffee shop for a red baseball cap and see three scattered throughout. It's not exactly a unique qualifier in Phillies country, and I approach the closest.

The guy doesn't seem enthusiastic about my advance. I smile and keep walking. Number two has a laptop, awkward approach for what's supposed to be a casual introduction, but this is a Jonas-setup so anything goes.

"Chris?" I ask, reaching for the chair across from him.

"Uh…"

Yeah, not Chris.

"Jesse?"

I turn and stare at Red Hat Number Three. The only one I'd ruled out because…

She grins. "Let me guess. You weren't expecting someone so short?"

I swallow and force a smile. "I didn't know what to expect. Jonas isn't exactly great with details. He said Chris would be here at ten wearing a red hat."

The woman laughs and ushers me toward the counter. "What are you drinking? My treat."

She stops my protest with a look, and I obediently place my order. We wait at the counter, making small talk about important topics like other hot beverages we've tried at this establishment and why the current selection is the best. I think I get her strategy. By the time we get to the table I'll be begging to discuss my *deepest darkest* if it means no more caffeine-related insights.

"So I finally get to meet the famous Jesse Everett."

"Famous?" I hold back the snort.

"Jonas talks about you non-stop."

"Really." I don't know how to feel about that. Hell, I don't even know what that means.

Warm brown eyes scan my face before resting on mine. "He was a shit father, huh?"

Somehow, I manage to swallow my coffee instead of spit it all over the table.

Her lips turn up as she watches me recover. "I'm assuming that reaction isn't because you disagree."

"No." I take another sip to save further explanation.

"He also thinks you're the world's greatest gift to music."

I almost lose my drink again and smirk. "Right."

"I don't know. He's got a case. Your stuff is pretty sick."

"You've heard it?"

"Limelight? You kidding? The guys and I have seen you play a few times. We would've sold our souls to open for you."

I laugh and shake my head. Now I know she's bullshitting me. "Jonas said you had your own band. King something?"

"E-Z Kings."

"Ha, yeah, that's right."

"It's also probably why you assumed I'd have a penis instead of boobs."

Damn I love this chick. "The thought might have crossed my mind."

"To be honest, I don't even remember where the name came from. I think it was Louie's brilliant idea. Anyway, it's a shit name and probably why we'll be playing the Tunnel for our entire career."

I laugh again. "Hey, we love the Tunnel. We just played it not too long ago."

"I know. We were there."

"Really?"

"Jonas invited us. Invited the whole damn group, he was so proud."

I pick at an imperfection on my mug. "What kind of music do you do?" I'm not trying to be subtle. She hasn't earned that conversation yet.

She leans back and studies me. "Bluegrass."

"Bluegrass?"

"Why the shock? Because I'm a woman?"

"Because this is Philly."

She shrugs with a smile. "Maybe another part of our problem?"

"Ever thought of trying your luck in Nashville?"

"Of course—ten years ago. I'm thirty-six. Music is a passion, not a career."

Is it weird that a twinge of jealousy shoots through me? "So what's your career?"

"Keeping musicians alive."

"Ah, so you're a masochist."

"I'm a fighter. Someone saved my life, just returning the favor."

"Is this where we talk about rehab and therapy and all that?"

She smiles. "This is where we talk about how much I get it and why I know you won't accept any bullshit."

"Well, I'm not an addict."

"Okay."

"I'm not. I don't need to use to function."

"So just recreational?"

"Pretty much."

"So you've never gotten wrecked to the point of unconsciousness? Your use has never impacted your career or relationships? You've never found yourself in a dangerous situation as a result or did something you regretted?"

I take a long sample of my coffee.

"Addiction comes in many forms, Jesse."

"Yeah, well, it's not that simple."

"It's never simple. It's messy and ugly."

I nod. Even look thoughtful to get her off my back. "When are the meetings?"

"Thursday nights at seven. Your father knows all the details. We'd love to have you."

"He's not my father."

ooooo

For the second straight day I find myself on my bed, clicking through the *Mila Taylor Archives*. I'm not the only one she's fucked over. That doesn't surprise me, but what keeps me moving through the backlist is the remarkable level of insight behind her acerbic tone.

Truth is, she's not wrong most of the time, and I'm surprised at the number of positive posts strewn among her infamous artist-bashing. She may have destroyed a few careers, but she's made plenty as well.

Could I be the first to have both?

It gets harder and harder to ignore those alluring eyes each time I click back to the landing page. My body burns with the memories, but it's my heart that gets charred from the blaze.

I glance down at my phone. No new messages since the original e-mails. Mila isn't the type to beg and has already given me more chances than I deserve.

Chris' words have been flooding back since our meeting. *Your use has never impacted your relationships? Made you do something you regret?*

She did it on purpose; those questions were meant to haunt me.

I dial Mila's number before I can stop myself.

"Jesse?"

Just her voice rushes a calming breeze through my chest.

"I've come up with a few arrangements for the wedding prelude." I have. That's not a lie.

"Oh? Is that why you rang?"

"Yeah." I clear my throat. "Plus, we have band business to discuss."

"Sure. What's up? Is Parker with you? I have time for a conference."

"Uh, no. I told him I'd take care of it."

My fingers tap the edge of the bed. The tempo intensifies with each second of silence.

"Hmm, that's strange because he already called with an update. He told me about Jonas' offer as well."

He did? Right because I begged him to.

"Ah, okay. A miscommunication. Yes, we have some money now if we need it."

"That's great, Jess. I'm glad Jonas is finally taking ownership of his mistakes."

A twinge spikes through my heart. "Are you coming to our show on Saturday?"

"Do you want me to?"

I swallow. "We're going to try my new song."

"You have a new one?" So much excitement and admiration I haven't earned.

"Yeah. The one I was working on... that night."

Her silence is more loaded. "Ah right. Well, I will try my best to make it then. I'd like to sit down with all of you and start formalizing plans for the Alton wedding and the Smother show. Both will be high-profile events, so we need to do them right."

Tell her. Tell her that your insides are ripping apart!

"Sure, makes sense." I clench my eyes shut. "Hey, uh, if you want to come a day early and stay with us, you can. Might make things easier." The long breath on the other end...

"I don't think anything could make things easier for us."

Shredding. Tearing. Echoing through new voids.

My eyes slip closed again as her latest truth smashes through.

"I'm sorry," I whisper.

"Me too. I'm sorry for breaking my promise."

"You never promised."

"Yes, I did. But you were making me break a promise to myself. My feelings for you weren't helping either of us."

"So you left."

"No. This time *you* left. I care about you so much, but you care about escaping your demons more. Until you fight them instead of running away, you'll never have permanence. You'll always find yourself alone because you're always on the run."

What does she know about it? Everything.

What do I know? My bed is so cold now. Colder than a dark basement.

I draw in a lungful of air. "What will it take, Mila?"

"For what?"

"Everything."

"You want everything?'

I squeeze my lids together. "Maybe."

"Stop running."

20: AGITATOR

Not sure which is stranger: the fact that we're playing a school or the row of recovering addicts looking on from center right. I spot Jonas and Chris among them when I peek out for a view of the crowd.

"Jonas here?" Parker asks, leaning past me. "He said he'd come."

"He's here. Along with all his friends."

Parker grunts at my tone. "He's being supportive. He's proud of us."

"Not now, Park." I let the black curtain drop, and grab a bottle of water from the case.

"Cool place," Reece says. "Looks nothing like any school I've ever been to."

"No bells," Derrick explains with a corroborating point to the ceiling.

Right. No bells.

Truth be told, it looks more like a warehouse than anything with its high ceilings, cement walls, and industrial fixtures. Big too. I'm guessing we've pulled over two thousand tonight.

Still not sure how we got this gig.

"They know our music, right?" I ask Parker.

"Yep. Tickets were open so a lot of these seats are our fans."

I nod. *Our fans*—just not Mila. Two thousand minus one is way less than 1,999.

My palms are slick and heavy as I shove them in the back pockets of my jeans.

Thump, thump, thump.

It's my heart this time, strangling out evidence of the fear I've gotten so good at hiding. From the outside, I may look *profound*. But my skeleton knows the terror.

Thump.

And like the pro I am, I put it away when we take the stage. Under bright lights and murky haze I can hide from anything. A show, right? Stage smiles, stage energy, and stage seduction. Look, but don't touch. Lust, but don't feel. Burn hot for the man no one can handle, including himself.

And I do. Burn. Seduce. Give the audience all and nothing because no one wants everything. They're here for the fantasy, to escape their ghosts and demons and shadows. I am slave and master.

Two women crowd the stage, their exposed, writhing bodies oozing Desire. I toss a wink to satisfy them. Another girl sways in a deep trance. She's here for release and gets a smile when our eyes connect. The dude to her left receives a nod for his supportive fist pumps.

Sex god, counselor, prophet. I can be anything for the hours I belong to them.

Then the lights go out. The crowd goes home, needs met, fantasy fulfilled. I step off the stage, headed back to the basement.

Back to the real Jesse Everett.

Back to nothing.

ooooo

"That was sick."

"Great crowd."

"Let's get wrecked. Where's the beer?"

"Check this out!"

Traitor, faker, promise-breaker.

"Is that tuna salad?"

"Sweet! Look at this!"

"Are you fucking dense?"

"Know what I miss?"

Fluorescent lights blast from above.

Echoes bounce from the tiled floor.

Should be

Won't be

Unless she collects

the lies she tells

I press my eyes shut.

An explosion of laughter.

Ha ha — cackle.

Ha ha.

Keep checkin' for clues, cuz I refuse your bait

"Jess, you have to see this!"

"It's not tuna. What is wrong with you?"

"Reee-eeece!"

"It's—"

"Dude, did you see—"

"Hell, yeah!"

Not bright enough to see my scars

Just enough to

That knife you hold is so damn pretty

"Hellooo. Jess?"

I shake my head.

Words. Inside. Outside.

Blinding lights.

Racing pulse.

I can't breathe.

My reaction time is lacking

No backtracking now...

"Be right back," I force out, stumbling toward the exit.

I rush from the green room, down the hall, to the right. Another left, several more steps, and I feel safe to rest my forehead against the cool metal of lockers.

Breathe.

In. Out.

My hands pat my jeans for a sign of impending relief. Just one small lump will do, but they come up empty. I'm out. Fuck Mila. Fuck Chris. They'll never understand why I run, and now I have to face this attack alone.

Breathe.

A fucking god beneath the fraud

She said

She said

So damn pretty

It's all right.

It's all right in the candle—

"Omigod, Jesse Everett?"

"Ahh! Will you sign this for us?"

Fuck! Not now. No no no.

I open my eyes and twist toward the voices. Both intruders are young, cute, and decorated with every sign they intend to fuck a rock star tonight. Their grins say it's time to cash in, and my dick wants to escape my head at the moment.

Fuck!

"How did you get back here?"

"We know our way around."

Shit. "Are you students here?"

"Please." She takes a bold step into my personal space. "We graduated last year."

"We're over eighteen," the other assures me, joining her friend.

Gusts of girl scent wash over me and fill my head with sex. My body reacts on instinct—I don't want this nearly as much as I need it.

Escape. Comes in multiple forms.

No backtracking now that you've got me on the prowl
I'm looking at you
Traitor
Shut up!
Breathe.

"Great. So what do you want signed?"

She holds out... panties? Is there a cliché they haven't researched?

They giggle while I scribble my signature like thousands of times before. On panties, bras, bare skin.... I won't remember them like they hope.

"You were so good tonight." Her hand rests on my shoulder. Slides down my arm.

"So good." Her friend is pressed against me.

"Thanks."

"We were hoping... you know, if you wanted to unwind a bit?"

"See the area?"

"There are lots of great clubs."

In Lancaster? No.

"Appreciate it, but...."

A palm shoves into my chest and pins me against the wall. Blood pounds with violent need when she pulls a bag from her purse. "We'll make it worth your while."

My gaze locks on the contents. Salvation. Escape. Hope that never lasts.

I'm no god, just a piece of hell
A fraud

Too hazy for a spotlight

Hot lips latch onto my neck. Fingers surge down my abs, wrestle with my belt buckle, a stubborn button. The one latched to my arm suddenly cups my hand over an eager breast. With a gasp, she leans into the contact, guiding my fingers. Pressure builds against the zipper of my jeans.

Fading pain. Escape.

"Let's go somewhere."

"Please, baby?"

Painted nails trace the bag over my skin.

Take it.

Escape.

Run to the clouds.

Forget.

Thump. Thump. Thump.

I clench my eyes shut.

Do it!

Everyone leaves!

Run to the clouds.

Everyone leaves.

Everyone.

A crystal stare flashes through my mind.

STOP RUNNING.

My back stiffens.

Stop running.

What if I can't?

I crush my fingers into fists. "I can't."

You can't what?

What?!

"C'mon, baby. Party with us."

Pale yellow pills scream from her palm.

One last time.

Thump. Thump. Thump.

Destined for rejection, binding imperfections, nothing but objections

They said, they said

"I have to get back."

"You don't mean that."

I shake my head. I don't. I do. My pulse hammers.

Stop running.

What if I can?

I push away from the wall. A hand grabs my arm and jerks me back.

"I believe he said he wasn't interested. Thank you for understanding."

I freeze.

Wouldn't be if not for helping hands that cower under streetlights

The apparition in my brain stands a few yards away. Smooth dark waves reflect light in a crown. Penetrating eyes cut through my chest, straight to my lungs. I pull in a painful breath.

"Mila."

My legs move first, the vacuum of her absence sucking me toward her. No thoughts, no plan because I'm completely consumed.

I'll trade a slap for a touch.

Her gaze is on mine. So many questions. So many fears. Hope? Not yet, but not despair either. I pull her in, breathe her for whatever seconds she'll allow before remembering what I am.

Instead of a slap, her arms tighten around me. Her breath against my neck warms my entire body, and the blood that resisted two gushing fangirls explodes for the woman who will never worship me.

"I missed you so much." My voice cracks. She makes me want to...

Stop running.

"I missed you too."

Fuck etiquette.

I guide her toward the wall and devour the lips I've been craving. She meets my attack, hungry palms shoving up my chest and locking around my neck. Her hips rock against me, and I wedge her against the wall.

"You said no to them," she breathes through our kiss.

"I want to stop running. Help me stop?"

She pulls back, fingers framing my face. I let her look, let her see my sincerity, my pain, my shattered mess of a soul that had no chance two minutes ago.

"Then we stop." She states it, makes it more than a possibility. Tears shine in her eyes. My beautiful rock, my witness, my champion ready to fight.

"How?"

"We go to the people who know."

The muscles in my shoulders constrict. "You mean Jonas?"

Her eyes soften. "I mean whomever and whatever we need."

With a hard swallow, I tear my gaze away.

Not bright enough to see my scars. Just enough to...

The hallway is empty when I look. The girls are gone, and with them...

No escape.

I made a choice I'm not strong enough to make.

Oh god, what am I doing?

I can't. I can't.

She won't forgive me when I fuck up again.

She'll leave.

They'll all leave.

Everyone leaves.

Thump. Thump. Thump
Breathe.
What have you done?!
"You okay, babe?"

"Of course." Her gaze is too intense to believe my smile. I push it brighter. "Let's go find the guys. We're overdue for a band meeting."

"You sure?"

I throw my arm around her shoulders and start guiding us... away.

Attractive fraud, where's your army now to defend the legend that only exists in
Could have beens
Would have beens
Should. Have. Beens.
"Jesse?"

My heart races, with fear, guilt. A mind reader? "Yeah?"

"That new song." Her eyes fill as she reaches up to take my hand resting on her shoulder. The way she squeezes... "It's amazing. What's it called?"

I glance over. Draw in a deep breath.

"'Agitator.'"

21: HEA

Life is rosy now. Happily ever after and all that shit.

Oh wait, no. That was the stupid cable movie Derrick made us watch because it had some chick from his high school in it.

My life? Fucking sucks.

Even my ocean ceiling mocks me from its perch. Majestic art to crappy paint job. Well done, sobriety.

"Brought you some coffee. You hungry?"

I try for a smile, manage a muttered "thanks."

Mila has that look as she hands me a mug. She understands, and she doesn't. Sympathetic and pissed as my head pounds and tries to ignore her.

"The lads are waiting for you in the rehearsal room."

"It's not even…" I check the time on my phone. *Shit.*

"The wedding is in three weeks. You need to finalize your set. I've been in touch with the coordinator about logistics. They're going to take care of you."

"Great."

"Jess."

I swing my legs to the floor and force myself up. "I'm gonna shower then head over."

Lips that are usually so kissable press into thin lines as I strip and make my way to the bathroom.

"Have you rung that counselor yet?" she shouts through the door I didn't close fast enough.

Water thunders from the tub faucet.

"I will," I call back, pulling the lever to force the stream through the ancient showerhead. Can we do a bathroom remodel for twenty-six grand?

"You've been saying that for a week now!"

I pretend her intense volume is so I hear it over the pound of the shower when I step in, not her anger. Eyes closed, heart thrashing against my ribs, it feels good not to breathe.

Fifteen, twenty, twenty-five. My chest burns. *Thirty, Thirty-five.*

Thirty-six.

Thirty-seven.

If I never breathed again…

If I never breathed again.

Five

Four

Three

Two

One more second to break.

I step back and gasp in a torrent of humid air.

Amazing.

The far portion of the curtain shoves back, blasting me with icy air.

"What the hell?"

"The deal was, I come back and you get help. I came back. When are you going through with your side of the bargain, Jess?"

She's pissed, but it doesn't stop her gaze from traveling over my body. I lean back and wring my hands through my hair to give her a full view.

"And I haven't used since you've been back."

Her arms fold across her chest.

Fine, let's play. Shampoo next. I work the lather through my hair, trying not to smirk at the thought of every cheesy softcore movie I've seen. By her expression, Mila isn't amused.

"You can ignore me, but I'm not going away."

"No? Can you do my back then?" I ask, eyes closed as I rinse the suds from my hair.

"You're being a wanker."

Damn she's cute. I keep that to myself.

"Mila, I'm fine."

I'm guessing she's even more irritated that she can't stop watching me rub soap over my skin. Maybe I have a future in porn? I keep that to myself also.

"Really? You woke up terrified again last night. That's fine?"

My shrug gets lost in the violence of my rinse. I'm done playing porn god.

"I know you can hear me."

I yank the faucet handle. "Pass me the towel?"

"Not until you talk to me."

I reach past her and grab it.

"I'm fine."

"You're not."

"I'm not a junkie. Look at me." I hold out my arms. "Fine."

"What do you know about PTSD?"

"Oh fuck me." I step out, shove past her, and wrap a towel around my waist. I don't remember my room being so far from the bathroom.

"You're a textbook case, Jesse Everett!"

I shake my head, cold droplets of water spraying folded clothes as I hunt through a drawer.

"The nightmares? The flashbacks? The panic attacks? You survived some serious trauma and you—"

"Just. Stop." The fire in my stare halts her barrage. "I said I'd call, okay?"

I'm not lying. I *will* call. Doesn't mean shit because she has no fucking clue about the *trauma* I've survived. Neither will the name on that useless piece of paper. I'm not using. I'm not running. You won. Take your trophy and leave me alone.

Her gaze turns hot as she reads my mental tirade. "Coffee's ready," she snaps and storms to the kitchen.

Air releases from my chest in a long exhale.

Abuse her, use her, refuse her love.

You're going to lose her.

Traitor, faker.

Wanker.

This one makes me smile. And feel like *shite*.

"Mila." I stumble toward the kitchen while I work my legs into a pair of boxer-briefs.

She straightens from behind the fridge door, eyes brutal with indignation.

"You're right, okay? I'll call after rehearsal."

Her expression relaxes into a hope I can't stomach.

"This afternoon?"

"Yes." I close the gap and shut the door. Securing her face with my palms, I search her eyes. "I promise."

To call.

To play the part until everyone believes.

"Thank you."

Those kissable lips finally use their power and harden my body into a carnal distraction. I kiss her back, losing my fingers in her hair as hers spread fire over my skin. Sorcery it is, the way every muscle responds to her and tightens in her hands. I groan when her grip on my ass shoves our hips together.

"The guys are waiting." She teases my lower lip with a gentle bite, torments the rest with a cruel grind that shoves me against the fridge.

Fu-uck.

"Just some inspiration?" Am I begging? I force her grin to a gasp. We both gasp.

"Maybe if... ah, Jess." Her head falls back, eyelids fluttering in the most poetic plea.

"What's that, babe?"

"Ahh."

Yeah, I don't stop. Not sure I could if I wanted to. I flip us around and trap her against the stainless steel. Her hands slide up, grasping the edge of the freezer door as I slide down. Down. Slowly. Slower than she wants by the way her hips buck against my grip. I hold her steady with one hand and clear a path of bare skin with the other.

"Jess, just..."

"Just what?"

"Now."

"Now?"

"I'm ready, okay?"

"For?"

"Stop being a twat."

"Not a wanker?"

"That as well."

I grin up at her, brush my lips along the edges of some seriously erotic satin panties. My girl, so strong and confident in her desire. There's nothing hotter than being her prey.

Hate her.

Love her.

I burn for her.

Fire.

Heavy choir of flame

Dire anthem of consuming fate

Writhing in mutual desire
Burn, my candle. Blaze into demanding...
She gasps out a moan of pleasure.
Burn, my candle.
I push her through another.
"Oh god, Jess." Her hands rake through my hair.
Burn.
Burn.
She collapses against the door in desperate appeals for air.
Burn.
Sear away the pain that remains
Of those ghosts from hell
Bent on drawing blood
Over and over and over and.
Over.
I close my eyes. Pull her into my arms on the cold tile floor.
"Thank you, love," she breathes. "That was... Your turn—"
"No."
"Jesse—"
My lips rest against her hair, now scented with a layer of beautiful scarlet. "The guys are waiting."
She twists back a glance, and I force a smile.
"Yeah. Later then?"
"Later."

∞∞∞∞

Fucking ghosts, man.
"What's he doing here?" I let the door to our practice space crash shut behind me.
Parker steps between us. If only blocking my view would make the intruder go away.

"I know, man, but if we told you he'd be here, you would have freaked."

"Damn right I would have." I start opening the clasps of my guitar case.

"He has a lot of good ideas."

I glare up at Traitor Two, then over to One. "So do we."

"Jess, you said it yourself. We'll need a shitload of production on this album, and he's one of the best."

"Was."

"Is," Jonas corrects. "I've been back, working mostly with Seamless, for six months now. I'm booked with projects again."

"Great. Congratulations."

Parker sighs. "Jess, can we just—"

"Are we practicing or what?" I sling the strap over my shoulder and move to my mic.

The door creaks again, drawing our attention to... Mila. Fantastic.

Her gaze settles on Jonas long enough to reassure me that she wasn't involved.

"Mr. Everett," she says, way politer than I was. Their stares have a conversation we all can follow.

"The boys have informed me that you're representing them now," Traitor One says.

"I am."

"I'm hoping we have a chance to work together."

Her brow lifts in a comforting level of doubt. "If the band has interest in that possibility, I'd be happy to discuss it."

"We're interested," Parker says at the same time I say "we're not."

We exchange a long look that results in a stalemate.

I woke up impatient of this bullshit. "Okay. Prelude. For flow, we'll run the 'Water Music Suite: Air', 'Ave Maria,' 'A

Midsummer Night's Dream,' then the bridesmaids' processional."

"That's the German song?" Derrick asks.

"Will you stop calling it that?" I say. "It's Canon in D. Every person on the planet knows it as that."

Derrick shrugs. "Sorry, *sweetheart*. Didn't realize you were so protective of old-people songs."

I shake my head. "Moving on. After the bridesmaids are in, we signal Wes and Tracing Holland to come out for the processional. Then we don't play again until the recessional."

"The leaving music," Reece translates for Derrick, who gives him a middle finger.

I glance over at Mila. "Also Luke will be there and we're planning to cover 'Greetings from the Inside' with him at the reception."

Her forehead lifts again in surprise. "Luke? At an Alton wedding?"

"Holland Drake's plus one," I explain.

"Ah. That's a good collaboration for you," she says. "Let's talk to Jay about grabbing audio of that. In fact, maybe we can get the entire opening set for some special releases. What's on the setlist for the reception?"

I take her through our plan, and she nods. After a quick glance at our *guest*, she clears her throat. "I just have one suggestion. The bride is a fan, isn't she?"

"Sophia? Yeah."

"Okay, then she will really appreciate" — another look at the man — "'Jonas.'"

I follow the exchange as well and lift my chin slightly in challenge, waiting for him to protest his anthem.

He doesn't flinch.

"Move it earlier in the set to make sure she hears it," Mila continues. "Maybe get her attention first with a lead-in?"

"I have some ideas for the track," Jonas adds, eyes finding me. "I'd be honored if you allowed me to work on it."

Reece and Derrick try their best to shrink into the floorboards. Parker's face brightens with hope. Mila remains stoic, her attention shifting to my studiously casual stance behind the mic along with everyone else in the suddenly too-small space.

I run a slow chord to test my tuning. And another as I work on the slightly-flat B string. Closer. The high E is out too.

"We'll get back to you." My voice doesn't sound like my insides are exploding beneath my shirt.

∞∞∞

I spend the rest of our rehearsal pretending Jonas doesn't exist. When he speaks, I let Parker respond. When we wrap, I bolt from the room without so much as a glance at the man who seems to think he's earned a seventh shot at my trust.

My streak continues when I call the counselor and learn he doesn't have openings for a while. I assure them that's fine and I don't need the alternative references or emergency numbers they offer.

Check.

Check.

And check.

I'm golden by the time I toss back a few shots of the cheap shit stashed above the fridge. 26-K should be enough to get us decent alcohol. Note to self and my cheap-ass roommates.

Mila enters on the tail end of the burn. I don't know why I feel guilty.

"I have an appointment with *Seth* for two days after we get back from Toronto."

"You called him?"

I nod, force a smile. "He's booked until then."

"That's great, Jess. Did he sound decent?"

I shrug. "Didn't talk to him. Just the intake person."

Her gaze lingers on the bottle and my incriminating shot glass, but I would have looked worse trying to stuff it out of view.

"So your father made an interesting offer." Glacial eyes sear a hole through the liquor label.

Is that why you're drinking? Would you be high if I wasn't standing here?

"Interesting? That's one word for it."

"What do you think?"

I shrug. "Let him have the damn song."

Clearly not the answer she was expecting.

Are you drunk already?

"Are you sure?"

"I have nothing to gain by fighting this. Parker's got his heart set, and who knows, what if he actually comes up with shit we can use?"

My eyes find the amber ring staining the bottom of the tiny glass.

Remnants.

Remnants of relief so vicious to refuse.

"That's a very mature perspective."

I snap my stare to hers, fist clenching. "Don't."

She shrinks a bit. "Don't what?"

"Treat me like a child."

"I'm not."

"I haven't been a child since I was five years old."

"Jesse."

I shake my head. Pour another shot because I'm done pretending for today. I slam it back, pour another, until a warm hand reaches out and stops its progress.

Remnants of belief so vicious to pursue.

"Jesse, what are the scars?"

A boulder slams into my chest and rips down to my leg.

"Not bright enough to see my scars." Her gentle voice betrays the violence of those lyrics.

Needles pierce the veins beneath my skin, flow with savage grace from one limb to the next. The numbness in their wake spreads to my lungs.

Air. There's never enough of it in this house. I yank my arm from her grip and toss the contents of the glass down my throat.

"I don't remember," I lie.

Shut up, you little shit! No one wants to look at you.

Not bright enough to see the scars.

Burning scars.

Burning.

Sizzle of hot flesh, stench of melting skin.

Shut up, you little shit!

"I'm going for a run."

Five shots in, not the best idea. My brain already has to force extra neurons to the project of keeping me steady as I brush past her to my room.

Oh you're going to cry now?

Cry! Go ahead. See what tears get you!

I kick off my jeans and yank on a pair of shorts. It's still pretty damn cold, but my blood is simmering and keeps me warm. After throwing a hoodie over my t-shirt, I leave Mila's protests as a distant ringing in my ears. I'm on a mission. To forget. To pretend. To not think about the time my own father held me down and watched me burn.

∞∞∞∞

The ground swerves and bounces in mounds I don't remember from my former navigation of this park track behind the house. A few stumbles in, and my lungs already hurt. It's a different race when you're running *from* instead of *to*. When it's about the starting line, not the finish. The gravel swells in a sudden hurdle, and I land with a sickening *thud*.

I force my palms against the stones and cringe at the pound of footsteps approaching from behind.

"Oh my god! Are you okay?"

A college girl drops to a squat beside me, and I nod back like I'm a normal guy who fell going for a run. *I have a dog at home and a boss who rides my ass, and damn these shoelaces that got tangled up. I sleep and do normal things like see the man on my birth certificate without having a panic attack.*

"Here." She pulls on my arm, and I let her guide me toward a bench. My fingers circle the backrest as my chest inflates with air. Burning. This is the burning I crave, a pain I can control, start and stop, feed and soothe at will.

"You're bleeding."

"Yeah."

I don't tell her I love watching the red puckers balloon from my skin. I'm already sighing at the thought of the future sting of hot water.

Sting.

Water.

My head floats with pleasure.

"Wait, are you…?"

Drunk? I don't say that either. Only smile, for real—because how funny is this?—and straighten myself as best as I can.

"Thanks for your help," I say as I jog-stagger off.

Blood coats my shins and sleeves by the time I reach our stoop. Would Parker believe another mugging?

Pain has a sobering effect, so I'm hoping the inebriation angle can stay between me and the pretty girl who will probably think twice about jogging alone on that track.

Mila and Parker blast glares at me from the kitchen table when I pass, followed by heated muttering to each other. A chair scrapes the floor and warns me of a confrontation. Parker gets the honor this time.

"I sent the tracks to Jonas." Daring me, he crosses his arms as he leans against my doorframe.

My chest tightens, limiting my response to a casual shrug. I grab the towel drying over the closet door and gingerly apply it to my bloody knees.

Parker straightens, smugness melting into concern. "What happened?"

"I fell."

Traitor. Promise-breaker.

"Need help? Looks bad."

I shake my head and force myself up. "It's not bad. Excuse me." I brush past him toward the bathroom.

"We have to keep moving forward, Jess. I get your issues with Jonas, but we—"

"No. You don't," I say and slam the door.

22: WEDDING BAND

Truce. That's the best description of the weeks that follow. Mila, Parker, even Jonas, are numb footnotes in my exhausted existence. After twenty-three years, I'd eked out a rhythm of survival. Maybe it wasn't ideal, but I could function. Life and I had come to an agreement of sorts. Now? All those hands trying to fix me are shoving me in too many directions.

The music has become a tumor in my head, blasting its lyrics and melodies with debilitating fury. I scribble violently, always at night, in the privacy of darkness so I can polish and paint a different story with the sunrise. The nightmares return. The day terrors. The voices, the demons, they all slice through undefended walls, lodging beneath my skull until it's everything I can do to lift my head off the pillow in the morning.

Any remaining strength is spent on hiding.

Mila leaves. Not for long, she promises, but her time in the States has already been extended beyond what her schedule can accommodate. She returns to the UK to manage the part of her life that doesn't involve babysitting an unstable rocker. I pretend well enough to convince her she's safe to leave me alone.

Li is my first call when she does.

∞∞∞

It will be different this time.

My ocean ceiling blurs through the mist soothing my head. I'll be careful, responsible, which is why I don't have to feel guilty about breaking my promise to... everyone. But promises are complicated, simple in their construction, muddied in the execution. Those same champions need me to function. That's the part they forget.

"Hey, we're going to start loading the trailer. You coming?" Parker asks, ducking his head into my room.

"Yep, just give me a sec."

He nods, narrows his eyes a bit.

"You okay?"

"Fine, why?"

His shoulders lift and drop. "I dunno. Just... Okay, see you out there."

He claps the doorframe and disappears. I blink away as much of the fuzz as I can and force myself up. Like I said, responsible, which means getting my relief *before* crossing the border into Canada.

∞∞∞

The Alton's clearly spared no expense on their daughter's wedding. After an uneventful journey north, including a trailer inspection at customs, we pull up to our Toronto gig four hours early. We may need every minute if we spend more time gawking at the Greek-inspired edifice. Columns, fountains, and "statues of fucking gods and shit" (Derrick), guard the premises as a silent marble army.

"Dude, we need one of these for the porch," he says, palming a poor goddess' head. "By the door?"

"I'm gonna check in with the wedding coordinator and find out what's up," Parker says. Zero interest in landscaping design, that guy.

Reece is already climbing back into the driver's seat. "Let us know where we should meet you to unload." I guess I can't blame him when the alternative is watching Derrick... Wait, where the hell is Derrick?

I squint through the marble forest and find him attempting to ride a minotaur. Hope he knows I'm not spending the second influx of Jonas cash on broken bull parts.

"Yo, D! Want to explore with me?"

Derrick lifts a hand and slides to the ground. He never made it further than the minotaur's butt anyway.

"Bet they have a chocolate fountain at the reception. Like the expensive shit from Sweden."

"You mean Swiss chocolate?"

"S'what I said. Dude, look at that!"

Derrick explores every feature of the grand foyer while I check the message on my phone. Luke and Holland want to know when we arrive so they can meet us. I'm about to pocket the device when it rings.

The name both chills and warms me.

"Hey, sweets."

"Hey, babe. How's Yorkshire?"

"Great. Are you at the venue?"

"Yes. Parker is tracking down the coordinator so we can setup."

"Fantastic. I wish I could be there for you fellas, but I'd hardly be welcomed."

"I get it. We're fine."

"I found out one of my contacts will be there. I've asked her to shoot some video we can leak."

"Our manager wants to bootleg her own band?"

I've missed her laugh. "It's a new era, babes. Jess." Her tone turns serious, and I drag in a deep breath.

"I'm sorry for leaving. I hated going away, but I need to sort a few things and set us up for a longer-term situation. I'll be back soon, I promise, and then we'll focus on you and the band."

Great...

"I have a lot of ideas I want to discuss with you when I get back. Plus, I have some updates on the Smother event."

"Sounds good."

"Okay. I still feel guilty. You've kept your promise and I feel like I'm breaking mine."

I clench my eyes shut. Another long inhale.

"Jess?"

"Yeah."

"I'm so proud of you. You know that, don't you?"

"Thanks."

She quiets, and I wait for a distraction. Lies are easier in silence.

"Anyway, Parker says you've been writing again?"

I swallow the panic that rises every time the music hits. Sensory memory's a bitch. "A little."

"Anything good?"

"Probably."

My brain is too cloudy to recall it.

"Jess, I just want you to know how much it means to me that you're trying. I know how hard it has to be for you."

"Thanks. Hey, listen, I have to go find Derrick before he gets us arrested."

She laughs. "Course. I miss you."

"Me too."

I really do. I'm also relieved she's not here to see me.

∞∞∞∞

The coordinator wants a stripped-down setup for the ceremony and the full deal for the reception. *Accousticy,* she said. With our antique gold and mahogany instruments, I'm guessing? Yeah, she doesn't know our music. Or the evil plan for the bride's brother to play his forbidden rock anthem processional. We accept the brunt of her wrath by insisting on a full kit, amps, two vocal mics, and our decidedly *not* pretty gear. Wes and the Tracing Holland crew will need it for whatever magic he has planned.

We compromise by allowing flower shit to be wrapped around anything that can handle it. Including Derrick's head, apparently. By the questionable gaps lining the kick drum, I'm guessing his lily-crown came from that.

"Nice, dude. You wearing that for the ceremony?" Reece snorts while strapping on his bass.

"Just trying to fit in."

"With the forest nymphs?" I mutter.

"We could braid some into your sexy locks," he calls over.

"God, it'd be breathtaking," Reece adds, eyelashes batting in all kinds of unpleasantness.

"Fuck off." I pull my own strap over my head and tuck my messy hair behind my ear. I kinda smile too because maybe that'd be hilarious. "You good for sound check?" I shout back to Jay.

He sends a thumbs-up, and we run the first song of the prelude. Our second stops mid-way through when some serious industry star power shadows the entrance to the room.

"Hey, man." My grin spreads through my voice into the mic.

"'Sup?" Luke separates from his girlfriend to trek up the aisle. I step down from the platform to meet him in an embrace that's way more forest nymph than jaded rocker, but who gives a shit when it's Luke Craven? He steps back, and I watch his brain decide how to handle this complex situation. Our last reunion wasn't exactly a clean break.

"You got plans for lunch once you're set?"

I shake my head. "I think they're putting something together for us here, but I'd rather go out."

He nods. "Let's grab a bite. Just you and me." He says this loud enough for the rest of the room to hear. No one even follows up with a smartass comment. That's Luke. His word is law, even for Derrick.

"Sounds good, man."

He claps my shoulder before looping a protective arm around Holland. It's hard to believe that man was once almost as messed up as I am.

"We'll let you finish up. We've got some details to sort out as well," Holland says.

"Heya, Holland. Good to see you too."

She smiles and waves as they fade back through the door.

∞∞∞∞

Luke chooses a low-key deli near the venue. My guess? He wants me to be comfortable. Partly, it's a nice guy thing. Also, I brace for tough love.

We make small talk while we wait for the food and get settled at a table. The place is almost empty at this hour in mid-afternoon, which works well for us. The last thing I need are a bunch of eavesdropping fans listening to our heart-to-heart.

"So our last meeting was interesting," he begins, popping a chip in his mouth.

I stab at my sandwich with the toothpick. "Yeah. Sorry about that. It was... yeah."

He keeps his position. So casual. Like it's totally okay for a guy to have a panic attack in front of you for no reason.

"That happen a lot?" he asks.

"What?"

"The flashbacks."

I clear my throat, force a shrug. "Comes and goes, I guess."

"Yeah? What does your doctor say?"

Casual Luke again. Conniving, casual Luke. I almost laugh at his smoothness. "Not a lot."

"You're seeing someone for that, right?"

Another shrug.

He quiets, his brow creasing in concentration on his sandwich. "Thirty-eight," he says finally, looking up at me with those crazy-deep eyes.

"Thirty-eight?"

"The number of times I tried and relapsed on my own before I got professional help."

Thirty-eight.

"What are you at, Jess?"

Ouch.

"Not sure."

"You know. No bullshit."

"You counting booze?"

"I'm counting any substance that blocks the pain you don't want to deal with."

My gaze cuts an intricate pattern on my rye bread.

"I love you, man. I care about you. Hell, I've been there, and I'm telling you, you can't fix it by yourself. You can't."

"I have an appointment with an addiction counselor on Wednesday."

He leans back, eyes testing my evidence. "Yeah? That's great. You gonna show for it?"

I don't know.

No.

Maybe.

I don't know.

"Of course."

I can't tell if he believes me. Now, *that's* a poker face.

"Good. Let me know how it goes."

"I will," I lie.

Another long look. "How are things with Mila?"

Awkward. Why can't we talk about sports and shit?

"Good, man. She's back in the UK right now, sorting stuff out, then she'll be here. She's still helping us get back up, did you know that?"

"Wow." The word draws out in a surprised sigh.

"Yeah. She believes in us. In me." Why does it come out as an accusation?

"Of course, she does. So do I. So do a lot of people."

If you get your shit together.

The qualifier lingers in the air around us.

If.

If.

If.

Talent-wasted.

Failure.

Wasted.

Overrated.

Not.

Now.

I suck in a huge gulp of water and let it release slowly down my throat.

"You okay?"

"Yeah. Spicy," I say before realizing I haven't taken a bite yet. Luke, man. Throws a guy off-kilter. So maybe I have a man-crush. What about it? Who doesn't get flustered over Luke Craven?

"What's so funny?" he says with a smile.

I shake my head and finally bite into my not-at-all spicy food. "You know Derrick almost broke his ass trying to ride a minotaur in the courtyard?"

He delivers that rare, million-dollar laugh, and I feel like I can breathe again. "Not surprised. By the way, Eli and Sweeny are still pissed about that prank you pulled on tour."

A grin slides over my lips. "They deserved it."

"Not arguing that. Hey, we still on for 'Greetings' at the reception?"

"Absolutely. We wanted to open with it if that's cool with you?"

"Sure. Wes will love that."

I snicker. "So you guys haven't become besties yet, huh."

"No," he huffs. Then relaxes. "But... eh, never mind, it's complicated. The dude has his own shit right now, so ours is on hold. Plus, Holland?"

"Yeah." I return his grin. "She's hard to ignore."

"Understatement."

"Things are good there?"

"Really good. She's it, man."

Glacial eyes framed by long, dark hair flash through my brain. My blood pressure spikes, my body flooding with adrenaline that wants to pour its wrath into a woman.

Not *a* woman, one woman.

One smartass, difficult, impossible woman who challenges the hell out of me and ignites a fire for life that died years ago. *Is Mila...?* No. Not possible. Cupid must be laughing his ass off right now. *Arse.* I smile to myself, then stifle a painful stab of longing.

"When's your next show?" Luke asks.

Right. Luke. Sandwiches.

I swallow a mouthful of food. "Not for a month. We're doing some big promo gig Mila cooked up that's supposed to relaunch our career and put us back in play."

"Really? Sounds interesting. Mind if we come by?"

I almost choke on a swig of water. "Seriously?"

"Of course. Shoot us the details. We'll do our best. Casey still talks about that track you showed us when we stopped by. He wants to see what you've been working on."

"Okay." My heart hammers. Luke and I go back, but this doesn't happen. Not to me. Not to disgraced, overrated garage-band frontmen who can't keep their shit together for more than five minutes. I clear my throat. "Awesome. We'd be honored."

He sees pain where others see stars.

How far will you get with infected scars?

He lets them linger, fester, devour.

Gives them power over future hope.

A tangled rope that binds to Hate.

What will it take to break...

"That was a damn good sandwich. You ready to go?"

I blink myself back to Luke. "Let's do it."

∞∞∞∞

I'm no wedding connoisseur, but I'm pretty sure this affair is the exception not the rule. The sea of guests flaunts black-tie attire like an Oscars audience. Accessories, hair, makeup— It's nearly impossible to tell who's getting married here.

Thanks to Mila, even we're dressed for the occasion. All of us wear some version of the required tux, albeit unconventional adaptations. I may have left my shirt untucked and tie loose. Derrick's wearing what can only be described as a top hat with his jeans and tailored double-breasted jacket. Parker of course looks the *right dapper chap* that he is in a classic ensemble that would make any congressional candidate drool.

So yeah, more than a few eyebrows lift when we take the platform in the front left of the room and strap on our guitars. I guess they're afraid marriages without a strings ensemble aren't valid?

I glance at the clock and watch another rush of guests being escorted to their seats. Our contract calls for a twenty-five-minute prelude, so I shoot a text to Holland that we're starting. I'll send her another one when it's time for Wes and her band to storm the stage.

Maybe I get a rush of pleasure imagining these faces grimace at the shock about to come. They think electronic Beethoven is hardcore?

Derrick counts us in, and we launch into our take on wedding music. Thing is, it's pretty damn fun. With no lyrics, I perch on a stool to fingerpick my way through some pretty sick melodies those old guys put together back in the day. Parker backs me up with power chords and Reece adds a modern rhythm to the classic basslines.

Yeah, Mila was right. Jay has us tracked to separate channels so we can get a good recording. With some production and mixing, we could have a pretty sweet EP on our hands.

The time flies. When we hit our last song, the room is packed. The best part? A lot of those eyebrows have softened into smile creases. Guess they don't call these songs classics for nothing. I like to think Pachelbel would approve of our version.

As planned, Parker takes over the lead when the wedding coordinator signals that the bride is ready. I shift in my stool for a discreet text to Holland letting her know they're up as Parker and the guys draw out the longest outro in history. The poor planner is fuming when I dare a glance in her direction. Don't we know her word is law? When she says it's time for the processional…

Her silent tirade transforms into horror as the door on stage right opens. This was not in her binder, in her notes, in an email, text, or voicemail. We just exploded her flower-crusted universe.

I'm grinning like a kid when Wes and the Tracing Holland musicians take over our positions. Parker and I exchange an amused look as we lean against the wall and wait for sparks to fly. If I know anything about Wes Alton, it's that his song will blow this place up. I'm surprised when another woman I don't know joins him front and center, but whatever. This twist only adds to the epicness.

The main doors open, the bride appears in all her glory, and the man escorting her looks about ready to combust. The music starts and yeah. This is officially the best wedding ever.

∞∞∞

It's not enough to say the tone is awkward when Wes finishes his surprise processional, accepts an elated hug from his sister, and is not-so-subtly shoved from the room by security. Clumsy? No. Gauche. That's it. As much as I've enjoyed plenty of the festivities so far, nothing compares to the restrained madness of this moment. Guests murmur to each other, twisting in their seats to catch a last glimpse of the drama as it rushes through the door and out of view. The father-of-the-bride looks about ready to charge after him. Pissed enough to miss his own daughter's wedding? Only Wes Alton has the ability to provoke such wrath. Say what you want about him, the guy's got balls times ten.

The stuffy ceremony officiant drones like a pro through his checklist of *thous* and *thees*, but frankly, I'm not sure even the happy couple is paying attention. I suppress a smirk watching the bride's gaze continually drag from her beloved toward the door. She's concerned for her brother. That much is clear. I spot Holland whispering feverishly to Luke and pushing him from his seat. He looks less than pleased as he follows his girlfriend's orders. I can't wait to harass him about that.

Eventually, the vibe settles and things get boring. The rest is stale wedding fare. Overly sentimental poetry, some opera song in French that makes the lady in row three with the peacock hat sob, and a bunch of other rituals that I can't accept are real things. Something with knots and sand and I don't know. I'm definitely going to a justice-of-the-peace if I ever get married. Air catches in my throat at a sudden image of Mila, and I push it away. Weddings make people insane. Clearly.

Speaking of insane, I have to fire several warning shots at Derrick throughout the marathon. Put sticks in his hands and the guy cannot *not* bang them on shit. Dude is worse than a three-year-old. Should have checked to see if they had childcare at this thing.

Finally, the coordinator signals for the recessional, and we get back into place. I almost call an audible to launch "Jonas" instead of our planned piece but manage to restrain myself. This crowd has been through enough shock for one event, best save some juice for the reception.

Derrick counts us in, and it's official: Limelight can now call itself a wedding band. Dreams do come true.

23: VIRAL

Going viral in three easy steps:

1. Watch your world fall apart in a highly publicized tanking of your career.
2. Perform a surprise duet with a superstar of his hit song at a private event.
3. Leak said performance to the masses.

Mila is damn proud of herself. I see it on her face when I meet her at the airport, on the ride home, as we cross the threshold into our humble Mt. Airy townhouse. Yes, Limelight is back in the industry conversation, slamming into radars left and right, and I try my best to play the role of hungry frontman.

This is what we wanted, right? Our dreams coming true with our image in the same frame as Night Shifts Black. The guys are freaking ecstatic, already talking labels and tours. So many new albums I have to muster the energy to smile about. This is what you wanted.

This is what you're supposed *to want.*

"I'm emailing you a schedule of the upcoming publicity events I've arranged to keep the momentum while we've got it." Mila barely shoved her belongings into my room before calling a band meeting. Her long, dark hair is twisted up at her neck, all business. Hell, she's even dressed the part with some tweed getup that includes a silk scarf and everything. Even our passionate reunion at the airport felt... managed.

I study her as she speaks, glacial eyes scanning her tablet, elegant fingers tracing the screen with expert grace. The others lean forward in rapt awe of our fairy godmother, but I'm not sure about this version of my girl. *Is* she my girl when she's in business-mode?

"What's going on with the Smother show?" Parker asks.

A slow smile spreads over her lips. "Actually, there's been an interesting development there. Leon and Arianne contacted me with their concerns. Apparently, interest has been so high in your appearance at their club, they've had to take the unprecedented step of ticketing the event. We're in the process of renegotiating the contract in light of the change, but this is excellent news for you. Promoters are already calling with requests. If we keep this up, we should have no problem putting together a formal tour. Once we leak 'Jonas' after the Smother gig, the sky's the limit for us. I can feel it."

A rumble of excitement spreads around the table, and I hate that mine is forced. Grins, high fives, that's the normal response to manifested dreams.

This is what you're supposed to want.

Fame.

Money.

Prestige.

Legend.

I swallow the mass suddenly pressing on my chest.

This is what you're supposed to want.

"Jess?"

I blink and return to the conversation. They're waiting, and I know I've missed something.

"Yeah?"

Mila's eyes darken with concern. For her or me?

"I asked if you thought you'd have enough material for a full album," she says.

"Um..." My brain does a quick inventory.

Spotlights.

Late nights.

So many nights in the.

Darkness.

Loneliness.

Expectations.

Failure.

Their dreams, your burden to carry.

Your burden.

Your hell.

Your eternal basement to sweat, bleed, scream.

Who owns your soul, Jesse Everett?

"Yeah, we should have enough."

I feel Parker's gaze. *Really? You control the music now? You can make it come?*

"I didn't know you had new stuff," he says, translating our private conversation.

"Yeah. It's there, I think." The lie slips through my lips before I can stop it. Parker is the only one not reassured by my announcement.

"Excellent," Mila says before he can argue. "I'll start putting together a schedule." She sighs a content, encouraged expression of everything I'm supposed to feel. "It's happening, boys. The train is moving. I hope you're strapped in."

∞∞∞∞

The first thing I notice is the smell. Damp, organic death. I twist my head to find rotted underbrush and thick mud. Insects poke and

*claw through the filth. Then pain. An awkward pressure against my
back. Stiff, jagged patterns push into my flesh.*

*How long have I been locked in this position? I try to adjust,
but my wrists snap back in a painful jerk. Shit! I pull harder against
the restraints and crane my neck to see the other ends attached to…
long steel bars? I stare ahead, and sure enough the ladder of a train
track extends past the horizon into infinity. My ankles are bound as
well, tightened with the same throbbing tension and…*

A rumble shifts the planks beneath me.

No. No!

*I yank against the restraints, the rope slicing into my skin.
Blood leaks from torn flesh, but I barely notice as I strain for another
look—back this time. It's there, closer than I feared. Bright, burning
headlights force my eyes into a squint. My muscles instinctively
tense, fighting the ropes, and the rattling sends my lungs into a
frantic search for air.*

*"Stop! I'm here!" My cries are drowned out by the blast of a
whistle, the thunder of engines and countless wheels.* Chug-chug.
*The train rockets forward with relentless speed. What's missing is
the squeal of breaks, any desperate attempt to alter its course.*

The conductor doesn't see me.

"I'm here! Stop, I'm here!"

*Tears burn down my cheeks as my body lurches into a frenzied
explosion of violence against the ropes.*

Stop! Stop! I'm here!

*The rumble is a growl now, reverberating through my pores
with each decaying second. Suddenly, the ropes tighten, pulling my
wrists and legs into bone-crushing alignment with the side rails.
This scream is from pain, but the conductor can't hear that either.
No one hears me. No one sees me. No one even knows…*

This is my death.

*"I'm here." My voice is only a whisper, the tears streaking into
my hair as I still.*

No one hears.

No one sees.

No one cares.

No one even knows.

No one.

"Jesse! Wake up. Jess!"

My eyes snap open. I shoot up from the bed as oxygen plunges into my chest with a deep gasp. Heart racing, my gaze shifts in terror around the room. A hand moves to my back, rubs gentle circles over the etches of train tracks. I hold up my wrists and squint through the dim light. No bloody wrings, so why does my skin throb?

"I'm fine," I lie, forcing my legs over the side of the bed. I lean my elbows on my knees and fight for consciousness, the return of order.

It's all right in the candlelight.

It's all right.

It's all right.

"Another dream about the basement?"

I shake my head and run a hand through my damp hair. "I'll be right back."

I make it to the bathroom in time to throw up.

∞∞∞∞

More "great" news awaits me in the morning. Jonas sent over what he came up with for our song, and it's fucking good. Like, out-of-this-world-the-guys-are-flipping-out good.

Parker replays the track, and Derrick does his teeth clenched over fisted knuckles happy dance around the room. Mila leans against the doorframe, eyes locked on me as I concentrate hard on the worn throw rug. I feel her stare, Parker's too, because as much as he says he'd go on without me, we all know he won't. He can't, and he wants me to love this collaboration as much as I hate that I do. Jonas may be a dick father but he's a damn good producer.

"That synth line though," Derrick squeals, clapping like a hyperactive seal.

Even Reece is bursting at the seams to contain his delight over the brutal drops and rich layering of bass for a killer dubstep vibe. I don't know why I'm surprised that the man who manufactured my DNA would get our music so intensely. Worse than that, he took it to a place I hadn't even considered.

A place you couldn't have gone.

You need him.

"It's good," I breathe into the silence when the track clicks off.

Derrick fist-pumps the air. "Hells yeah!"

"We need to get him into the studio with us and do this for real," Reece says.

He's right. They're all right. I bury the nausea ripping through me.

"Shut up, you little fucker!"

"Stop crying!"

Thump.

"Things will be better this time. I promise, Jess."

Traitor. Promise-breaker.

Earth-shaker.

Fuck!

I scrub my face with my palm. "I need a drink."

Pushing up from the couch, I make my way to the kitchen. Mila follows at my heels, probably because *drink* isn't ambiguous enough for her comfort.

"Jesse…"

"What?" The tequila bottle is getting low now that I'm hitting it harder than usual. One shot. I clench my eyes shut and enjoy the burn sliding down my throat and coating my stomach. Two shots.

"Jesse!"

I slam the glass on the counter and glare over at her. "What?!"

Her gaze narrows into Manager Mila: firm, frustrated, fucking *judgmental*.

Shot three.

Shot four, and the bottle is wrenched from my hand.

My glare can cut glass too. "What do you want from me?"

"You know."

I shove away from the island and storm to my room.

Door locked.

Mic dropped.

Gun cocked.

Forgot what I came for.

Shell shocked.

Head blocked

Can't stop

The sound of failure.

No no no. Not now! I shake the words from my brain.

Stop

The sound of failure.

I drop to the bed and press my palms over my ears. I can't. I *can't*!

No knock.

Scene dark.

Don't start!

With a frustrated cry, I slam the first thing I find against the wall. Brochures flutter through the air, debris from the lame-ass folder Counselor Seth forced on me.

You're still running.

Seth didn't say that. Seth didn't say much because I gave him nothing at our first meeting.

Box checked.

Regrets?

Maybe. No. No!

Li has minimums.

My body goes cold, then hot.

Li has minimums!

I rush for the bag hidden in the pocket of a hoodie at the back of my closet.

You promised, phantom Mila warns me. Phantom Mila who's fully present just a few yards away. I glance at the door.

You promised.

A promise I already broke. I'm already a liar.

A fraud. A…

Promise-breaker.

No better than him. Worse than him?

Liquid burns in my eyes, sears down my cheeks.

Stop running.

I tried. God knows how hard I tried. I want to. I can't. I have to. I won't. Everyone knows I won't.

I glance back at the door.

Dropped.

Cocked.

Forgot.

Shocked.

Blocked.

Knocked.

Can't stop can't stop can't stop can't stop.

You're already a failure.

I empty the bag into my hand.

24: Decisions

I stare out the giant glass window, studying the toy cars weaving through the maze of parked vehicles below. Small human ants crawl among them. In, out, up, down. There's something unsettling about the fact that I can study them and they'll never know my name. Never even know we had this moment together and they starred in the thoughts of a desperate stranger.

A quick knock taps my door, and a nurse pokes her head in.

"Good news." Her face is all smiles and expectation when I turn. "We're working up your discharge paperwork. Now would be a good time to inform your ride that you're ready."

"Thanks, but I'll be taking a cab."

Her smile falters, fades into... pity.

Don't! Don't look at me like you understand why. Like suddenly it all makes sense.

"Okay. Well, you have the information from the social workers. Sure you won't consider checking into a program?"

I answer with a return to my window, and the door clicks shut after a few seconds of silence.

Discharged. Maybe I'd be relieved if I had anything to go back to.

"I'm glad you're okay, love, but I'm returning to my flat in New York."

Arctic gaze heavy with pain. Elegant fingers clasped in a tight knot.

"I desperately want for you to get well. Please seek help. But I can't do this, Jesse. You're not living; you're functioning, and quite honestly, sometimes you're not even doing that."

Deep breaths do nothing in a vacuum. A void so dark the fires of hell couldn't spark a flicker.

"After we fulfill our commitment to Smother, our relationship ends, both personally and professionally."

Ends.

Forever this time, her tears said. Glacial melting dripped down her cheeks and collected on smooth skin I'd lost the right to touch. Her gaze brushed over me, lingered on my eyes, pleading. She waited. Five, ten, fifteen seconds for another promise we both knew I'd break. Just a few simple words to save the fairytale we'd built. It was right there. The golden path to life, legend, and love.

God, she loved me. She'd never said it, how could she, but we both knew it. That I loved her too, *needed* her, and we belonged together in a way that only cosmic jokes can invent.

I needed her so much I couldn't do it to her again, so I let the silence speak.

I'm a promise-breaker, Mila. I'm a fraud.

Somewhere in her delusion of hope she'd always known that. She'd known the truth about the Philly boy who'd let fate sucker-punch him. But she'd been cursed with hope. With success and a history of making her dreams come true. And that's all I am. A dream. A ghost. *Her* demon.

She believed I was more than I am.

Wasted talent is the name of the game... means bugger all if you can't handle your own gift.

My spark of life.

Over.
And.
Out.

∞∞∞∞

The house is dark when I go inside. No note, no text. I figured as much. The guys are beyond shattered that I blew their second chance.

Because you're not worth the pain.
Because you are the little shit they said you were.
Because.
Because.
YOU!

I sink into my mattress and close my eyes just as the tears come. Hot, agonizing lava flows down my face.

Why did you think you could be anything?
What joke were you playing?
The music is laughing. Hear it? Laughing!
You're nothing.
No one wants you.
No one.
No one.
Do the world a favor and...
STOP!

Broken sobs echo through the darkness. They have to be mine. I press my fists against my face. To block them? But they echo louder in my head.

Yes, Jesse. Just... stop. Stop before you do any more damage. Before you break them for good. You should *be alone. You're poison. That's why they leave. You're cancer. You're the traitor. The overrated promise-breaker rearranger of truth. Composer of lies! Author of failure, sobbing little shit—that's you, Jesse Everett. That's you.*

That's you.

That's you.

"Hello?"

My eyes snap open, heart racing.

"Jesse? Parker? Anyone?"

Did I not lock the door?

Footsteps clap toward me.

Thump, thump, thump.

Closer now. Doors swing open and close again.

"Jesse?"

I shake my head. Sink lower into my sheets.

"Jesse, are you here? The hospital said—"

He stops. Stares. Watches the pain flooding from my eyes. His own expression melts, and I can't look.

I clench my eyes shut.

You don't deserve.

Life.

Legend.

Love.

"Jesse." His voice is soft as it drifts closer. "Hey, it's okay."

Arms pull me up, wrap around, and settle me against a chest I've never felt before.

"God, Jess, I'm so sorry. I'm so, so sorry." His voice breaks with his own tears. I turn into the scent of detergent. The smell of *clean.*

"They left," I breathe, pressing against a warm heartbeat. The one that stayed.

His grip tightens around me. "This is my fault, son. *I* did this to you."

I shake my head again, and he stills it to his chest.

"It *is* my fault, but what you do with that truth is up to you."

No!

My throat closes, crushing my voice.

"It's too late, Dad," I force out. "I'm already broken."

The gasp of his sob rustles my hair.

Dad.

Is that what he is? What do you call the man who destroys you, then insists on stitching you back together?

"No, son. You're not! You're a fighter. You've survived so much. You're stronger than—"

"You don't know what I've survived." Instinct spits the words, starts to pull me away. That's what's real. I tug and they let me go. They run, escape, like they should. Like he will, but... no. He holds tighter?

"I do, Jess. I know. And I also know that if a fuck-up like me can find his way back, a warrior like you definitely can."

You can't know that.

You can't.

"You know how I know?" His voice firms through the tremor of tears. "I know because I'm not giving up. Never again, son. I will never leave you again."

∞∞∞∞

Jonas makes coffee now. The real kind, with a French press and everything. Eggs too, apparently, and I wonder what other firsts I'll experience before the day is through.

I rest my head on my arms as I watch the strange scene from the table. Even after ten minutes of sifting through memories, I can't remember that man at a stove. Meals were always a scavenging event for Parker and me. Sometimes it was fun to use our combined ingenuity to cobble together a full stomach. More often it was brutal when we couldn't. Eventually we negotiated a deal with Old Lady June in the neighboring apartment to keep an extra box of granola bars on hand if we came up too short for too long. She was responsible for Jonas' first strike with the state.

"Do you have any bacon?" he asks.

I shrug. "No idea. Three roommates, remember?"

He smiles and pulls open the fridge. "How do you take your coffee?"

"Black is fine."

"That's my boy."

I flinch, and his smile fades.

"Sorry, Jess."

He turns away to fill two mugs and two plates. Two. Such an odd number when it involves Jonas Everett. He slides one of each to me and takes a seat across the table.

"Thanks." I inhale the aroma and stare at my reflection in the small ripples.

"I'm sure you have a lot of questions," he says, carefully arranging eggs on his fork.

I push my own around the plate. "Not really."

He quiets, and I almost feel a twinge of regret.

"Where are you living now?" I ask.

"I have a place in lower Bucks."

"Really? A house?"

He nods. "It's not fancy, but I wanted space to set up a decent studio."

I lower my fork. "For live recording too?"

"Working on it. The contractors are still finishing up, but hopefully, in a month or two I'd be able to do it all in-house."

"Wow. You think you'll have enough artists to support that?"

"I already do. Seamless has been sending more work than I can handle. I could do more if I didn't have to travel so much."

"Maybe we can be your first official in-house project," I joke too fast for the words to register. *Shit.*

His eyes change. "I'd love that, Jess."

The coffee in my mouth drains down my throat. I take another swallow so my lips don't do something stupid like smile.

"What did you think of my work on 'Jonas'?"

If he's hurt that he inspired such an ode to resentment, he hides it well. "It was dope."

His lips turn up behind his mug. "Yeah? Well, you know where to find me if you want to move forward with it."

"What really happened to Mom?" I blurt out. He wants to play? Well, game on.

He squirms under the weight of our past, and his voice sounds distant when he finally responds. "Honestly? I don't know. I never heard from her after she ran off."

"Why didn't she take us with her?"

"I don't know. She was—"

"Is that why you started using?"

"That's when it got out of control."

"Did you know that what happened on Halloween when I was twelve left permanent scars?"

Strike two. The old marks burn through my shirt as I watch his face shatter.

"Jesse, I—"

"Do you know what happens to third degree burns that don't get treated?"

"Yes, but—"

"Did you know I was the one who found you when you OD'd for Strike Three? I thought you were dead. I wished it too until they sent me to NEC and I learned there are worse things than having a junkie father."

"Jess—"

"Did you know they used to beat the shit out of me and lock me in the basement? Do you know what a starving kid is willing to do for something to eat? To get out of a basement? Do you?"

His eyes clench shut, head shaking in tortured arcs.

"Answer me, *Jonas*. Do you know?"

I hadn't even realized I was crying until the molten drops land on my skin. The air is saturated with our breaths. Me, on my feet, leaning forward with fists tightened around the edge of the table. Him, looking as broken as I've ever seen a man.

My voice falters almost to a whisper. "Do you have any idea how much I wanted to love you? How little it would have taken for that to happen? One look. One touch. One fucking moment of feeling like I mattered."

I collapse to the chair and lock my hands in my hair.

"The answer is no, Jess," he says quietly. "I don't know, but I do know I don't deserve another chance."

"I gave you another chance!" I fire at him. "I let you back in, and what did you do?"

Fucked me over, his look says, but his confession brings no comfort.

"I'm working two jobs so I can give you every penny I earn from producing. I swear to you, I will keep burning the candle at both ends until I pay back every cent I stole from you."

Candle.

Light.

It's all right...

Not bright enough to see my scars.

God, they hurt so much. Candle flames burn too. Did you know *that*, Jonas?

"Have you heard from Parker?" I snap.

"Jess—"

"Have you? Are they coming back?"

He studies me closely, searching for something. "They're in Manhattan," he says finally.

"Manhattan?" Air rushes from the room again. "With Mila?" Just saying her name guts me.

He nods.

"What could they have to discuss with her? I thought she was dropping us."

His expression falls, and I know he's fighting between loyalty to each of his sons. He owes me way more than Parker.

"She's agreed to help them explore options for moving forward without you."

Wham! Oxygen blasts from my lungs. Painful. So horrendously logical.

"I'm sorry, Jesse," he says as I stare at my uneaten food.

"Yeah, well, that's what happens when you blow second chances." I push myself up from the table.

"It's not over. You can't look at this as the end."

"Yeah? What is it then?"

"Rock bottom."

Another blow. This one harder, deeper.

His eyes soften. "Don't let this moment be the end. Make it the starting line. Today can be the beginning."

He waits. I look away and drag myself up from the chair. "I'm tired."

∞∞∞∞

I wake to warm, soft arms. Peace. Relief.

"Mila?" Heat burns through me as I turn toward that flawless smile. My heart, oh god. I pull her close, crush her against my chest.

"I'm sorry. So so sorry," I whisper against her neck. Her arms tighten around me.

"Me too, Jess." Is she crying?

"We have to figure this out. Please don't leave me again. Please." A sob escapes my lips as I press them against her hair. "I'll do anything."

"Good, because I sent your songs to some people I know and they're beyond excited. It's happening, Jess. Everything you ever wanted. Life, legend. Love."

Her mouth reaches for mine, hungry. My body is already charged, tensing with every press of her fingers. She grips the edge of my shirt, and I roll back. Ready, waiting, wholly hers.

"I love you," I say, searching those brilliant eyes.

"Shut up, you little shit."

I jerk up. "What?"

"You heard me. Fuck you, junkie."

Stunned, I cry out at the sudden pain in my chest. I crane my neck to find the handle of a knife protruding from my skin.

"How does that feel?" she hisses. "Strike one."

Paralyzed, I can only stare in horror as a second blade hovers above me.

"Mila! Please—"

I gasp as another searing pain floods through my abdomen.

"Strike two."

"Parker!"

I scream to my brother who ducks through the doorway. But instead of subduing Mila, he accepts the dagger she hands him.

His lips curl in a grotesque twist, teeth white in the sudden darkness. Only a small candle illuminates the room. Just enough to see the glint of metal as it rushes toward me.

This time I have no air left for protests.

"Strike three, you overrated piece of shit," he growls.

"Four."

"Five."

"Six."

Jesse. Jess! Wake up! Jess!

I gasp and open my eyes. Sunlight streams through the windows. My hands fly to my chest as I search for blood, gaping wounds. The pain. The pain is too real.

"Hey," a voice says.

I draw back in alarm, pushing as far away from the intruder as possible.

"Don't. No more. I'm sorry!" I scream, holding up my hands to block the knife. Seven, eight? *I'm dead! Why are my eyes open?*

Why are his eyes open?

Other details slowly bleed through the veil. My messy desk. The pile of dirty clothes in the corner. And...

No Parker.

No music.

No Mila.

No future.

The pain is deeper than a knife cut.

I choke on the words in my throat. "I lost everything. There's nothing left." This time the arms that tighten around me are hard. Strong. Drenched with a sense of permanence.

"So did I, Jess."

I shudder at his tone, tender and deliberate at the same time.

"I want it back, Dad," I whisper.

Dad...

There's something new in the way he bolsters me against him.

"Then we get it back, son. We go get it back."

∞∞∞

"Getting it back" feels impossible until we break it down into a list I can see.

I stare at the page in my notebook as Dad makes us coffee.

1. *Work with Counselor Seth to deal with the mental shit.*
2. *Attend group with Dad.*
3. *Accept Chris' offer for one-on-one mentorship and accountability.*
4. *Investigate inpatient and outpatient rehab programs.*

"You're going to be able to do this, Jess," he says, placing a mug in front of me. "Trust me."

I swallow the rising panic in my chest.

Trust me.

What about the music?

Trust me.

Who am I, what *am I if the music doesn't come anymore?*

"What's going on in that head?"

I flinch and hide behind the cup.

"Nothing. Just trying to figure shit out."

He leans back in his chair, gaze reflective. "I know you don't want to hear this, but you and I are a lot alike. It seems as though our art is in the darkness."

"Isn't it?" I grunt.

"Maybe. But I promise you'll learn to access it in a healthier way. Parker told me the music wrecks you when it comes. Wouldn't you like to be the one in control?"

I'd do anything to breathe when the words come.

I'm sure Dad has more in the arsenal but he's cut off by the clamor of returning roommates. The ruckus skids to a halt when they see us. Their faces slide from surprise to guilt.

My violent dream floods back, this time as a lie. Parker wouldn't stab me; I stab *him.*

"Jesse. Hey, man. Welcome home," he says.

"Thanks. You too."

His gaze ducks away. "Look, about New York and not picking you up—"

"Don't. I get it."

Four sets of eyes follow me from the table to the fridge. I rip the page from my notebook and slap it on the door with a magnet.

"And now we're getting our future back."

25: GETTING IT BACK

This time when I meet Chris at the coffee shop there are no awkward stranger ambushes or red hats. She smiles when I enter and waves me over to a table.

"Good to see you, Jesse," she says, pushing a cup toward me.

"You too." I raise a brow at the surprise gift.

"I remembered what you ordered last time. Hope that's okay."

"It's great. Thanks." I take the seat across from her and wrap my hands around the giant mug.

"I'm glad you called."

"Me too." The too-hot coffee doesn't stop me from singeing my lips and tongue.

"How have things been going?"

I release a long breath. "Honestly? Shitty, but that's why I'm here. I want my life back. Scratch that. I *need* it back."

"Yeah? What's your motivation?"

I swallow another scalding draught. There's a question. Are we here for coffee or a weekend retreat? "Simple answer? I'm not really living. I have no control of my life, no future on this path."

"That's a scary place to be."

"I've lost everyone," I mutter to my drink.

"Not everyone."

I glance up and meet her warm smile.

Not everyone. Even at my lowest.

Rock bottom.

"Are you in control of your substance use, Jesse?"

I clear my throat. Another great question. Why does everything have to be so damn complex?

"I'm not physically dependent, but mentally..." My fingers twist a path through my hair as I study the table. "There's so much... I need breaks. From my head. From life. I can't handle it without help."

"Chemical help."

I nod.

She leans back in her chair. "And that's not working for you."

It's not a question. Of course not. My coping strategy sounds ridiculous out loud, even if it's a truth I lived inside and out my entire life.

"No. I need to find a better way. I'm ready to ask for help."

I expected some kind of jubilant eruption from her when I finally committed. Don't they have t-shirts and name badges or something? Instead, she stares back with a solemn nod.

"I'm so happy to hear that. What you have is a substance use disorder, and like many diseases, the path to healing is difficult but possible. Are you prepared to work hard toward recovery?"

Work hard. Harder than fighting the demons alone every second of every damn day only to lose again and again? Harder than watching your friends, your brother, the woman you love walk away? Harder than being an overrated, garage-band wasted, *crying little shit*?

"I'm ready," I say. "Whatever it takes."

Her gaze settles on me, punctures deep into my resolve. And suddenly, there's the smile I'd been waiting for. Better than a t-shirt.

"This is a great day, Jesse. We'll be seeing you Thursday night?"

"I'll be there."

∞∞∞∞

Seth's office isn't as lame as I remember. His hair is still slicked back in an unnatural assault on gravity, but the arch of his brows is probably concern, not disdain like I originally thought. He waits as I squint through the blinds and consider his latest request.

Tell me about the demons.

The words slither through my head and lodge in my stomach. The demons just *are*. Like oxygen. And brain cancer. I pull a long stream of air into my lungs. How do you talk about something you don't even understand?

"They scream," I say finally. My eyes trace the outline of a tree through the window. Spring flowers fill the branches in an alarming explosion of pink.

"When?"

"All the time."

"That must be difficult. How do you make them stop?"

"I can't."

"Never?"

I shake my head. "Not without chemicals."

His brows are arched again when I dare a look.

"Do these voices ask you to do things?"

"I'm not schizophrenic," I huff.

"I'm not suggesting that. What do they say to you?"

"That I'm a worthless piece of shit."

"Do you believe them?"

"A lot of the time."

"When don't you?"

"When I'm high."

Exactly, Counselor Seth. Good luck with this case file.

"Would you like to be free of them?" His tone is gentle like he knows the answer.

"No."

Those brows again. "No?"

"They bring the music."

"I see. That's quite a dilemma then."

Quite. "I'm pretty fucked up, doc."

He doesn't like my joke, though his lips crinkle into a polite smile.

"Actually, you're not. Your situation makes perfect sense to me."

My gaze shifts from the window, locks on his.

You make sense.

I make sense?

"You suffered severe trauma in an environment that modeled addiction as a coping behavior."

A heavy knot gathers in my stomach. I cross my arms to hide it.

"And the demons?"

"Sounds like a cerebral manifestation of depression in a highly perceptive and creative individual."

My throat closes around my response. *I'm telling* myself *I'm a worthless piece of shit.*

"Jesse, it's obvious that you are extremely gifted. You have an awareness of your existence and the world around you that's different from most people. Combined with your musical talent, this gives you access to a host of creative insights others could only dream about. It's also a huge burden to carry. Your brain will process and interpret stimuli at a profound level that can be overwhelming and exhausting."

I smirk. "So you're saying I'm not fucked up but gifted?"

Not even a polite smile this time. "Do you find auditory stimuli more heightened and distracting than others seem to?"

Yes.

"Do you feel overwhelmed by your own creativity and a pressure to make sense of yourself and your world?"

Yes.

"Do you find yourself seeking solitude for reflection and daydreaming?"

Yes.

"Ever face silence from humor that's often too subtle for others to appreciate?"

Similar to the silence he's facing now? I focus back on my window, loving the way the setting sun forces its orange streaks through the slats. Ocean ceilings, sunset blinds.

"Do you see the intricate complexities in the world around you? Find yourself lost in the beauty of ordinary things? How about risk-taking? Do you feel confronted by an overwhelming host of possibilities, problems, and complex relationships that make it hard to choose a course?"

Fuck.

"Jesse, do you find it difficult to connect with others because they seem to be living in a different world than you do?"

Point made, I sense his stance soften across from me. His chair creaks as he leans forward.

"You're not a mistake, Jesse. Your brain is special, and instead of being nurtured, it was assaulted by trauma. It's no wonder substance use got a foothold in your life."

The glowing blinds are nice, but suddenly I'm struck by the corresponding slices of light adorning the opposite wall. How did I miss that?

Daylight candlelight. What if there's beauty beyond the darkness?

"Interesting theory, doc."

"Do you disagree?"

No. I pull my attention from the wall-candles and focus back on him. "So now what?"

"Now we help your brain process the interfering obstacles and set it up to thrive."

∞∞∞

I'm exhausted by the time I return to the house. The guys want to do a full rehearsal for the Smother gig, but I'm not sure I can handle that right now.

Strange that the place is dark when I climb the front steps. I mutter a curse to myself. Guess they're already setting up in the practice space. So much for a rest.

I push through the front door and stop at the barrage of deliciousness wafting from the kitchen. Is Reece expecting Gina again?

"You cooking takeout, dude?" I call out. Smells too divine to be an authentic attempt. At least he's trying.

"I hope that's okay."

I freeze. Heart in my lungs, brain skipping all over the place. She comes around the corner, and now I know I'm dreaming. Maybe I *am* schizophrenic after all. How else do you explain the most beautiful woman on the planet, in my hallway, encased in a glow from the kitchen?

"You look like you've seen a ghost," she says, perfect lips curving into a devastating smile.

"An angel, maybe."

"Not an *alabaster queen*?"

My heart can't take it, the weight of her presence. I've missed her too much, and the void starts to swallow me again. I'd come so far and now—

"What are you doing here?" My voice trembles, caught in the battle between pain and ecstasy.

God, I miss her so much. She must really hate me to show up here looking like that.

Her smile fades as she reaches back through the doorway and pulls something off the fridge.

"Is this for real?"

My hurried scribbles glare illegibly in the patchy light.

I swallow the host of explanations, defenses, and apologies that rise in my throat. "Yes" is the only word I let out.

Suddenly the dark hallway is alive with sparks and color. Her warm body molds against mine as I sink my face into her neck.

"You have no idea how much I wanted you to say that. How hard it's been to stay away until you did." Her words are thick with tears. I feel them soaking my shirt, and I pull her tighter.

"I'm not running anymore. I promise."

Her arms slip under my shirt and lock around my waist. "Then neither am I."

∞∞∞

Mila wasn't kidding. The woman can cook. I lean back in my chair and it's hard to argue this isn't the happiest moment of my life. Is this what it's like to live? To want something? To chase a future because you crave more of the present?

"You've got that far off look again," my alabaster queen says.

My attention settles back on her along with a smile. A genuine one. A content one.

"I'm just happy," I say, and wish I could say it again to see her face light up like that.

"Me too. Jess, I…" She blinks. Blushes? I didn't think I'd ever see Mila Taylor blush. She clears her throat. "Parker said you were at counseling today. How is that going?"

I smile to myself, disappointed, but I can't exactly blame her for backing down from those three words. I haven't had the courage to say them either.

"It's going well. Hard, but well. You'll laugh," I add, mentally reviewing this past session.

"Why?"

I shake my head. "Only because of what Seth told me today. He thinks I'm gifted."

She does laugh, forcing a shine to her eyes I haven't seen in a long time. "My professional opinion? No shit, Sherlock."

"An *I-told-you-so* would suffice."

"Really… what about this?" She leans forward and presses her lips to mine.

"Even better. Should I list more things you were right about?"

"Please do."

I grin and steal another kiss instead. "So you still never told me what you're doing here."

Her eyes wrinkle into a coy expression. "Maybe I was just in the area."

"And decided to pop in and cook Italian for two?"

"I was hungry."

"And the guys?"

"They went out."

"Uh-huh."

I draw her in for another kiss. A long one this time so she knows this is where she belongs.

"You want the truth? Jonas rang me and said you were committed to turning things around."

"And you believed that? I screwed it up before."

Her gaze becomes serious. "I believed *him*." She sucks in a breath. "The man loves you, Jess. Like it or not."

Her words strike hard.

"I know," I say finally.

"Do you?"

I nod, and our mood lifts with her sudden grin.

"Then you should also know that I'm leaking the 'Jonas' footage tonight. By tomorrow morning Limelight will have blown up the internet again."

26: SMOTHER

"Jerky?" Derrick swings the package in an arc over the back of the seat.

"No, man, we're good," I say. Mila shakes her head when he slides it over to her side of the seat.

"No thanks, love."

Derrick snickers. "Love. Heh. She's so British," he tells no one.

A smile tickles my lips, then flares into an all-out grin at her expression.

Don't encourage him, her look warns.

It's killing her that we're only halfway through the eleven-hour drive to Smother and we have no more band business to discuss. She's already recapped, summarized, and picked apart every one of the torrent of industry responses to our now-viral "Jonas" video. We've discussed the plan, venue, and crowd at Smother so many times, even Derrick is crystal clear on the highlights. We've even reviewed, one-by-one, each of the many requests for shows, interviews, and appearances, including SauerStreet's apologetic bid. Mila handled the thanks-but-no-thanks rejection of their offer.

Now my high-energy, go-getter girl is stuck in a van with five laidback dudes who are perfectly content trying to identify various likenesses in slices of beef jerky.

"Hey, Jay! Who's this?" Derrick holds up a large chunk so his friend can see it from the seat two feet away.

"I dunno. Kinda looks like a strip of dried beef, dude."

"No, Mrs. Hall! Remember? From sixth grade?"

Parker and Reece exchange a glance from the front seats, and I hold in my snicker. He drives you insane, but we can't imagine not having the guy around. Life is so simple for him. I would benefit from studying the Derrick Rivers manual for human existence.

"Eh, look at this," Mila says. She twists up in my arms and slants her screen toward me.

"Seamless is sweetening the pot?"

She nods. "That's a pretty good offer."

"What about Seamless?" Parker calls back. The dude has rabbit ears when it comes to shit he cares about.

"Seamless sent another deal," I say.

"You think Dad had anything to do with that?"

I shrug. "Why? You ready to do elevator rock now?"

He throws a dirty look to the back of the van, and I grin in response.

"I was thinking we should do another new one besides 'Jonas' tonight," Parker says. "Thoughts?"

Which in Parker-speak means if you disagree you better have a damn good reason.

"What are you thinking?" I ask.

"How about 'Agitator'?"

"Ooh, yes. This crowd will love that one," Mila says.

"Okay." The word no sooner slips out of my mouth than the entire van zeros-in on me. Even Reece peers in the mirror from the driver's seat. "What?" I ask.

Parker clears his throat. "Nothing. I mean, that's great. I'll pencil it into the set."

"You never agree to anything without a fight," Derrick says, much less tactfully.

A collective cringe registers from front to back. Of course. It's eggshells and tiptoes around the unpredictable Jesse Everett powder keg. I have some epic friends and bandmates to still be here after everything I've put them through.

"I love you guys," I blurt out, and now the stares shadow with concern. "I'm serious! It's way past time I tell you that."

Derrick, who's closest, leans even further over the edge of the seat. Is he staring into my eyes? Oh my god.

"I'm not high, loser," I say, shoving him back to his zone.

He shrugs, and relieved chuckles drift from the front seats.

"You all are impossible," I mutter, settling back into the cushion.

"Hey, Jess," Parker calls out. "We love you too, man. Good to have you back."

∞∞∞∞

Now, this is a club. We know the second we pull up to Smother that we're about to have an experience for the ages. A reverent hush falls over us at the approach of a man who must be the owner—when he's not modeling for underwear commercials. Damn, if I were a chick... I'd react just like Derrick.

"Oh my god," he whisper-shrieks to me. "He's so hot!"

I smack his chest. "He's married, dude."

"Leon, good to see you again, love," Mila says, taking his hand and initiating two posh cheek brushes.

"You too. We're really looking forward to this. Arriane has gone all out for Limelight Night. I'll introduce you and she'll take it from there."

"Great." Mila turns and waves us after her.

"We sure about this?" Parker mumbles to me.

"Playing a club?" I ask.

"Becoming superstars."

I glance over and exchange the smile with my brother we've been waiting over twenty years to share. God, I love that man, and at the risk of turning all Derrick on him, I swallow the emotion and focus instead on taking in more of the venue.

The club is even more impressive on the inside. A DJ booth overlooks a nice-sized dance floor, and the space has obviously been reorganized to accommodate a large platform.

"Looks like you'll have room for both basses," I quip to Reece.

He's too excited to take the bait, and huddles with Parker and Jay to discuss logistics instead. I check for Derrick, but he's already off exploring the sick-looking patio bar. A beautiful woman by the main bar directs employees with a calm authority, making it obvious who runs the show at Smother.

"Arriane," Leon calls over, and she turns with a breath-taking smile. On her approach, we catch a glimpse of a little human following shyly behind her. The kid is a devastating mix of his parents, and there's no doubt he'll be breaking hearts in twenty years.

"We're so happy to have you. Welcome to Smother," Arriane says, shaking each of our hands.

"Thanks for hosting us. I'm Jesse." I point to the others. "Parker, Reece, Derrick, and Jay who will be running front of house."

She nods. "You said you'd be bringing your own audio equipment, correct?"

"Yes," Mila says. "Hiya, I'm Mila. Nice to finally meet you." The women exchange greetings, clearly evaluating, then approving of each other. We'd be a mess without Mila, and I suspect Limelight Night would not be happening without Arriane. I relax knowing they're in charge.

"As we said, the night sold out quickly. We'll be at capacity, but we've rearranged some things to better accommodate the crowd. Would you like to taste the signature Limelight Margarita for tonight?"

"Hell yeah!" Derrick cries.

"Later," Mila warns him. "Please just show us where to set up, and we'll get started."

"Great." Arriane turns and waves at a ripped dude behind the bar. "Christian, can you come over here a minute?"

The guy slings the rag he'd been using over his shoulder and approaches with a confident smile. "Christian runs the bar and helps manage things around here. If you need anything at all tonight, he's your man."

"Good to meet you," he says. "Get me a list of your drinks, and I'll be sure to keep you stocked."

"Thanks, man," Parker says.

He nods.

"Oh my god!"

Our ears bleed from the loudest shriek in the history of sound. We turn toward the wail to find an adorable blonde-haired pixie who couldn't possibly have projected such volume. The guy behind her snickers as he tries to hold her back.

"It's Limelight! They're, like, supernovas!"

"Superstars, Inga."

"Whatever. A nova is a star."

"Okay, but—"

"Ahh!" She tears away from her captor and bolts across the room toward us. "I'm Ingela," she announces. "Inga. Yes, call me Inga. I love you guys! When Arriane said you were coming I lost my shin!"

"Your shit," the guy mutters, approaching behind her. "You lost your shit."

She shoots an annoyed look to her (boyfriend?), and crosses her arms. "Shut up, Cameron. You're just jealous because I said I'd leave you for Jesse. Didn't I?" She stares right at me. "I did. I would."

"You would not," Cameron grunts.

Her glare melts into affection as she throws herself into his arms with a thud. He lets out an *oomph* and barely catches her. "You're right. You're my eleven-incher. But I'd do both of you. You always wanted a threesome, right, baby?"

My night just got very interesting, apparently, and I haven't said a word. Mila's gaze creeps over my face as I maintain oblivion. I'd crawl through a pit of poisonous spiders before reacting to that offer.

"Thank you for your support, Inga, but if you don't mind we have a lot of setup to do," Mila says like the professional she is. *Also, no threesomes with my boyfriend, thank you.* That look is for me, and I shrug with a grin. Not sure how I'm in trouble for a conversation I'm not even in.

"Inga, Cam, please finish setting up the patio." Arriane points her employees toward the glass door. "Sorry about that," she mutters to us. "You will love them by the end of the night, I promise. Okay, again, if you need anything at all, please don't hesitate to ask myself, Leon, or any of the staff. While you're setting up, I'll check on the refreshments and make sure your green room is ready."

I glance at the guys and their faces mirror mine. Yep, it's good to feel like rock stars again.

∞∞∞∞

The night lives up to the hype. The lights, the haze, Jay blasting us through the stratosphere, it's no wonder the crowd is going ape-shit for our music; *I'm* a freaking animal in this cloud.

Everything about this moment is right, and it's not the present but the future that has me wound to a new notch of energy. We could do this every day. We're on the doorstep of dreams, and the best part? I'm here for completion, not escape. Running to, not from, makes all the difference as I pull the mic from the stand and yank the crowd into my ecstasy.

"My reaction time is lacking
No backtracking now that you've got me on the prowl
Hey hey
I'm looking at you, traitor, faker, promise-breaker,
Re-arranger of the lies we've tried to bury
Hey hey"

Voices rise up in unison to lyrics they can't possibly know but feel the urge to sing anyway. Bodies rock together with my words, the bass pumping EDM waves beneath adrenaline-fueled drops from the track. At the last one, a cheer erupts with the lights when the music jumps back to life. Damn, even I have chills.

This college club crowd is the perfect vessel for our music, and I know Mila will be gloating plenty. She's up in the booth now, grabbing as much bootleg footage as she can. Hell, I wouldn't be surprised if she's planted pros throughout the room for some real film.

This is the magic musicians talk about. I never thought it could be mine, but here we are: sweat dripping down our faces, music blaring through a veil of exhilaration so pungent we've all been transported to a higher plane. This is the moment where life, legend, and love combine into an irresistible mantle of hope.

It's happening.

Lights flash blues, whites, and yellows.

It's actually happening!

My eyes connect with Parker who returns a grin that tells me everything. We've made it, bro. After a lifetime of fighting through the darkness, we've finally pushed through into the light. *Parker and Jesse*, two names that are more than case files and entries in the foster system. More than hungry children and forgotten youth. This is what life feels like. This is what joy feels like. I want this, my reason to fight.

Parker launches into the intro of "Agitator," and for the first time in as long as I can remember, I'm excited for tomorrow.

∞∞∞

The green room Leon and Arriane set up for us is great, but we find ourselves gravitating toward the main area of the club after the guests go home. How could we possibly hide in a back room with the vibrant personalities floating around Smother? We have a blast with the staff who seem more intent on drawing out the party than clearing it.

Parker and I chill on barstools watching that chick Inga tear up the dancefloor to a phantom song in her head. Her boyfriend is helping with the makeshift stage when he's beckoned to the floor by her ear-splitting demand to "get his groovy on!"

Even Leon cringes and interrupts his conversation with Mila to shoot an irritated look in her direction. Arriane points Cameron to the dance floor, probably to keep his girl under control more than anything.

The entire circus is beyond entertaining.

"You know, if the music thing doesn't work out, I'd take a job here," I say, swallowing a mouthful of club soda and lime. As delicious as those bottles of tequila look, I don't trust myself yet, and Christian has stayed true to his word and kept us well hydrated — me with seltzer — all night.

"Think they have space for two employees?" Parker asks. "You're not leaving the band without me."

"Better make that three," I say, pointing to the dance floor where Derrick has another employee attached to his hip. "We can't expect him to fend for himself."

"What about Reece?"

"Gina has him covered, right?"

We exchange a smirk and relax into the moment. The night was perfect. The club, the vibe, the crowd, everything was exactly what we needed to boost our current hype. Once Mila edits and posts the footage, we'll have our pick of futures, she says.

My heart swells at the gift of this moment. I'm right where I'm supposed to be with the people who matter. With the three of us together, there's no chance in hell we won't find our way.

"We did it, bro," I say quietly. "No matter what happens next, we already did it."

He turns and flashes the joy he's always deserved. How many times have I stripped it away from him, and he still stood there, tall, alone, against the storm? God, I stole so much from the one person who gave me everything.

And yet he's the one who says, "I'm proud of you, man. Proud of us. *We* did this. Jesse and Parker. Life tried to break us and we kicked its ass."

I smile back. "We did. Ready to make history?"

"Let's do it."

I hold up my glass. "To kicking life's ass."

He clinks it with his bottle. "To kicking life's ass."

∞∞∞∞

Mila hasn't stopped talking since we walked out of the club, rode in the van, checked into our hotel, and found our rooms. She's bursting with details about this PR company, that blogger, this label, and that promoter. She already has us doing stadium tours on the moon, and I'm too turned on by the excitement on her face to dash it with a hit of Jesse Everett Realism.

She's the best kind of dreamer. Intelligent, driven, and connected, her dreams are goals, not fantasies, and if my alabaster queen has us going platinum by this time next year, who am I to argue? What I can't tolerate is the amount of clothes she has on.

"I've already sent a message to my contact at—"

The rest comes out muffled against my lips. I back her into the closed door of our room.

"Can you be my girlfriend for a few hours? Just a few." I grab her perfect ass and shove her into me. She gasps out a surprised moan, and I love that it takes so little for me to distract her.

"Jess, I have to..." She full-on whimpers as I hike that tantalizing dress up her thighs for better access.

"What's that, babe? I missed that."

"Shush your mush," she breathes.

I pull back and snort a laugh. "What?" My grin earns me a playful slap. "Shush your what?"

"Mush! Argh. You heard me, you arse."

"I thought I was a wanker?" I try for the accent and cover my face to block the blows.

"Tosser. Dickwad. Prick. Twat!"

I lock her wrists to stop the assault, and she erupts in giggles as I pull her onto the bed.

"How about fit as fuck?" I tease, securing her on top of me.

Her nose wrinkles as she shoves my shoulders, then softens into intoxicating alignment with my body. "I prefer *lover*," she says, singeing my lips with a hungry kiss.

A groan rumbles from my own throat. This woman... "Okay, you win. Claim your prize." I pull off my shirt with a playful smirk.

"Arse," she mutters again, and shoves me back to the mattress.

∞∞∞∞

I stare at the passing cars, trees, all the interesting things that fly by a back window when you're in a van going 70mph. Mila is still "updating" us on the upcoming *everything* she's booked in the last twenty-four hours. That woman can get more done over a continental breakfast than I accomplish in a decade. I have no clue what she sees in my lazy ass—besides the fact that it's *fit as fuck*.

Thing is, I'm happy. Yeah, I said it. I'm freaking content.

"What's so funny?" she inserts mid-sentence into whatever news I was ignoring.

I glance over, making no attempt to hide my smile. "Nothing."

"Not nothing. You're grinning."

"Can't a guy be happy?"

Her eyes narrow into a skeptical appraisal. "Not you. What is it?"

"Seriously, Mila. I wouldn't push it," Parker calls back. "He's probably thinking about your boobs."

"Shut up," I laugh. "I am," I say to her just to get the smack she lays into my arm.

"Ouch." I rub my bicep with way more gusto than necessary, and she rolls her eyes.

"Don't be a sissy."

"A sissy? That's not what you said last night."

Her glacial eyes grow to their full size as snickers scatter throughout the van.

"Jesse Everett!"

But she's not too mad. "I love seeing you like this," she whispers.

"Like what?"

"Like—"

"Fuck!"

The last thing I remember is screeching breaks and the darkest basement in Hell.

27: Voids

"We did everything we could."

No! Bullshit! What's everything? What *the fuck* is everything?!

I stagger to a chair, shrug off the useless hands reaching for my shoulders. Numb fingers comb through my hair as I process nothing. Everything! I don't fucking know. How can you know?!

Whispers scratch the air around me, and I clamp my eyes shut. Try to control my breathing.

Don't they know?

Someone fix this. Tell them it's supposed to be me. Tell them how they got it wrong.

No, no, no. My head is shaking, the numbness in my limbs sparks into tingles and shallow breaths.

You bastards took the wrong brother! How can you not understand that? Fix it! God, please fix it! Please!

I can't breathe.

I'm going to be sick.

I clutch my stomach and barely make it to the trash can before my gasps become retches. Suddenly, I'm the center of attention. Stealing from my brother even in death.

Selfish bastard. But oh god, there's no air in here.

My eyes search for him. My rock, my sanity for twenty-three years. *Parker, I need you! Please please please. Oh god! I can't. It can't—*

Arms guide me to a gurney. I hear words like anxiety attack and other phrases that make it sound like keeping me alive is important. Why didn't they care this much about saving the worthy brother? The necessary one? The strong one who dreamed and believed and fought enough to pull us through hell and back?

Why are they wasting resources on me?!

I throw up again.

"Jesse, you have to breathe. Deep breaths, hon."

Sobs wrack my body, sucking the little air that's left from my lungs.

Everyone leaves!

You promised! You fucking promised me!

I hate you!

My fists pound my eyes.

"He promised! He promised he wouldn't leave!" That voice can't be mine. The pain in those words draw echoing tears from other eyes. I feel them burn my skin as more arms fold around me.

"Jesse." This voice is familiar, laced with pain too. Trembles with loss and fear.

"I did everything he wanted. I followed the rules. The list. I did everything…"

"I know, love. I know."

"You don't understand. I can't do this without him," I plead, turning into her embrace.

"You can. I promise."

"No promises. Don't make promises."

Life tried to break us and we kicked its ass.

Fuck life. Fuck promises. A cry explodes from me as I rip myself away from Mila and bolt for the exit.

∞∞∞∞

One smile you could hold onto.
I run. Legs stumbling along a blind path.
One embrace that made things okay.
One heart that forgave.
Believed.
Sacrificed and fought to give you a future you didn't deserve.
A ragged hiss of air burns through the hole in my chest. Another. In-through-out. In-through-out. Never lingering long enough to soothe the swell of panic.
One giant void that will...
Ache.
Shake.
Break you into the nothing that you are.
You're the traitor, faker, promise-breaker and you're not enough!
Not enough.
Never enough against fate's prank to take
The one person not afraid to hope.
Nope, you're the joke, Jesse Everett. The tragic hoax no one wants to touch without the protection of Parker's connection. Because he's the sun and you're the one
Afraid of light.
Scars reopen.
Fester and bleed!
I cry out against the voices and fall to a bench.
"It's all right. It's all right." But there's no candle here. No, it's too dark in this basement. The van. Coffins, everything— everywhere. No flicker. No oxygen to feed a flame.
Just blame!
Plenty of that.
"Stop!"

Bright lights flash. A horn blares. Eyes flare wide as they turn to me for a final plea.

"I'm sorry," they cry. "I'm sorry for breaking my promise."

"Goodbye."

Five souls walk away without a scratch.

Ha. Ha. Ha.

Five souls steal from one.

"I love you, brother. You're going to be okay," vacant eyes say. They lie as he dies and sucks away everything left in me.

My body shakes from the details crashing in. A steel monster smashing through the front passenger door. The van spinning, flying. Screams. Such a chorus of broken glass and terror. We're all going to die. No one will die. Only one.

Oh god. Only one.

"Parker!" I reach through the shattered van. Sobs, the wet stench of tragedy. It's so thick around me as I flail blindly for my anchor. My brother.

"I need you. Please, please." I'm sobbing again. "I need you, Parker! Where are you? I can't see! I can't…"

Suddenly, warmth. Relief.

Parker. It was all a nightmare. Thank you, God!

Trembling, I fall against the steady rise and fall of another's breath. He breathes for me. In. Out. In. Out.

Slowly, the air starts to circulate in my lungs.

In. Out.

Parker.

My rock.

My protector.

"Just breathe," my father says.

∞∞∞

Just breathe.

Impossible when your rock is gone and your phone blows up with validation of fate's mistake.

"Parker will be missed."

"One-of-a-kind, that guy."

"So sorry for your loss."

"It wasn't his time."

"The good die young, right?"

Right.

I toss my phone on the pile of clothes in the corner of my room. Mila's cooking something that makes my stomach lurch like everything else they've tried to force down my throat since we returned home. Two days and I've managed to swallow a bowl of cereal. My stomach is too bloated with pain.

Dad, Derrick, and Reece? I don't know. At the funeral home probably, pinch-hitting for the train-wreck brother of the deceased.

"You're gonna hate your funeral, dude," I mutter to him. "It's your own fault for leaving us in charge."

You're the micromanager, so who the hell is supposed to coordinate the fallout of your death?

"Didn't think about that did you, genius?"

A sharp wave of agony fires through me, and I roll to my side to absorb it. Body folded over itself, I have nothing left to fight this attack.

It's just forever, right? Just one crushing cosmic hole that siphons oxygen and nails you to a mattress in a shitty Mt. Airy townhouse.

How long is forever?

How long for this crushing ache to fester?

You promised me!

No joke.

No hope.

No… dope.

Li.

Li can fix this. Only Li.

You promised him.

Fuck promises. No one else keeps them.

"I'm proud of you, man. Proud of us. We did this. Jesse and Parker. Life tried to break us and we kicked its ass."

Nausea climbs in my throat.

You promised.

He promised! *He* fucking promised so where does that leave us?

Huh, Parker? Us! Parker and Jesse. "We" had dreams. "We" kicked the world's ass. We, we, we. You know I can't handle "me." That's your job! Didn't think about that either, did you?

I clench my eyes shut, cutting off the hot sting of tears.

A rhythmic buzz climbs out of the pile of clothes. Another call I can't handle.

Li can fix this.

I roll off the bed and drag myself across the room.

Peace.

Oblivion.

I need to fix this.

YOU PROMISED!

The voice screams so loud in my head, I almost trip over my guitar. I catch the neck just before it crashes off the stand.

You promised.

I stare at the instrument in my hand.

Promises...

Parker deserved a promise not me. Parker deserves the music. He deserves everything, and he got stuck with me instead.

He—

Rewind back to the start

And your heart would still be too big for me

Love is a game
For some a lie
For you an epic tie that bound you
To the one who cries
When the lights go out
When the chill seeps down
Through cracks you always mended

My guitar starts to sing with the words. My body inches back to the edge of the bed.

Arms that braved the fiercest storms
Swarmed, warmed a broken boy
Who never had a chance
To dance with fate
Who lived afraid of himself

That's love in a city of demons
A pity they never saw you coming

Rewind back to the day
A superhero roared,
"It's okay
To fly, to dream, to spread broken wings
To scale a mountain in spite of it all."
"Brother," he said.
"I'll catch you when you fall."

∞∞∞∞

Bloodshot, glistening orbs: Mila's eyes as she places a tray of food on the dresser. I lower the guitar to the floor and wipe my sleeve across my face.

"That's beautiful, Jess. What's it called?"

"'Philadelphia.'"

Silence.

Glassy orbs widen, brighten with a spark of understanding. A sob escapes her as she rushes over. Her arms wrap tight; muscles tremble in sync with mine.

"Oh god, Jess," she whispers, burrowing her face in my chest. "City of Brotherly Love."

I close my eyes. "'Philadelphia.'"

28: PHILADELPHIA

What do you do in the City of Brotherly Love without your brother? Can't seem to figure that out.

So I play. *The Song* is a constant loop over the next three days. Perfection, that's my goal. Make this last link to Parker the one thing that's good enough for him. Somewhere in the house people whisper and clank dishes. They worry, they knock, they act like life goes on when it stops for one.

And maybe that's true for them. But my present is too painful without the music. When it goes, the ache returns in an unbearable weight, so I play for him. Sing to him. Honor him with the only good thing I am. I give him everything until the song becomes a lullaby to rock me to unconsciousness. Then it's awake, water, and more music. More knocks. More pleas. More whispers.

More music. Just the music until it's ingrained in my soul beside my brother. For three days I play, cry, and escape.

On the fourth I wake up and realize I faced the mother of all demons without substances. And won.

∞∞∞∞

And how do others cope with grief? Erect a giant plaster minotaur, apparently.

"What the hell is that?" I mumble to Mila as I walk past the living room on the morning of the funeral.

"Jesse." She throws her arms around my neck, and I close my eyes to absorb her warmth. Just like the music, maybe there's room for her beside Parker in my heart.

"Are you...?" Her gaze wanders through my head as she pulls back.

"Working on it." I force a half twist of a smile.

"Good." She hands me a mug, and I do my best to swallow something besides water.

"Now—that," I say, staring into the living room.

She leans against the island beside me. "What? The new tablecloth? The other was quite faded."

I toss her a look, and she smiles. "Oh! You mean the massive bull-man. Derrick's tribute to your brother."

I snort a laugh in spite of myself. It's the least painful reaction I have in me.

"Wow. If Parker wasn't haunting us before, he certainly will now," I say.

"Nah, I think it's cute. You could dress it up for each holiday. Parker would appreciate the thought."

"He'd freak at the damage it did to the hardwood. I'm guessing Derrick doesn't have plans to fix that?"

"Doubtful. But I saw him before he left this morning and he had trousers on and everything."

Another laugh leaks out, and I throw my arm around her shoulders. "God, I love you."

We still.

Time stops.

Three words echo and bang and shatter history as the present lies in ruins.

I feel her chest lift in a long inhale. Release in a longer exhale.

"Good," she says finally. "Because I love you too."

∞∞∞

I suck at funerals. Never understood them. Still don't as I stare at the box supposedly containing my brother.

I'm here, dude. You're still dead. Now what?

Closed casket. Too much damage for makeup to fix, and right now, I think I'm okay with that. Who needs to see my strong, take-charge brother all chalky and painted like one of those creepy wax figures?

An arm slips around my waist as a head rests on my shoulder.

"I'm so sorry, Jess," Mila whispers. It's different coming from her; those words actually mean something. Maybe everything.

"He'd hate this, you know," I say. "These flowers are ridiculous. And that photo Reece gave them?" We study the grinning man in a tux.

"He wore a tux?"

"Yeah, once. Last month for the Alton wedding. A real picture of Parker would have him at the kitchen table giving me the death stare."

"You probably deserved it."

"I always deserved it."

We quiet, and I swallow the emptiness rising in my gut. Blink at the box that has no business holding my brother.

"It was nice of the boys to sort out a lot of the arrangements for you."

"They're amazing."

"They are. Though I'm surprised by the lack of mythological beasts."

This girl. I squeeze her tighter.

"My guess is the funeral home frowns on plaster bull-men."

She chuckles softly and laces her fingers with mine. "You going to be okay to do your song?"

"No."

"Good." Her hand tugs mine to her lips.

∞∞∞

I learn a lot about my brother as the speeches rumble from the podium next to his coffin. I do a good job keeping my eye-rolls in check and pretending to be properly touched by the exaggerated stories of his brilliance. He *was* great, and also a smartass who would be snickering right along with me if he weren't locked in that damn box.

Mila squeezes my hand when the officiant calls my name and says I'd like to say a few words. Very few, really, because speeches aren't my thing.

Nervous rustling flutters through the room as I slide out of my chair. I don't remember the walk to the front being so long, the air by the casket so cold. I reach for my guitar, pull the strap over my head, and adjust the instrument that suddenly feels foreign in my hands.

A stab of pain cuts through me when I instinctively glance to my right for reassurance. No nod. No smile. No, *you-got-this* look from the face that's always been there. Shiny boxes do a damn poor imitation of my brother.

The coldness seeps through my pores and lodges in my chest again. My fingers vibrate on the strings. The audience watches, waits for the train-wreck brother to embarrass the legacy of the better one. I swallow the mass in my throat.

"This is for Parker," I say.

I close my eyes. The music starts, and suddenly he's beside me again. I hear his clean guitar in my ears, his perfect backing vocal. Never too much, always the right build and release to match my lead because that's what brothers can do.

They read minds and interpret hearts. They make it okay not to be perfect because they fill gaps and…

Mend cracks.

"Rewind back to the start
And your heart would still be too big for me"

I dare a look at the audience, and a rush of warmth spreads through me. Not just at the quantity, but the *quality* of the people who love my brother.

"Love is a game
For some a lie
For you an epic tie that bound you"

There's Luke, Casey, Callie, Holland, and even the other NSB guys looking on from a middle row. Can't believe they all flew in.

"To the one who cries
When the lights go out
When the chill seeps down
Through cracks you always mended"

Mila, of course. A swell of love gusts into my chest at her reassuring smile and the glisten in her eyes. I know it's for me as much as for Parker. Mila. Where would I be without her? Probably waiting for Parker in the ground.

"Arms that braved the fiercest storms
Swarmed, warmed a broken boy"

And there in the second row, my father—Parker's father—with Chris and his fellow in-recovery army of supporters. His face... My voice falters, my throat closes around itself. The next words barely make it out.

"Who never had a chance
To dance with fate
Who lived afraid of himself

That's love in a city of demons
A pity they never saw you coming"

My gaze pulls away to rest on the box where my brother should be standing. I know he's not in there because he's so firmly lodged in my heart.

"Rewind back to the day
A superhero roared
It's okay
To fly, to dream, to spread broken wings
To scale a mountain in spite of it all"

At this point I doubt anyone else can understand the lyrics. They blast in my head, though, so I know Parker hears them. He's even singing along, smiling because for the first time, I controlled the music. Instead of running, I dug in to face the greatest pain of my life and transform the mother of all demons into beauty.

"Brother, he said.
I'll catch you when you fall."

∞∞∞∞

Silence. No not silence. The whisper of sniffs and tissues spreads over the room as I stand immobile in front of the mic.

I have nothing else to give, but I can't bear the thought of ending my last conversation with Parker. My guitar hangs heavy on my shoulder. My pick—I don't know what happened to that.

This end, it's unsatisfying. Is it an end? A beginning? Both? What the hell is my life without him?

My father's sudden request to say a few words startles me from my daze. Startles everyone as a murmur filters over the rows of guests.

He approaches with somber, but sure strides. His hands grip my guitar and help lift it over my head. I watch as he places it on the stand with reverence before straightening in front of the mic.

"Some of you know, I stand here today as an intruder." His gaze flickers to me. "My name is Jonas Everett and I'm responsible for the conception of Parker and Jesse, but little else. Parker was the man he was despite me, not because of me."

Tears well in his tired eyes, bringing a burn to mine. He clears his throat. "I've thanked God every day since these boys let me back in their lives. I didn't deserve another chance, but Parker was the kind of man who believed enough to support those who didn't. Parker forgave when others forgot."

His eyes find me again, and I draw in a ragged breath. "My time with Parker got cut short. It crushes me to know I've only returned a fraction of what I owe him, but I promise you, Jesse, I will pour my heart and soul into being the father I should have been when you needed one.

"You may not recognize it yet, but Parker lives on in you. He was so proud of you. He believed in you and the man he knew you were becoming. He loved you beyond words, just as I do, and I swear I will fight for you until it's me in that casket."

My cheeks sting with tears as the man I no longer hate, the man I might *need* if any of his words are true, moves toward me. His arms reach out, and I fall into them freely. For the first time in my life, I believe him.

I believe Jonas Everett's promise.

How can I lose a brother and gain a father on the same day? My heart explodes.

"I love you," he says for my ears only. "We're going to make him proud."

∞∞∞

With reverent silence, the guests clear to a reception upstairs until only two remain.

Two. The strange number that involves Jonas Everett. It's become common lately.

An obscene flower arrangement cascades over the coffin as we stare in silence. The arm that slips around my shoulders is heavier than normal, and the weight I've been fighting so hard to sustain today crashes down around me. Crushes me. Pushes me to my knees and forces my face against the box in an avalanche of grief.

Dad drops beside me and wraps me in his arms.

I don't know how long we stay like that. Seconds, minutes, days? But with each release of painful tears, I feel lighter. Like maybe I'll find the strength to stand again. To walk from this room and leave that box behind.

I reach up and grip the smooth metal with two hands, my forehead resting between them. It feels wrong and so necessary at the same time. I clench my eyes shut and absorb my brother's cold death into me.

"I swear to you, too," I whisper, voice as broken and strong as my heart. "I'll kick life's ass for both of us, brother."

29: STEPS AND LEAPS

If ever there's a time to have a tough, take-no-prisoners woman beside you, it's when you lose your brother and need someone to keep your life running. While I grieve and stare at shit on my ceiling, Mila bustles around on her phone, maintaining and building a life we can go back to. She becomes the spokesperson for the band, the visionary, the advocate, the negotiator, and the planner. Even Parker would approve of her performance, especially the way she *manages* me by refusing to let me follow him into the darkness.

"Grieve, don't get lost," she says when I hide in my head for too long.

"I'm releasing the footage from Smother tonight." She pushes me over so she can join me on the bed with her laptop. "All anyone wants to talk about is Parker, but it's time for that to be a private conversation for you. We need everyone else focused on the future."

I nod and blink up at the blue swirls above us. "What *is* our future?"

A sharp glance cuts over to me, but she softens at my sincerity. "You told me yourself, you're kicking the world's arse, right? So that's what we do. The best way to honor Parker is to make Limelight the legacy he always wanted."

She taps industrious keys in the silence.

Tap. Tap. Tap.

The sound of my future.

The sound of a woman who loves me for reasons I still don't understand.

Not so long ago I wanted to murder this woman. Now I'd murder *for* her. How have I come to need the two people I hated most in this world in order to survive the loss of the one I can't live without?

"I don't know if I can do this, Mila. What if I can't?"

Her busy cadence stops, and I look up to meet gentle love.

She closes the laptop, slides down to the sheets, and slips her arm over my stomach. I cover her hand and hold on.

"I'm here for the long run, Jess," she whispers. "You can because I'm not letting you go."

I blink away tears and secure her fingers to my lips.

∞∞∞∞

A week later, I'm ready to brave the public again. Luke is my first call, and the selfless man drops everything to take me to lunch. He never mentions what he's sacrificing to be here, and I don't ask. I'm just grateful for his confident, calming presence.

"It's some rough shit, Jesse. How are you holding up?"

I shrug and fidget with the straw in my glass. "Not sure I am. Mila's holding my universe together."

"But it's being held. That's a big step for you."

Damn. Yeah.

I still haven't run.

I'm still living, fighting.

Look at Jesse Everett facing the greatest pain of his life stone-cold sober.

The slightest of smiles flickers over my lips.

I'm doing it, Park.

"Yeah, I guess it is."

He smiles back. "It was a great service, man. That song for Parker was extraordinary. Holland was a mess afterwards. You should consider releasing it."

"Thanks." I swallow the sudden surge of emotion. "How's everything with you?"

"Good. We're working on a world tour."

"Yeah? When?"

"Late fall."

"Wow." I let out a laugh.

"What's so funny?"

I shake my head and lean back. "Nothing. Just that a few months ago, I was convinced that was impossible for me. And honestly it probably was."

"And now?"

I meet his thoughtful expression. "I want it, man. I really do. Parker believed we could get there, and I want that for myself as much as for him now."

"Of course, you can. You just gotta play the long game. Take the small steps, and before you know it, you'll look back at the mountain you've climbed."

"You always make things sound easy."

"And you know they're not." He settles into a serious expression. "How's your head?"

I study my fingers as they tap an absent rhythm beside my plate.

"I don't know, man. I don't know much of anything right now except that I have to keep trying. I *want* to because I have a life out there waiting for me when I get through this."

I take a deep breath. "I'm thinking of checking into a program for a few weeks. You know, to deal with the psychological crap and get a foundation. Set myself up for real, you know?"

I dare a look up and breathe a sigh of relief.

"I think that's a great idea. I'll give you the info on where I did my recovery. It was an incredible place. Life-changing."

"Thanks, that'd be great." I pick at the straw again. "Mila has big plans for us. I need to fix my shit."

"You need to learn to manage it. Nothing ever gets fixed."

For some reason, I find comfort in that. Attainable goals, that's what I need. Someone like Luke who's lived through it, who fights and survives and is willing to drag my needy ass along with him. No wonder the world is in love with this guy.

"Keep me in the loop," he says. "I wouldn't be surprised if Mila has big plans for all of us."

∞∞∞∞

Luke was right. With Mila at the helm of our public narrative, everyone wants us. Labels, promoters, every fangirl and her brother. Once the word is out that Limelight isn't dead, but intent on shining bright for Parker, the requests go viral. Everyone wants in on our story, and Mila convenes almost hourly band meetings to discuss the latest options on the table.

"First thing's first," she says, once it's obvious we need more than updates; we need decisions. "What are you doing about a lead guitar player?"

My stomach twists as all eyes rest on me.

Of course, we have to…

"We can never replace your brother, Jess," Mila says gently. "But we can add a new member."

I swallow. "Yeah. What about Jay?"

Reece's eyes light up. "Oh my god. Of course! We used to play together all the time before he got into the tech side."

"He knows all our music. Probably better than we do," I add.

Derrick nods with excitement. "Plus he wears suspenders."

Also true.

Satisfied, Mila types something out on her laptop. *Click, click, tap, tap. Enter.* Back to us. "Okay. I'll have a word with Jay this afternoon and make an offer. Next discussion: label. At this point, you pretty much have your pick, so you tell me what you want."

We exchange long looks, and I warm at the silent agreement extending around the table. It's been a while since I've been so sure about anything. "I say, none. I say we do this our own way."

Mila's gaze jerks from the screen to mine. "What?"

"No one will do a better job with our future than you. We trust you."

"Really? Are you sure?"

"Positive."

"Thank you, that means so much, but I can still look after you as your manager while—"

"Labels let us down. You haven't."

Her smile is something I won't forget. I tuck it away for later when we're alone.

"Well, okay then. Now we need a studio so we can get you fellas back in the game."

I grin and lean forward. "Not a problem. I've got that covered too."

∞∞∞∞

Dad's house is nicer than I expected. It's no castle, by any means, but with four bedrooms, three baths, and a finished basement, it's obvious he bought it as more than a bachelor pad for a recovering addict.

He shows us around with pride, explaining his plans for each room, including a lounge for visiting artists and guest rooms for overnight stays when sessions run late.

The kitchen is fully stocked, and it seems like he'd be offended if we didn't help ourselves to the snacks and beverages he's provided. Derrick has no problem diving in. Reece and I grab a bottle of water for the trip downstairs to the studio.

Even with the warning, I'm not prepared for it. The scene at the bottom of the steps is straight out of any small, modern studio I've visited. The space is bright and clean, with glass and hardwood everywhere. Recessed lighting makes it shine, and when he leads us through the glass door, I instantly fall in love with the acoustics. From Jay's expression, he's rabid to play on this side of the window again. A control room looks on from the other side, and even from this distance I suspect it's a producer's wet dream.

"Wow," I mutter.

Mila smiles. Reece and Jay visually inspect every crevice in awe, and Derrick does his dolphin-seal dance. Yep, this is the place for our new beginning.

"Your studio time is free, of course. I'll deduct extras from what I owe you by submitting a weekly invoice for your review," Dad says.

Mila extends her hand. "Thank you. We agree to those terms."

Dad takes it, his expression brighter than I've ever seen it. "Excellent. Come, I'll show you the control room."

Sure enough, the engineer and producer's lair make the studio look mediocre. Two giant screens hang on a wall and display massive grids of tracks piled on top of each other in the recording software. It's so impressive, I can't wait to play with the production side of things.

"Wow, this is sick," Jay mumbles. His eyes are huge as he takes in the room like a starving cheetah at a steak buffet.

Dad crosses his arms, beaming. "Thanks. I'm hoping we can work together on the mix and production."

Jay looks ready to wet his pants. "Seriously?"

"Absolutely." He clears his throat. "Well, this is it. You want to give it a shot?"

"For sure," I say, warm, driven, excited for the first time in a long time.

"Great. What are we starting with?"

Our eyes lock. Producer and artists. Hope and second chances.

Father and son.

"'Philadelphia.'"

∞∞∞

"Oh my god!" Mila rarely loses her cool, so when she bursts into the control room and interrupts our playback, we know it's big.

"What's going on?" I ask.

Her eyes shine with excitement. This is what dreams look like when they come true on someone's face.

"I just got off the phone with TJ Barringer!"

"Night Shifts Black's manager?" I ask, my heartrate climbing to unsustainable levels.

She nods. "They've officially invited you to co-headline on their world tour this autumn!"

Our heads shake in unison. "No way," Reece says. "No. That can't be right."

"You sure they didn't mean we could open for them like last year?" I say.

Her eyes narrow in mock irritation. "I know how to speak English, boys. I'm telling you, Luke and Casey want you at the top with them. This is... in all my experience..." She shakes her head and demonstrates what we're all feeling.

This is the type of shit you don't even dare to fantasize about.

"Well, what did you say?" Derrick gasps out.

"I said we'd think about it," she quips in a dry tone. "What do you think I said?"

We all connect in one giant grin.

"Abso-freakin-lutely!"

I draw in a long breath, stare at the gap between my father and me. He's there. I feel him warming the cavities of my heart. Grinning an *I-told-you-so* so obnoxious, I'd punch him if I could.

We're doing it, Parker. We're about to kick the world's ass.

Epilogue

I keep my word to myself and my newly-formed family. I check in at Reflections and work my ass off to make the most of my time there. I have too much waiting for me outside to fuck this up.

My program and progress allow for visitors, and Mila and Dad stop by often. The weeks fly with productive sessions of individual and group counseling, physical and emotional training, and a general focus on holistic wellbeing. Slowly, my mental dependence on escape begins to transform into a healthier reliance on community and music.

I understand the truth right from the start. How what seems so logical now never would have worked before I was ready. I had to want this for myself. Like Chris warned, I had to be ready to work hard to make a lasting change I could trust. The thing is, it will never end. No, this fight is a marathon. Mila promises she's all in for the long haul, and that's becoming more significant the more I grasp the challenge I'm facing. Strange part though? I'm starting to believe them when they say I can do this. The demons still circle, but they've lost a lot of their power.

It seems like just yesterday I lost my brother and started on this path toward the future he always wanted for me.

I'd do anything to have him here, to see the fruits of his sacrifice that are helping me become the man he believed in. But the harder I fight, the more I understand how the best way to honor him is to keep him alive in my story. To include him in my success, my failure.

I'm here, man. Clean, hopeful, and surrounded by a bigger family than we've ever known. The flicker of a candle has become a blaring sun I can see even in the dark moments.

Mila meets me in front of the facility on my last day. We grip each other in a hug strong enough to finish one chapter and start the next.

"I'm so proud of you, Jess." Tears collect in her eyes as she leans against me in the cab. "I can't wait for the world to meet the real you."

My heart swells.

I'm armed, dangerous, and ready to kick some ass.

"*It's all right in the candlelight,*" I sing softly to her.

Arctic eyes shine with affection as she wraps her arm around mine. Her lips turn up for a kiss, and I'm already there. "You're my candlelight, Mila Taylor," I breathe against them.

"Yeah? Well you're my Burger Prince Charming."

∞∞∞∞

"Post." Mila drops a fancy envelope in front of me.

I set my mug on the table and scan the unusual letter. There's no return information, just old-timey calligraphy with my name and address.

"What is it?" she asks, and I shrug.

Sliding my finger, I break the seal and pull out some frilly, yet classy-looking, card.

As a dear friend,

Callie Roland and Casey Barrett request that you save the date of September 4, 2018 to join them as a witness and celebrant of their marriage. A formal invitation and details to follow.

Well, damn.

A giant grin spreads over my face.

"What is it?" Mila hovers over my shoulder, straining for a peek.

I glance up and push the card toward her. "Be my plus one for the wedding of the century?"

The End.
For now.

NOTE FROM THE AUTHOR

Addiction is a serious illness that impacts both the victim and their loved ones. Seeking help takes strength and courage, and there are many compassionate people and organizations devoted to helping those who struggle.

If you, or anyone you know, is struggling with addiction, help is available. Please know you are not alone and seeking professional assistance is critical to recovery.

American Addictions Centers
https://americanaddictioncenters.org is a great resource to find facilities and information for victims and their families.

Seek help, and know that you are important and you are loved.

Sincerely,

Alyson Santos

ORIGINAL LIMELIGHT MUSIC

Experience Limelight's unique alternative rock/EDM sound on Alyson Santos' YouTube Channel: Author Alyson Santos.

MORE NSB

LIMELIGHT continues the journey of several characters in the NSB universe.

For more NSB:

A special thank you to bestselling author Sunniva Dee for loaning her Deepsilver characters.
For more on Leon, Arriane, Inga, Cam, and Christian:

ACKNOWLEDGEMENTS

From the start of my journey, I've been blown away by the amount of support from new friends, readers, bloggers, and fellow authors. I can't possibly see this as my accomplishment, but as an incredible blessing thanks, in large part, to all of you. There are so many people in my heart, and I wish I could list every one of you, even though I know it's impossible. Please know that I treasure you all and take nothing for granted.

To my amazing husband who is always there to support me. Without you I would not be writing these words.

To Sunniva Dee: my amazing AB and CP. I'm so happy to share a brain with someone as amazing as you! Love being your Virgo.

To Nicola Tremere: Thank you for being my UK Consultant. Even more importantly, thank you for being such a good friend.

To Lynn Vroman, Hazel James, Darlene Avery, Nisha Reading, Evie Woods, and Kali McQuillen: Your friendship and feedback mean so much to me. You always help bring the best out of my writing.

To Jon Meckes: As always, thank you for lending your talent and music industry expertise.

To Seraquil/Nico: Thank you for bringing Limelight's unique rock/EDM sound to life. I absolutely love "Limelight" and had a blast working with you.

To Era Media Co.: Thank you for yet another beautiful cover.

To Megan Buisch: Thank you for your support and lending your medical expertise.

To the "epic" members of ABC (Aly's Breakfast Club): I can never thank you enough for your encouragement and support. You always bring a smile to my face and remind me why I do this. I love you hard!

To all my readers, I wish I could thank every one of you. Thank you for taking this journey with me and I would love to hear from you!

Alyson Santos
PO Box 577
Trexlertown, PA 18087-0577

Facebook: Author Alyson Santos
Facebook Reader Group: Aly's Breakfast Club
BookBub
Website: http://www.alysonsantos.com/
Instagram: AuthorAlysonSantos
Book+Main
Spotify: AuthorAlysonSantos
YouTube: Author Alyson Santos
Twitter: AuthorAlySantos

42830560R00179

Made in the USA
Lexington, KY
21 June 2019